BEYOND MIDNIGHT

D.J. MACHALE

*This is for KEM, for
whom I've dreamed up
dozens of stories.*

Here are a few more.

BEYOND MIDNIGHT

Seven Peculiar Tales of Mystery and Suspense

D.J. MacHale

The Tales

Foreword

Welcome.

We're about to set off on a new adventure together. For those who know my books, you'll find this one to be a bit different. For those who don't know my books (and why don't you? Hmmm?) let me thoroughly describe the difference.

I usually write novels. This isn't a novel.

That's pretty much it. What you're holding is a collection of short stories. As unusual as that may seem to readers who are accustomed to my epic adventures that play out over multiple books, for me it's about getting back to my roots. I discovered my love of reading through short stories. Supernatural stories in particular. That's a broad description that covers many types of stories, but the common denominator is that these tales are about characters who experience real-world conflicts that would be interesting even if nothing supernatural happened to them. Their plights escalate when they're also faced with strange, impossible, thrilling, and often frightening situations. Both conflicts usually resolve together, and the endings aren't always happy. Best of all, there's often a twist waiting at the end. I love the twists.

Edgar Allan Poe, Daphne du Maurier, W.W. Jacobs, Richard Connell, F. Marion Crawford, H.G. Wells, Sir Arthur Conan Doyle, and Agatha Christie are only a few authors whose stories were the bedrock of my early reading experience. I'm also a huge fan of Stephen King's short stories. These tales offer intriguing dilemmas, relatable characters, and a narrative engine that drives the story forward quickly with little fat to slow it down. What's not to like about that?

I have had a few short stories published, but my experience with the form goes far beyond that. I moved from reading short stories, to writing them when I forged the television series *Are You Afraid of the Dark?* Those tales may have been written and produced for TV, but each episode was actually a short story that followed the form I described above.

There is another aspect of this book that is different from my others. I always write stories that appeal to me, and it just so happens that they also appeal to young readers. (Not sure what that says about me, but whatever.) The stories in this collection were written the same way, though the concepts and characters are more mature than my norm. So…middle graders beware.

I believe these stories may hold special appeal for those who grew up with *Are You Afraid of the Dark?* I can easily hear these tales being told around a campfire. In fact, the title pays homage to the storytellers of my Midnight Society. I imagine that those characters have grown up, but still have a passion for sharing supernatural tales. The only difference is that their perspective is now more mature. Hence, they have gone *Beyond Midnight.* (Clever, no?)

As mentioned, I've had a few short stories published in previous collections. Two of them I've included here. *The Scout (Redux)* was originally published as *The Scout.* *The Weeper* was originally published as *The Green Grabber.* I've rewritten and updated both of these stories to better fit the tone of this collection. The novella *The Paper Trail (Vera)* is notable in that it's part of a larger story that I plan to write as my next novel. It's about the people of a small town who find themselves swept up in multiple frightening dilemmas. The novella here follows one of those stories, while teasing some of the others. Don't worry, it will make sense when you read it.

Along with those you'll find a variety of other tales. There are a few ghost-stories, a sci-fi adventure, one with a vampire (of course), and several uncanny dramas that I trust will keep you guessing…

…right up to the twist.

Hobey ho!

D.J. MacHale

INFLUENCE ISLAND

Desperate is a strong word.

Derrick was desperate.

It came down to money. Doesn't it always?

"I spent it," he said in an accurate yet pitiful plea over the phone to his literary agent. "What can I say? I can't give back what's long gone. Besides, it's completely unfair that they want it back."

"I'm afraid it isn't," Derrick's agent, Randolph, replied with strained patience, seeing as he had already gone over this ground with Derrick many times.

"An advance isn't a fee. Publishers give authors an advance on royalties in anticipation of receiving a publishable manuscript they can profit from. You have not delivered one, publishable or otherwise. The contractual deadline passed over a year ago. Therefore, they would like their advance back. It isn't rocket science."

"I'm not a child, don't speak to me like one," Derrick said, sounding very much like a chastised child.

"Forgive me," Randolph said, unconvincingly. "You know how it works."

Randolph didn't raise his voice. He had been in the literary agenting business for a thousand years and had seen it all. He never showed much emotion, whether he was delivering news to his clients about how their book had hit #1 on the New York Times Bestseller list, or that they were about to be sued for breach of contract. In Derrick's case, Randolph had delivered both those pieces of news.

"You're right, I'm sorry," Derrick said contritely. "But I'm in a bind. Alimony payments don't stop because I'm fighting writer's block. Nor do mortgage payments. And health insurance. I have to pay through the nose for that."

"As do I," Randolph said.

"I'm on the verge of getting tossed out of my house and hauled into court by Uncle Sam for back taxes on money I'm now being told I have to return, and my dear ex-wife's scumbag lawyer has just served me papers looking for back alimony. I'm not sure who I fear more."

"I've met our ex," Randolph said. "You'll have a better chance negotiating a settlement with Uncle Sam."

"Not funny," Derrick snarled. "True, but not funny."

"Perhaps you should sell the Tesla," Randolph offered. "Or the Porsche."

"Oh?" Derrick snapped back. "Perhaps you should refund me the fifteen percent commission I paid you on that money, seeing as I've got to give one hundred percent of it back."

"I delivered a high seven-figure deal for you," Randolph said dispassionately. "I did my job and earned the commission."

Derrick wanted to argue the ethics of that logic but needed his agent to be on his side.

"I'm sorry, you're right," Derrick said. "All I need is a little more time."

"They've already given you a year."

"I need another month, that's all," Derrick begged. "I've got a new idea. Finally. A great one. I know I can bang something together that'll satisfy them."

"In a month?" Randolph asked incredulously.

"Plenty of time to knock out a rough first draft. Hell, they owe me that much. I've sold a lot of books for them."

"Which is why they've given you a massive advance for the next one. I don't understand why you accepted that deal if you had no idea of what to write."

"Because it was a lot of money!" Derrick cried. "But creativity isn't something you can count on, like flipping on a light."

"I understand, but for whatever reason it appears as though your power's gone out and unless you get it re-connected, I can't protect you."

"But you can buy me a little more time. I'm desperate, Randolph. Name your price. Whatever I've got, it's yours."

Randolph didn't respond right away, which gave Derrick hope that he might be considering the idea.

Finally, Randolph sighed and said, "Fine, I'll try,"

"Thank God."

"God's got nothing to do with it," Randolph shot back as if bristling at the notion. "But I do. Promise me that if I go out on a limb for you, you'll deliver. A complete manuscript. You aren't my only client. I work with this publisher all the time."

"No problem," Derrick said.

"Then we have a deal. Again, I want a finished manuscript or there'll be hell to pay."

"I'll deliver," Derrick said emphatically.

To Randolph, Derrick sounded more relieved than confidant, like a chronic gambler who'd dodged getting his legs broken by a kind-hearted thug who took pity on him even though he knew there was no chance he'd come up with the dough he'd lost playing the ponies.

Randolph had been down this road before.

"All right then, get on it," Randolph said. "I hope you won't mind if I check in with you in a few weeks."

"Not at all, check away," Derrick said.

"Inspiration is a fickle thing, Derrick. You never know where it will come from. Relax and let the story find you."

"Thanks, Randolph. I owe you."

"Yes you do," Randolph said. "And I will collect."

He punched out of the call.

Derrick took a deep, relieved breath as if he had just gotten a stay of execution, because he had. His euphoria didn't last more than a few seconds as the reality-tide came rushing back in and he tossed his cell phone across the room out of frustration. Unfortunately, he hadn't closed the sliding door that led to his lanai. Rather than hitting glass with a dramatic and satisfying crash, it sailed outside, over the rail, and into the bushes.

"Perfect," Derrick said to himself. "I can even fuck up a tantrum."

Truth was, Derrick did not have a new idea that could be turned into a seventy-five-thousand-word manuscript in four weeks. Or eight weeks. Or thirty. He was a decent writer. He could turn a clever phrase, find an apt metaphor, and create snappy dialog with the best of them. Or at least with the better of them. Trouble was, he was like a talented carpenter with a gleaming set of tools who had no idea of what to build.

He had been blessed with one good idea. No, a fabulous idea. At least from a commercial perspective. After working for the past ten years making a decent living selling personal insurance policies, he decided to turn his experiences into a work of fiction. While many people think that the everyday dramas of their workplace would make fascinating reading, or a hilarious sit-com, they're wrong and wisely never pursue it. Derrick was different. He didn't necessarily think that he could mine literary gold from the thrilling adventures of a moderately successful insurance agent who peddles whole life policies. It was more about the fact that his clientele consisted mostly of wealthy Southern Californians who had more money than sense, and he was a surfer who spent most of his time at the beach. The dichotomy of his two worlds seemed like a ripe platform for an insightful novel about class distinction, wealth, entitlement…and sex. Lots of sex.

Titled *Sweet 30*, it was a semi-autobiographical tale of a debouched surf bum who found his way into the vacant yet glittery world of SoCal society by writing high value policies that covered yachts, Aston Martin's, multi-million-dollar properties, cosmetic surgeries and even pre-nups. In real life, Derrick was a nearing-middle-aged weekend warrior with a loyal wife who earned more than he did as an ER nurse while he scrambled for clients. But one can dream. Or at least spin a dream. That's what Derrick did.

The result was a cautionary tale about the rise and fall of a callous young man who, like Icarus, flew too close to the sun. It wasn't exactly The Great Gatsby, but what is? The book was equally reviled and praised. Critics called it trash, which immediately lured a crush of middle-aged women readers into the tent. Not since *Fifty Shades of Grey* had there been a book that was so titillating and naughty, with a handsome, young surfer at its core who attracted beautiful, wealthy women, used them (in graphic detail), and spit them out until he was finally brought down by a woman smarter than he, and after a short, tumultuous marriage ended up taking control of his business. In the end he was left back on the beach with only a surfboard to his name.

Yes, it was trash…trash that sold over fifteen million copies domestically, was optioned for a film, and landed Derrick a high seven-figure contract for his next book.

Unfortunately, Derrick had only one book in him.

His sudden fame, and the lofty royalty payments that went along with it, had turned him into a flesh and blood version of his *Sweet 30* character. He and his wife moved from a tiny, rented bungalow in Oceanside to an opulent home in the hills that overlooked the ocean and the bougey town of La Jolla. He stopped writing insurance policies and in between appearances to promote the book, spent his time surfing. Not writing. It wasn't as though he had a choice.

He had nothing to write about.

He didn't seek out the company of other women, they sought him, drawn to him as the personification of the bad-boy character from his book. But he wasn't a bad boy. He was a forty-year-old insurance salesman who knew more about the intricacies of an annuity than the specs of a Maclaren. But that was all right. He didn't want to spend much time with any of them for he knew they would eventually realize he wasn't the character from his book. He reveled in the attention and the no-strings sex, then moved on.

As did his wife, once she realized what he had become.

That left Derrick alone in his opulent seaside house with overwhelming debt and no hope. In that way, his life had mirrored that of his fictional alter-ego. The biggest difference was that there were two words at the end of *Sweet 30*: The End. Derrick didn't have the option to end his own story. He had to keep writing, though he had no words.

That's when the email arrived.

It was from a fan. A woman named Chloe224. It began like so many others:

"Dear Mr. Hensley, I don't normally write to authors, but in this case I had to so I could tell you how much I loved Sweet 30."

Derrick had read some variation of that opening line multiple thousands of times. Usually, he skimmed through the rest of the text, barely registering any of it, while looking for a unique grain of original thought or interesting comment he hadn't seen dozens of times before. He'd follow that by hitting "reply" and offering a dutiful, generic thanks. He never bothered to save the sender's email address to add to a mailing list that he could use for promotion. His book sold so well he didn't feel the need to do any self-promotion. Or maybe in the back of his mind he knew there wouldn't be a second book that needed promoting. But he always replied, which counted for something. The fan mail would then be deleted and dumped onto the massive cyber-barge of the planet's unwanted data, never to be seen or thought of again.

But this email was different. There was a polite request (prefaced by: *"I'll understand if you don't want to do this"*), for his opinion on a story she had written. Normally this would prompt an even quicker stab of the "delete" button. Derrick didn't consider himself to be an expert on publishing, or literature, and certainly didn't feel qualified to dispense editorial advice on a nascent manuscript written by an amateur. But as his finger hovered over the delete key, he saw something that made him hesitate.

It was the paper clip icon that signified the email had an attachment. Seeing it gave Derrick a pang of envy. Chloe224 was probably someone who had never written anything other than derivative poetry in high school, yet she had come up with an idea that she was so confidant in she was compelled to send it to an author who had just written a #1 bestseller. Whether it was any good was irrelevant. The fact that she had come up with an idea, any idea, made Derrick resent her.

What he needed to do, to salve his ego, was read this audacious submission if only to see how horrible it was. He needed to confirm that writing a novel wasn't something an ordinary civilian was capable of.

Rather than hit delete, he clicked on the attachment.

He had a fleeting thought that he had been scammed and by clicking this un-solicited link his computer would be infected with malicious Russian malware. He held his breath, then relaxed when after a few agonizing moments a PDF document opened. It was three pages long, single spaced, with the centered heading:

Deadly Influence
by
Chloe Bannister

Copyright © Chloe Bannister

His first thought was one of relief. It wasn't malware. His second thought made him snicker.

"Deadly Influence?" he said to himself with a scoff. "Sounds like a cheesy 80's movie thriller starring Michael Douglas".

He was already feeling better about himself.

Until he read it.

It wasn't a novel. It was a brief overview of the story she wanted to write. But even at three pages, Derrick knew it was good. Like all good stories, whether they be three pages or three hundred, if the words compelled you to keep reading, that pretty much told you it was solid.

It was a thriller. A "Who Done it". Or more to the point, a "Who's Doing It?" The premise had to do with a handful of young internet influencers who were invited to spend a weekend at a tropical island compound owned by a wealthy individual who amassed a fortune by investing in companies that manufactured various popular products. Clothing, cosmetics, footwear, music, alcohol, energy drinks…essentially everything that millennials lived for…and social media influencers made small fortunes off of by promoting. Eight of the most popular influencers of the moment were promised a weekend of hedonistic fun in return for Snapchatting, Tik-Toking, Instagramming, YouTubing and Twittering selfie images of them frolicking on the beach while using the products. It was a coup for this entrepreneur to gather such social media royalty together in one place.

But the host's true goal wasn't product promotion. The glorious weekend would turn into a nightmare as the lux compound became a violent playground when he turned the young visitors loose, daring them to try and survive as he hunted and killed them one by one. The last influencer standing would receive a prize of a million dollars. The rest would be dead. It was The Hunger Games…in bikinis.

It was ridiculous.

It was exploitive.

Derrick loved it.

It was silly, exciting, sexy, timely, and best of all, commercial. It made him not only envious of Chloe224, but resentful of her for having come up with it. The thought of some neophyte conjuring such a solid idea, where he, a bestselling author was struggling to produce even a bad idea, sunk him into an even deeper funk. He needed to shake himself out of it, so he grabbed his board and went down to the beach to get wet. The ocean had always been his refuge, but not on that day. He half-heartedly paddled out past the break but couldn't generate enough enthusiasm to fight for a wave. He soon gave up and went home, intent on getting drunk. Since he believed that alcoholism was a common malady of many successful writers, he often forced himself to work through a bottle of Johnny Walker (Blue, of course) to try and tap into his literary muse. It never worked, other than to reward him with a few numb moments of relief followed by a blistering headache. But that didn't stop him from trying.

When he got back from the beach he sat by himself, cradling a bottle while punishing himself by staring at the computer screen and the text of *Deadly Influence*.

The idea didn't come at once. Given the fact that he wasn't one for generating unique ideas, it's hard to say where it came from at all. Perhaps it actually did spring from the bottle. Or from the place that is often a rich resource for idea generation: fear. What was it that Randolph said? Something about not knowing where inspiration came from, but to relax and let it come to you. He did just that and was rewarded with an idea. An awful idea. A wonderful, awful idea, to loosely quote Dr. Seuss. Derrick chuckled at that thought. After all, Ted Geisel created the Grinch not far from the very house where he was now sitting, as he gazed down with contempt at the Christmas revelers in the town of La Jolla below.

The permutations quickly flashed through his head like a computer calculating possibilities. Could he do it? Yes. Should he do it? Debatable, but ultimately yes. Would it be worth it? Undeniably, yes, especially when factoring in the alternatives. Was it risky? Maybe, but not overly. The final question, how to do it, pushed him into action.

He sat forward, placed the half-empty bottle of scotch next to his laptop and hit "reply" to Chloe224's email.

"Dear Chloe. Thank you so much for your kind words regarding Sweet 30, and for sending me the brief treatment of the story you titled Deadly Influence. I truly enjoyed it. I can say that with complete honesty because it is uncannily similar to a novel I am writing myself. In fact, I'll be turning in the first draft to my editor very soon. I'm not accusing you of anything. There is no way you could have read what I've written. But you should know that if you decide to write this story, and manage to get it published, there would be copyright issues. I'm sorry to deliver that news. I'm sure it's disappointing. I have no doubt that you'll be able to put this aside

and come up with a new and wholly original story to be proud of. Best of luck! Derrick Hensley."

Derrick read it over once, twice and hesitated for a solid half-second before hitting the send key. That simple effort effectively lifted the weight of impending doom from his sunburned shoulders. He now had a concept that he knew he could write the hell out of. He even justified it in his mind that all this Chloe-person did was come up with the bones of an idea. There was no way she would be able to complete a novel, no matter how well-written her treatment was. He convinced himself that without his intervention this terrific idea would go unrealized. He was actually doing the world a favor!

And with that, he opened up a new Word file and titled it: *"Influence Island"*.

At least he was able to come up with a new title.

He was in business.

"Hi guys!" Alexandra chirped brightly. Her arm was outstretched, positioning the iPhone to capture a perfect close-up of her smiling face on the deck of a yacht behind which was a stunningly white-sand beach. "Wish all you babies were here with me because this is absolute paradise! Whooooo!"

She checked the playback and frowned. "Damn," she snarled, much less bubbly than a moment before. She had to do a second take because her enthusiastic "Whooo" knocked the sunglasses from the top of her head. That just wouldn't do as an effective product shot.

Derrick wouldn't go so far as to say that the story was writing itself, but with the template of an idea already in place, he felt more than capable of fleshing it out. He had set himself up in his house as if preparing for a long siege. He took an afternoon to stock up on enough food to see him through the grueling month he would need every second of in order to churn out a manuscript. He also scored a dozen Dexedrine tablets from one of his connected surfing buddies in case he needed a boost to keep working. His plan was to sleep no more than four hours a night.

He also took the step of contacting anyone (other than his agent Randolph) who might reach out to him, asking them to pretend that he didn't exist for the next month. He wanted no distractions, going so far as killing his Wi-Fi and leaving his cell phone in the bushes so as to avoid any temptations that might keep him from his work.

Thus prepared, he set sail for *Influence Island*.

None of them knew a thing about their host, other than he was the principal owner of many of the companies that manufactured the products that made them all rich before the age of 24. The concept of how such large companies functioned was alien to them. Their expertise was limited to the products that appealed to them, and therefore would appeal to their followers. The only substantive contact they had with any of the manufacturers was with their marketing departments. They were the only ones who mattered, for they wrote the checks, and paid for their travel to fabulous locales for photo-ops using their products. Pampering the influencers and paying them handsomely to share their images on social media wasn't cheap, but it was a bargain compared to the costs of traditional advertising. Laughably so. No one was complaining because everybody won.

Writing the first act of his story (Or Chloe224's story) was a breeze. He didn't bother with an outline. He simply dove into the adventure and allowed the story to take him where it wanted to go. If Derrick was good at one thing, it was the ability to imagine himself inside of a story in order to describe what was happening. He could slip into and out of the skin of multiple characters to imagine what each was going through and then describe it using accessible prose that wouldn't challenge the readers of such drama. It was almost as if he was living the story himself.

In less than a week he had created his eight influencer characters and landed them on the tropical island of the mysterious host. None of the characters were particularly unique or interesting, but he could justify that because as he saw it, no actual influencer had much more depth than a short glass of White Claw. For him, creating shallow characters was exactly what the story called for. It was also much easier to do that than to build multi-dimensional players. That would have taken far too long, and at this point, speed was everything.

In less than a week Derrick had gone from looking at a blank computer screen, to having a document that was twenty thousand words strong. And the fun hadn't even begun, for now that his fictional crew had their feet in the sand, the bloody shit would start hitting the fan.

He hadn't taken a drink for the entire first week and needed only one Dexedrine tablet to get him through a particularly long and fruitful day. He kept his head down and his fingers on the keyboard. But now, after six days of intense work, he sat back with the reward of a healthy glass of Blue.

"I got this," he said to himself with smug satisfaction as he raised his glass to toast his laptop.   The expensive blend went down well.

He later blamed what happened that night on the fact that he was operating on too little sleep and too much scotch. The dream was as vivid as any he'd ever had. He found himself on his imagined beach of *Influence Island*, walking across the sand with one of his influencer characters, a particularly handsome fellow named Tandee who he imagined as a young version of Johnny Depp. Tandee was stoked (Tandee lived in a perpetual state of stoke) to be there.

"Sweet, huh?" Tandee said as he led Derrick along the shoreline with his unbuttoned Hawaiian shirt flapping against his six-pack abs. "I don't know who the guy is, but he's definitely got beaucoup bucks. Give me another five years. I'm not saying I'll have enough to score my own island, but one of them yachts won't be out of reach and—"

His boast was cut short when an arrow flew in and embedded itself into his skull with a short, sharp crack. Tandee didn't utter as much as a peep. He actually took two more steps before his knees buckled and he hit the sand, face down.

It was a shocking moment, but not enough to wake Derrick up. His dream-self fell to his knees and rolled Tandee over on to his back to see that the poor kid had only one lifeless eye that was staring at nothing. The point of the arrow had taken care of the other one. Derrick didn't think it was worth looking for it. Tandee wouldn't be needing it. More gruesome was the sight of the arrow that was stuck halfway through his skull, like an arrow-through-the-head novelty gag.

Derrick pulled his hand away to see it was covered in blood. He stared at it curiously, noting that the tropical sun had already turned it a rich shade of barn red. Or was it cardinal red? He looked down at Tandee, who suddenly blinked and focused his remaining eye on Derrick.

"Well, that sucked," he said.

The talking corpse was more shocking to Derrick than the arrow strike, and it jolted him awake. It took him a few seconds to clear his head and realize he wasn't on a sunny beach in the Caribbean, but in his bed in La Jolla.

"Whoa," he croaked.

He glanced at his bedside clock. 4:45. Too early to get up; too late to go back to sleep. Not that he had any chance of dozing off after that shot of dream-adrenaline. He lay on his back, staring at the ceiling as his mind slowly came back on-line. Once he could focus, he laughed. Not that there was anything remotely funny about the dream, it was more that he now knew the manner in which his first character would meet his maker.

"Maybe the book really is writing itself," he said to himself, then hopped out of bed and headed to the kitchen to brew his first pot of coffee. It was a moment of total calm. While he may have been uncertain about finishing the manuscript in time to meet the new deadline Randolph had negotiated, he now felt certain it was possible. He was firing on all cylinders. The ideas were flowing, even in his sleep. The end was still a way off, but he felt confident that he could pull it off. He'd be able to keep the advance. He could pay off his debts. He wouldn't be going to jail and maybe, just maybe, this book would prove to be another bestseller. Everything was falling into place, until he looked at his hand as he filled the glass carafe with tap water.

Dried blood was caked under his fingernails. A lot of it. The rest of his hand was stained brown. The sight startled him into dropping the carafe. It shattered on the tiled floor, but Derrick barely noticed. He was focused on his hand. When did that happen? No, *what* had happened? He wasn't bleeding and the stain certainly wasn't there when he went to bed. Or was it? He had had more than a bit of scotch. Had he accidently cut himself and not realized it? No, a quick examination proved he had no injuries. He ultimately convinced himself that there had to be a logical explanation, though he had no idea what it could be. More important, how was he going to brew coffee? After a quick clean-up he found an ancient paper filter in the back of a cabinet, loaded it with coffee, and poured hot water through it into a mug like a cowboy on the trail.

By the time he had washed away the caked blood and finished his first cup, his mind had left the mystery of the moment and turned to what he'd be writing. He didn't know where the day's work would take him, but he knew where it was going to start.

Six-Pack Tandee was going to get an arrow through the head.

As Derrick once pointed out to his agent, creativity isn't something that can be turned on like a light switch. But apparently it can be turned off. Soon after he wrote the chapter where poor Tandee became the first victim of a mysterious archer, he hit a wall. He had no idea what should happen next. It wasn't like he could type: "and then she was killed" followed by "and then he was killed" and then the ever-so surprising "and then somebody else died". He could have done that, but it would have sucked. And how should they die? The deaths had to be clever and play into the concept that it was all a brutal game predicated by the temptation of shallow commercialism. Nothing he could come up with seemed right.

He felt the slightest tug of panic, which wasn't conducive to creative thought. He popped another Dexedrine, thinking it would sharpen him up and give him more time to think, but with writing there isn't a direct correlation between time spent, and results. An idea could spark to life in a single second, or fizzle after spending three days in futility. It's one of the few activities where hard work doesn't necessarily pay off.

After ten hours of banging away at the laptop (or rather banging his head against the wall) all Derrick had to show for the day was a few pages describing a murder that came to him in a scotch-fueled dream. He finally gave up, poured another drink, and convinced himself that it was simply a bad day. It happened. But given his deadline he couldn't afford many bad days. Rather than continue down another dead-end street he chose instead to go to bed early and get a fresh start in the morning.

It didn't cross his mind that he might be paying another nocturnal visit to *Influence Island*. He'd already forgotten about the previous night's adventure. His only hope was to rest and clear his brain for a run at the story the next day. Hoping for inspiration from his subconscious was the last thing on his mind…

…until he drifted off and once again found himself on the dream beach. He didn't think to look for Tandee's body. This was a new dream and dreams don't necessarily have continuity. Besides, he was much more interested in the two influencers who were playing in the shallow water.

Ree and Bindy were both blonde, both ridiculously pretty, both with 2% body fat which was made obvious in that they were both wearing tiny neon bikinis. Both carried iPhones that they were using to shoot videos of each other.

"Hi guys!" Ree exclaimed. ("Guys" was the universal term for the anonymous masses they spoke to). "Yeah, paradise. Water's deliciously warm, sun is baking me and I'm about to go to the cabana for my third PC!" (Pina Colada for the uninitiated) "Wish you could share it with me!"

She was totally flirting with the "guys" in Cyberland as she skipped through the shallows. She then pointed her phone at Bindy because it was her turn to tempt the "guys" and perhaps to convince some of the girl-guys to follow her link to the site that sold the bikini she was wearing. "I brought about a hundred bikinis. If you wanna see them all, follow my links. And don't forget to like the video!"

Derrick thought, "Nice. Seamless product placement".

The two girls left the shore and bounded straight for Derrick. He had assumed that he was an invisible observer in this particular dream, but the girls proved otherwise.

"C'mon Derrick," Ree called. "Let's play."

Derrick didn't question why they knew his name. Or why he was on the island for that matter. That's not what you did in dreams. You just went with it.

Ree scooped a football up from the sand and tossed it to Bindy. Bindy caught it awkwardly and tossed it back with equal awkwardness. As the two laughed and played catch, Derrick wondered why it was so cute and sexy to see two girls who didn't know how to throw a football, throw a football. He also wondered why they were laughing so much. It didn't look like much fun, but they were sure acting as if they were having a blast. It felt like a forced show, but who was he to question? He decided to take them up on their invitation and ran over to join them.

"Here you go Derrick!" Bindy said and tossed the ball to him. "I'll go long!"

She took off, running across the soft sand like a happy gazelle.

Derrick didn't want her to get too far before he threw the ball, or he'd have to put some juice on it and there would be no way she could catch it. He let her go for about ten yards and tossed it softly with a high arc.

Bindy turned around and stayed focused on the ball as she kept running backward. It hit her right in the hands, and she actually held on.

"Whooo!" Ree yelled and threw her hands in the air. Ree "Whoooed" a lot.

Bindy's momentum took her a few more steps backward until she stumbled and fell on her back. When she hit the sand, she disappeared.

"Bindy?" Ree shouted with a laugh. "What are you doing, girlfriend?"

Derrick and Ree ran to the spot where Bindy had fallen to see a four-foot-deep pit. It was roughly a six-foot square that had been concealed by a thin layer of gauze covered with sand.

They looked down into the pit, and Ree screamed.

It wasn't a "Whooo!" kind of scream.

Bindy lay face up, impaled by a dozen bamboo Punji Sticks. It was a camouflaged booby trap. The foot-long sharp stakes stuck up through her stomach, both thighs and her neck. It was the neck-stick that did her in. Or was about to do her in because she wasn't dead yet. Her eyes were open in shock as she struggled to speak. All that came out was an eruption of blood that cascaded down her chin to add to the pool of blood that was slowly expanding beneath her pierced body.

Derrick noted that she hadn't dropped the football. Impressive.

Ree was less impressed. She instantly went from gleeful to panic stricken.

"Who would do that?" she screamed. "Why?"

She backed away from the death-pit, only to stumble and fall back herself…into a second pit.

She disappeared below with a horrified scream, which was instantly cut off as Derrick heard the sound of multiple spears tearing through flesh. He chose not to look into the second pit. It didn't take a writer's imagination to know what he'd see. His thoughts turned to what he should do next, and the sick realization hit him that he was standing in the middle of a minefield of camouflaged booby traps. How many more were there? Where were they? How could he get off the beach without meeting the same fate as the two girls?

He cautiously made his way back the way he had come. It was the only route he could be certain was clear. He held his breath with every step. There was no way of knowing how close he had come to the same fate as the girls for there was nothing about the expanse of sand that showed any hint of where hidden danger lay. If only he could get back to where the girls had been tossing the football,

He took another tentative step, directly onto the edge of another trap. He didn't lose his balance, but his foot slipped off and plunged down into the pit with all his weight on it. For a brief second he prayed it would land in a space between spikes.

It didn't. The sharp spear shot up through his foot like a piece of shish kabob meat. Derrick had to lean on his other knee in the sand above the pit to stop himself from falling in. The sight of the bamboo skewer that had pierced his foot was gruesome, but there was no pain. After all, this was a dream. Dreams were pain-free. He looked at his foot with the same dispassion that he looked at the football clutched in Ree's almost-dead hands. This wasn't real life. Normal rules didn't apply.

He heard a high-pitched whirring sound that compelled him to look skyward. Hovering overhead was a drone that looked to be observing the gruesome events unfolding on the beach. Was this being controlled by the mysterious host who had lured the influencers to his island?

"Hello Derrick," said a synthesized voice that was broadcast from the drone.

Derrick couldn't tell if it was a man or a woman or a freaking robot.

"I trust you're getting some useful ideas for your book."

Reality came crashing down. Dream over. His eyes sprang open. He was in bed. The clock once again read 4:45. He forced himself to focus and blow away the cobwebs of sleep.

It had happened again. The Gods of Fiction had visited his dreams and given him the next chapter of his book. Derrick chuckled. He didn't think for a second that there was any such thing as Gods of Fiction. Anything that came to him in dreams was his own creation. Who cared if they made themselves known in strange ways? Whatever magic unlocked his subconscious creativity during sleep, he had once again conjured it and he knew where to go next with his story. As frustrating as the day before had been, he was now energized by the knowledge that his next bit of writing would be all about two cute and doomed girls named Bindy and Ree. Though it was still the wee hours of the morning, he was ready to get to work.

He threw off the covers, sat up, jumped out of bed…and crumpled to the floor in pain. The searing hot sensation started in his foot and shot right up his leg to the pain receptors in his brain. Derrick fell to his knees and rolled over onto his butt to take the weight off his foot. He struggled to climb back up onto the bed and turned on the light.

His right foot was covered in blood. He gingerly lifted it onto his opposite thigh to see that a large piece of glass was stuck in the soft underside. The full force of his stepping on the jagged shard had embedded it deep into his flesh. Without thinking, he pulled it out which only increased the blood flow. Unlike in his dream, this hurt. He grabbed one edge of his bedsheet and held it against the painful wound.

The piece of glass was a large chunk that came from the base of the shattered coffee carafe. But how did it get in his bedroom?

Derrick felt nauseous. He hobbled into the bathroom, sat on the edge of the tub, and ran water over the wound. It stung like hell, but the last thing he needed was an infection. He couldn't afford a trip to the emergency room. That would take all day, and he didn't have the time to spare. Instead, he found some gauze and adhesive tape in the medicine cabinet and did his best to slap on a bandage. There was going to be a nasty scar, but who cared about scars on the bottom of your feet?

Derrick limped back into the bedroom like a wounded John McLain and saw that his bed looked like a crime scene. Blood was everywhere. It wasn't until that moment that he made the connection between his accident, and the incident in his dream. It was a grisly coincidence. That was the only way to look at it. What mattered more was that he now had direction. He had to write it before the details of the dream faded.

He only had a week left to deliver.

"Who are you?" yelled Popo12. "Why are you doing this?"

He stood on the sand between the two pits that held the bleeding bodies of Ree and Bindy, staring up at the drone that hovered overhead. He had pulled his injured foot up from the pit and off of the bamboo spear that had skewered him.

"You have a choice," the amplified voice called down from the drone. "You can be a victim, or you can take control."

"I won't kill my friends," Popo12 cried.

"Are they truly your friends?" the voice asked. "Or rivals? There's a million dollars at stake. And your life. Good luck."

The drone powered up and flew away, leaving Popo12 to cradle his damaged foot and cry like the little boy he was.

Derrick finished this last paragraph and saved it with a feeling of satisfaction. It was a good chapter with a couple of nice surprises. It would make for a good read. But as much as the story was progressing and the word count rising, he was writing with the growing fear that he was about to hit another wall. He had killed off three of his eight influencers, which meant the story needed to take a turn. He was running out of victims. Not only was he unsure of where the story was headed next, he hadn't come to grips with the ultimate question. Who was the host? What was his agenda? Was he even a "he"? What would the end game be? It was time to start laying the groundwork for the climax and he hadn't yet come up with one.

As strong of a premise as Chloe224 had come up with, she hadn't finished the story. She wrote a treatment that deliberately didn't answer the question as to why it was all happening. If he resented her for having come up with such a solid concept, he hated her for not finishing it. Did she leave it out intentionally in order to tease potential publishers? Or perhaps she didn't know where the story was headed either. Whatever the reason, Derrick had to come up with his own conclusion and none were coming to mind.

He had the fleeting thought that he could email her and ask in an innocently casual way what she had planned for an ending. Just two writers talking shop. But he ultimately decided it might raise her suspicions, especially if his book came out with the exact same ending she came up with.

His anxiety grew as he hobbled around his house, limping on his damaged foot, wracking his brain. He needed a killer ending. Literally. One that couldn't be predicted. He needed inspiration. He needed to go back to sleep and hope that it came to him in another dream. That's how desperate he had become. He actually felt that his best hope of finishing the book was to have it appear to him in a dream. But anxiety and the lingering effects of the amphetamine weren't conducive to sleep.

As he pace-limped about, an odd sound caught his attention. It was faint, but unmistakable. It sounded like a music box. It took his clouded brain a solid thirty seconds to realize what it was. His cell phone was ringing from the bushes outside his house. As much as he didn't want to talk to anybody, he seized the moment if only to get his mind on to something else for a brief moment of relief. It was a painful walk outside and around the house to get to the phone, but at least he was thinking of something other than his maddening writer's block.

By the time he found the phone it had stopped ringing, but he saw that the call had come from his agent, Randolph.

"Shit."

He knew that whatever Randolph was calling about, it wouldn't be good. There was no way he would announce: "Guess what? The publisher wants to give you another month! And a gift basket!"

He had no intention of returning the call.

The phone rang again. Derrick didn't want to answer but figured he had better not piss off the only guy who was on his side, so he answered.

"Randolph! What's up?" he said, trying to sound upbeat.

"That's what I'm calling to ask you," the agent replied. "Are we on track for next week?"

"Uhhh, yeah sure," Derrick said without much conviction.

Randolph immediately sensed trouble. "Why am I not convinced?"

"No, I'm doing good. Hard to say how far along I am because I don't know how long it'll end up being, but I'm in good shape."

"I'm glad to hear that," Randolph said.

"Seriously, it's good," Derrick said. "I'll definitely make it, but if I had another week or two beyond that it would allow me to really polish it and—"

"Listen to me Derrick," Randolph said in his usual emotionless manner. "Getting you this extra month was unprecedented. I wasn't going to tell you this because I didn't want to load on any more pressure, but they were about to serve you papers. They were ready to sue, and I know who represents them. You do not want to face that individual in court. He'll not only go after the advance; he'll go after damages. I got them to back off because they don't want to drag a bestselling author into a high-profile court battle and it's not because they like you. They don't want the negative press. But at some point they won't care. They gave you a lot of money. A *lot* of money. At this point the bean counters have figured that the advance they get back from you will be greater than whatever sales might still come from *Sweet 30.* So, they chose to sue. I got them to hold off for a month. But legal papers are sitting on somebody's desk, ready to be served. If you miss the deadline by even a day, a call will be made, and you will be going to court. Who knows what will happen beyond that? They will certainly cut off the royalty flow from *Sweet 30* which means you will have no income. There will probably be a settlement but at best you will be ordered to return millions which you apparently no longer have. On top of that there will be the legal fees. This is best-case scenario. My suggestion to you is to forget about being polished. Forget about making it the best it can be. Get the damn manuscript finished so at the very least we can say you delivered. It's your only hope of salvaging something out of this mess, and your life. Do you understand?"

"I understand," Derrick said, barely above a whisper.

"Good. I can't wait to read it. Now, back to work."

"Right, back to work," Derrick said and punched out of the call.

The world was closing in. His brilliant plan, his wonderful-awful idea, was going to fall short. All for the lack of an ending. Being so close to the finish line, the idea of falling on his face this late in the game was gut-wrenching. He had no illusions about suddenly being hit with a brilliant masterstroke of an idea. That simply didn't happen to him.

Or did it?

Desperation drives people to extremes, and as much as it was a dramatically strong word, Derrick was desperate. To the point of irrational thinking.

He limped back inside, grabbed his car keys, and drove his Tesla down to the beach where he once again found his surfer buddy with connections. The guy always bragged about being able to get anything that anybody wanted. From what Derrick had seen it wasn't just a boast.

What Derrick wanted was Butisol. Or Secanol. Or Amytol. He didn't care which as long as it would knock him out and send him back to his other beach. His dream beach.

"Dude, you sure about this?" his buddy asked. "Didn't I just score Dex for you?"

"You provide medical advice too?" Derrick snapped at him. "That part of the service?"

"I'm just saying you don't look so good. You been sleeping?"

"Why do you think I need the drugs?" Derrick said, impatiently. "Do you have anything?"

He did, and soon Derrick was speeding back up the hill with two dozen capsules that he hoped would be his golden ticket into the candy factory.

Soon he was sitting on the edge of his bed, staring at a handful of red pills, unsure of how many he should take. It actually made him chuckle, thinking he probably should have asked his friend for a little of that medical advice. He probably knew the right dose that would put him to sleep, but not knock him out for so long that he wouldn't come back to reality in time to write the rest of the story. He took a wild guess and downed two capsules.

He sat in bed, with his laptop open for one last ditch attempt to come up with an original endgame while he was still conscious. He didn't. Soon the effects of the strong barbiturate kicked in, and Derrick was gone.

"Who the hell is this guy?" Artemis cried out in frustration. He was the outlier of the group. Unlike the others who were chiseled and tanned and low body-fatted, he was a short, pale, tech geek with jet-black dyed hair who excelled at Minecraft and had a legion of followers who loved to watch him play…while paying for the honor.

"The voice coming from that drone sounds kind of like Siri to me," Alexandra said.

"I wish," Cash said with a snicker. "Hey Siri, tell us who you are and then kill yourself."

The five remaining influencers were huddled together, sitting in a clearing not far from the beach, surrounded by thick, tropical foliage. They knew the situation. They had discovered the bodies. But they didn't know what to do about it.

Derrick stood back from the group waiting anxiously to see what his brilliant and creative subconscious would concoct as the endgame for these idiots. It was different than before. In the previous dreams he took part in the events, though the idea of it being a manifestation of the story he was writing didn't play a part until he woke up. This time he was an unseen observer and fully aware of what was at stake. He knew the players. He knew the situation. He needed to learn from it. He wished he had a way to take notes so as not to forget a thing.

Most of all, he hoped he wouldn't wake up before he got his answers. He wished he had taken another pill. Or two.

"We'll stay here, together," Cash whined. "That way he can't pick us off one by one."

At least Derrick thought it was the character he named Cash. He didn't look much different than Tandee. Except that Tandee was missing an eye and had an arrow stuck in his head.

"We're supposed to be home tomorrow," Alexandra said. "Somebody's going to come looking for us."

"They're going to find bloody corpses," Popo12 cried. "We're all dead."

Popo12 was a muscular six foot two with long, beach-blonde hair who looked as though he could be in the WWF but was more known for his make-up tutorials.

"Shut up, Popo," Cash barked.

"For the last time, it's Popo TWELVE!" Popo12 whined.

"Oh, for fuck's sake," Cash said. "What is your real name?"

Popo12 dropped his head and whispered, "It's Frank."

"Frank?" Cash said with a snicker. "What are you, sixty?"

Sailor, the youngest of the group who was eighteen but looked and sounded no more than twelve, was also the most mature. Her followers looked to her for dating advice, and break-up advice. She jumped to her feet.

"Stop!" she shouted in frustration. "If we fight each other we definitely won't survive."

She circled the sitting group, establishing her position as the alpha.

"Popo's right—"

"Popo TWELVE!"

"Or Frank," Cash said with a smirk.

"Shut…the fuck…up!" Sailor bellowed.

Derrick chuckled. This was all character gold.

"Whatever his name is, he's right," Sailor said. "When people come looking for us they're going to find a bunch of good-looking bodies if we don't get smart, fast."

"So, what do we do?" Artemis asked.

Sailor continued her loop around the group.

"He wants us to fight each other like this is some kind of Hunger Games," Sailor said. "I say we do the opposite. We fight back. Like Cash said, if we're together he can't pick us off one by one. Let's stop acting like victims in some cheesy horror movie who make all the wrong choices and start acting like—"

Sailor took another step, her foot triggered a snare that wrapped around her ankle and yanked her up into the air, feet first. The others watched helplessly as she was swung across the clearing, upside down, and was violently impaled on a long spear that had been camouflaged on the edge of the trees. The spear pierced her small frame directly through her heart, which was now on the outside of her body and stuck on the end of the spear, still beating. She died with her mouth open as if ready to complete her last sentence.

Sailor would no longer be giving dating advice.

It made Derrick absolutely giddy.

"Awesome," he said to himself. "Sail on Sailor."

Cash lost it.

"I am not going to die on this stupid fucking island!" he screamed.

"What are we going to do?" Artemis said with remarkable cool, seeing as they'd just seen someone impaled only a few short yards away and who still hung there with blood pooling beneath her.

"I don't give a shit about what you all are going to do," Cash screamed. "I'm taking care of me."

"What does that mean?" Popo12 asked. "Are you going to try and kill us?"

"I don't know what it means," Cash whined. "But whatever I have to do to stay alive, I'm doing it. Screw you all."

A short sharp popping sound made everyone jump. Everyone but Cash. He stood still, frozen in place with a red hole in the middle of his forehead where the bullet had entered. The back of his head wasn't as clean. His skull had been blown open into a gaping-red flower of an exit wound. He stood there with wide eyes as if stunned by what had just happened. In truth he had no idea. He was already dead. His knees buckled and he fell in a heap.

Artemis and Popo12 looked to Alexandra.

She stood with her feet planted wide, holding a Walther semi-automatic in both hands. She was still pointing it at the spot where Cash once stood, as if ready to fire again.

"Nice shot," Derrick thought. "Right between the eyes. Poetic, sort of."

There was a long, frozen moment. Alexandra's hands started shaking. Whatever adrenalin had given her the juice to pull the trigger was draining quickly. She was in shock.

Artemis and Popo12 exchanged, "What do we do now?" looks.

"It's okay," Artemis said soothingly to Alexandra. "I get it. He totally lost it. It was either him or us."

Alexandra nodded quickly.

"He…he…was going to come after us," she said. "I didn't have a choice."

"It was totally the right move," Artemis said calmly and took a cautious step toward her.

"W… where did you get the gun?" Popo12 asked.

"It was in my welcome basket," Alexandra said with a quivering voice. "Underneath the oranges and the tanning butter."

"How come I didn't get one?" Popo12 said petulantly.

Artemis slowly reached out toward the gun.

"You did good," he said. "But I think you're in shock. Let's be safe, okay?"

Alexandra looked to him, grateful that he offered some sense of sanity. She nodded.

"I didn't want to kill him," she said. "But I don't want to die."

"None of us do," Artemis said. "We're going to get out of here."

He gently touched the gun. Alexandra looked at him and didn't give it up right away. Artemis smiled as if to assure her that everything was going to be okay. She relaxed and let him take the gun from her.

"Thank you," she said with relief. "We're going to get out of here, aren't we?"

"Well," Artemis said. "Some of us are."

With one smooth, quick move he took the gun, stuck the muzzle against Alexandra's temple, and pulled the trigger.

And then there were two.

"Ahhh!" Popo12 screamed and fell to his knees.

Alexandra had no idea that she had been betrayed. The last thought she had was that they might have a chance to fight back and get home. Then the lights went out and she hit the sand a moment after pieces of her skull and brain.

"Excellent," Derrick thought. "Did *not* see that coming."

Popo12 backed away in fear. "Why did you do that!" he cried out.

Artemis stuck the pistol in his waist band.

"She was unstable," he said, all business. "She killed Cash. You don't think she'd do the same thing to either of us?"

"No! I don't know. Maybe."

"Take a breath Frank," Artemis said. "It's just you and me now."

"And you've got a gun," Popo12 said.

"I'm not going to shoot you. This is for protection. With just two of us we've got a better chance of getting out of this."

"How?"

"Let's get to the dock. If the yacht is still there we'll take it."

"You know how to drive a yacht?" Popo12 asked.

"Seriously?" Artemis asked. "That's your biggest worry? We'll figure it out."

"Yeah, yeah, you're right," Popo12 said. He was still in shock and trying to gather his thoughts. "Let's just get there."

"There's no telling how many other booby traps are between here and the dock. We gotta move, carefully."

Popo12 nodded in agreement. He had no choice. Either he went, or Artemis would turn the gun on him. Together, they walked cautiously out of the clearing, away from the kill zone and three dead influencers.

"Gold," Derrick thought as he followed the two along the jungle trail. "Absolute gold."

His enthusiasm was quickly tempered by the fleeting thought that if he woke up at that point, he wouldn't know how the story ended. He somehow had to make sure he'd stay asleep. But how? All he could do was keep going, and watching, and hoping that the ending would be as exciting as the last chapter and that he wouldn't wake up before the conclusion. He once again wished he had taken more pills.

"We're done," Popo12 cried as he stepped out of the jungle and on to the long dock.

The yacht was gone. He and Artemis had made it to the dock without incident, much to Derrick's disappointment. He kept expecting another surprise to pop up and catch one of them in a snare or trigger a deadly booby trap, but the journey across the island was uneventful, even with Popo12 limping on a damaged foot.

"There's a motorboat," Artemis pointed out.

Sure enough, a small speed boat was tied up to the dock.

"I can drive that no problem," he added.

He went straight for the small boat. Popo12 limped after him while constantly glancing back over his shoulder, expecting an attack. He didn't see or acknowledge Derrick, which wasn't surprising. Derrick's role in this dream-drama was omniscient observer, not player.

Artemis put the pistol down on the dock and leapt into the boat.

"Yes!" he exclaimed. "The key's in the ignition. We're outta here."

"To go where?" Popo12 asked.

"We passed a couple of small islands on the way in. Hopefully one of them will have cell service. Or a land line. The main thing is we've got to get out of this kill-zone. The gas tank is full so—"

Artemis looked up to Popo12, and square into the muzzle of the Walther.

"Oh, yeah!" Derrick exclaimed with glee. "End game."

Popo12 had picked up the weapon and had Artemis in his sites.

"Seriously?" Artemis asked, more annoyed than afraid. "We're about to get out of here."

"Only two of us left," Popo12 said. "Whoever is left will be a million dollar's richer. I don't know about you, but I don't plan on making TikTok videos the rest of my life. We've all got a short shelf life. Some of us shorter than others."

"Think about it," Artemis said with remarkable calm. "Even if the host makes good, how are you going to explain this to the authorities? There have been six murders. Seven if you pull that trigger. You think that guy's gonna write you a check for a million bucks and let you go? Even if he does, you'll be the only survivor with seven bodies. If that guy is as powerful as he seems, he could disappear and leave you holding the bag. Or the smoking gun. Don't do this, Popo Twelve. Frank. Put the gun down and let's leave together so we can back up each other's story."

Derrick looked between the two of them. The tension was electric. It felt like the perfect climax to the thriller, and he was ecstatic. He couldn't wait to see how it would play out.

"Don't wake up," he whispered to himself.

Popo12 softened. He nodded slowly.

"You're right," he said. "This is going to be a mess no matter what happens."

He lowered the gun.

"Good move," Artemis said.

Popo12 then quickly brought the gun back up and added, "But I'd rather have to clean it up with a million bucks, so I'll take that chance."

He pulled the trigger.

Click.

The gun was empty.

He pulled the trigger two more times. Two more clicks.

Derrick laughed. "Oh man, this just keeps getting better!"

Artemis calmly climbed out of the boat and onto the dock.

"I didn't trust you, Frank," he said. "I emptied the clip. Guess I'm a pretty good judge of character."

"I'm sorry, man," Popo12 said, trying to laugh it off. "That wasn't me. I was desperate."

"You sure didn't seem desperate," Artemis said. "Sounded like you had it all figured out."

"I was out of my mind. I'm sorry, I really am."

"Give me the gun, Frank," Artemis said.

"Here, here, take it," Popo12 said and handed him the weapon.

Artemis took it and stepped back a few paces. While he moved, he popped the clip, loaded a single bullet, and slammed it back into the grip.

"Whoa, wait. Are you going to shoot me?" Popo12 asked on the edge of panic.

"No. You're going to get in the boat and go."

"I am?" Popo12 asked, confused. "What about you?"

"I'm pissed," Artemis replied. "I'm staying here and I'm going after that guy. The prey is about to become the hunter."

Derrick couldn't believe the luck. What a twist! This story wasn't over! There was still another chapter to be written! Or for him to write.

"You're crazy," Popo12 said.

"Maybe," Artemis said. "But you're right, we have a short shelf life. If I've got to go out I'm going on my terms. Now go!"

Popo12 didn't have to be told twice and quickly boarded the small boat. He turned the engine over and the powerful outboard growled to life. Artemis unhooked the aft line from the cleat on the dock, then the bow line. Popo12 was free and floating.

"Where do I go?" he asked.

"Do I look like I give a shit?" Artemis asked. "You tried to murder me."

"That's fair," Popo12 said. "At least point me in the right direction."

Artemis thought about it for a second, then pointed north.

"We passed an island about a half hour north of here before we sighted this one. That's a start."

"Thanks man, As soon as I get somewhere I'll start screaming and get help for you."

"You do that," Artemis said without much enthusiasm.

"Good luck," Popo12 said.

He gunned the throttle. The engine roared and within seconds the small boat was speeding away from the island. Artemis stood on the edge of the dock, watching the wake spread as the craft grew smaller. He calmly put his pistol in the waist band of his belt, and reached into a front pocket, pulling out a cell phone.

Derrick didn't understand what he was doing. There was no cell service on the island. What was the point? He hoped it wasn't one of those dream-incongruities that defied logic. He would have to somehow justify how cell service had suddenly appeared.

Artemis held up the phone, made some inputs with his thumb, then looked up at the departing Popo12. He hesitated a moment, held the phone up high, and made one more input.

Instantly, the boat exploded as if there was a bomb on board. Because there was. A pillar of fire shot straight up from the doomed craft as a spray of fiberglass, plastic and Popo12 blossomed out to either side. The blast was so intense that when the smoke dissipated there was nothing left but small debris and some random gore floating on the water's surface.

Derrick watched with wide eyes. It was a complete surprise, and a great twist.

"I freaking love it," he said aloud.

A whining sound came from overhead. The drone had returned. The brutal game was over. There was a sole survivor. Was the host coming to offer congratulations? To wire the million bucks into Artemis's bank account? Or maybe Artemis was as doomed as the others?

The story just kept on getting more interesting.

The drone appeared from over the palm trees, headed for the dock. It went straight to Artemis and hovered above his head. If Artemis was worried about it, he didn't show it. He lifted his phone, input something, then spoke into the phone.

"And then there was one," came the robotic voice from the drone.

Artemis' voice.

Though the events were being created by Derrick's subconscious, he didn't understand what was happening until Artemis turned toward him. He spoke into the phone again, and his robotic-filtered voice came from the drone.

"You look confused, Derrick," the drone voice said. "Why? This is your story."

Derrick was no longer an unseen bystander.

The drone landed on the dock and the propellers stopped spinning.

Artemis lowered his phone and gave Derrick a big smile.

"It's a good twist," Artemis said. "Congratulations."

"A celebration is in order!" came another voice.

It was one Derrick recognized, but not from the story. He spun around to see a man stepping on to the dock with a silver tray that held a champagne bottle and three crystal glasses.

"Randolph?" Derrick exclaimed.

"I'm so happy to be sharing this triumphant moment with you," the agent said.

The gray-haired gent placed the tray down onto the railing and proceeded to pour the champagne.

"You can't be here," Derrick said. "The story isn't over yet."

"But it's so close," Artemis said. "This could go so many different ways. You've already got a classic twist. One of the victims turned out to be the villain. Question is, why? Was I some anti-social nerd who never got the respect of the popular kids and wanted revenge for a lifetime of ridicule? Or maybe it's a cautionary tale about the shallow world of on-line influencers who don't actual produce anything of value, but simply reflect the work of others? Maybe it's as simple as an aggressive influencer wanting to get rid of his competition. Or it might be about what Popo Twelve said. We have a short shelf life. If we want to make a lasting impression, we have to do something that's actually memorable…like mass murder. It's not exactly noble but it's certainly not a disposable concept that's quickly forgotten. So many classic tropes could work. You just have to figure out how to work one into the story. You can do that, right?"

"Sure," Derrick said, sounding anything but.

Randolph handed out the glasses of champagne.

"Of course he can, but I don't think he'd use one of those trite denouements. Derrick is going to come up with something completely different. Something original. Something meaningful that won't be forgotten the moment after the last page is turned. Isn't that so, Derrick?"

"Uh, yeah, of course. Exactly."

"After all, this is your story, right?" Randolph asked.

Derrick looked the old gent straight in the eye. The look he got back was steely, and oddly knowing. Did Randolph know the truth about where the concept of the story came from? They held each other's gaze for a long moment, then Derrick laughed. Of course, Randolph knew the truth. This wasn't reality. This was his dream, so everyone involved knew what he knew. But that wouldn't change things in real life. He was very close to completing the story. All would be right with his world, as long as he came up with the ending.

"Yes it's my story," Derrick said.

"And therefore, you know how it will end, don't you?"

"I do," Derrick said.

Randolph held eye-contact with Derrick as if searching for the unspoken truth.

"As I suspected," Randolph said with a sigh, then raised his glass. "Let's toast. To the completion of the triumphant second novel of the bestselling author Derrick Hensley."

Randolph's comment gave Derrick pause. Could he come up with a worthy enough ending? Or any ending?

"Drink up, Derrick," Randolph said with rare joviality. "Enjoy the fruits of your hard work."

Derrick lifted his glass and downed the champagne. The effervescent drink burned his throat, as champagne always did. It also went straight to his head. Derrick felt himself getting lightheaded and faintly nauseous. The dock seemingly upended beneath his feet, and he had to fight to keep his balance.

His final conscious moment was the sight of Randolph looking down at him with a smile and saying, "Take solace in the fact that no one will ever know."

With that unsettling thought, the dream was over.

"I'm his literary agent," Randolph said. "He had a manuscript due today. I came by to make sure he sent it. I had no idea this had happened."

If Randolph was upset, he didn't show it. Then again, Randolph rarely displayed emotion.

"Was there a note?" he asked.

"Nope," the Coroner said. "Could have been intentional. Could have been accidental. The toxicology report should tell us more."

Derrick Hensley lay still in his bed. The caked vomit around his mouth was a solid giveaway as to his fate. The envelope next to his bedside had two Seconal capsules left...out of the two dozen he started with.

"Would he have had any reason to try and off himself?" the Coroner asked.

"He's been under a lot of pressure," Randolph said. "I suppose he could have handled it this way. He was a passionate man. He put his entire soul into his work."

The Coroner zipped up the body bag and two assistants hefted Derrick's remains onto a gurney for the beginning of his final journey.

Randolph's cell phone chirped.

"Excuse me," he said to the Coroner and backed away from the grisly scene. He answered the call with a perfunctory, "Yes?"

He listened, while keeping one eye on the Coroner and his assistants as they wheeled his ex-client away. When he spoke to the caller it was with the same dispassionate tone that was his trademark.

"I understand, it's disappointing," Randolph said. "It was a wonderful idea, but I have no doubt you will come up with another."

As he listened to the caller, he stepped back to the bed where Derrick's laptop rested, still open. He sat on the edge of the bed and tapped the touch pad, bringing it back to life.

"Inspiration is a fickle thing," Randolph told the caller. "You never know where it will come from. Relax and let the story find you. I have no doubt that you'll hit upon an equally wonderful idea. Perhaps even better than your last."

Randolph scrolled through Derrick's files until he came upon the one titled: *Influence Island*.

"Be patient. Let the idea come to you. Have faith that it will. Who knows? It might even appear to you in a dream."

Randolph highlighted the *Influence Island* file and deleted it. He then searched for any emails to or from Chloe224.

"No need to thank me," Randolph said. "My thanks will come when you hit upon your next wonderful idea. When you do, I'll be waiting."

Randolph highlighted every last one of the Chloe224 emails, including the one with the *"Dangerous Influence"* attachment, and deleted those as well.

"I look forward to hearing from you…Chloe," Randolph said and punched out of the call.

The Coroner returned and Randolph stood to meet him.

"There's nothing good to say at a time like this," the Coroner said. "But if he was as troubled as you say, let's hope his soul has gone to a better place."

"His soul is most definitely in another place," Randolph said. "Though I doubt he would agree that it's a better place. Good day."

The Corner gave Randolph a puzzled look.

Randolph responded with a quick smile, then skirted around the coroner and exited the home of Derrick Hensley for the final time.

<u>THE END</u>

THE
BLOOD CODE

The elderly man stepped into the sparse, darkened room and was instantly hit with the musty smell of a damp basement. He hesitated a moment, letting his eyes adjust to the dark, as the heavy door was shut tight behind him. The sound of a lock being thrown into place gave him a familiar and uncomfortable chill.

"No need for that," he called out. "I ain't leaving until the job is done."

He scanned the large basement room to see a narrow cot, a table with a small lamp that gave off just enough light to create shadows, and hundreds of books that were neatly stacked along one wall. For a dank basement, it was remarkably clean.

"You got a library down here," the old man said to no one. "Not enough light to read by, though."

"I manage," came a soft, friendly voice from a dark corner.

The old man jumped in surprise and shot a look behind him to see a young man sitting in a comfortable easy chair tucked into a corner, with his legs crossed casually. His elbows were perched on the arms of the chair; his hands rested on his lap.

"Wouldn't hurt to open a window," the old man said. "Let in some light."

"Wouldn't it?" the young man asked.

Even in the gloom the old man could see that he was smiling. The guy looked as though he had stepped out of an L.L. Bean catalog. He was thin, clean shaven with neatly groomed hair and wore a polo shirt and jeans.

"Nice place you got here," the old man said. "Not sure why you're spending time in the basement."

"Tell me sir," the younger man said, ignoring the comment. "Why is it that you've come here?"

His formal way of speaking felt odd to the old man, but he wasn't about to question the younger man's diction as well as his living habits.

"Fella said he needed a strong back to help move some things. I'm guessing it's these books. Though you look plenty capable of doing it yourself."

"You're telling me that out of all the sturdier men who loiter outside of the Home Depot looking for work, he chose you?"

"I ain't as frail as I look," the man said with a touch of indignance. "Not as old, neither. I'm forty-two."

"Forty-two?" the younger man said, not hiding his surprise.

"And each year's been harder than the last," the old (ish) man replied. "Life takes its toll."

"Ah," the young man said as if he'd heard an answer that made everything come clear. "I'm guessing you don't have a permanent home, or a family to rely on."

"Good guess."

"And perhaps there's been some drug use?"

This made the man stiffen. Who gave this college boy the right to judge him?

"Never," the old man snapped. "I may have fallen on hard times and knocked back my share of the grape, but I ain't never touched that shit. Never will, neither."

The young man stood up fluidly, as if floating out of the chair. He walked slowly toward the visitor.

"Forgive me, I wasn't passing judgement. I simply need to know. The alcohol I have no issue with. But pharmaceuticals disagree with me. I now understand exactly why you were chosen."

"Let's stop the chit-chat so I can get to work," the man said curtly.

"Agreed," the younger man said. "No more chit-chat."

He leapt forward with such a sudden burst of speed that the older visitor had no time to react or register what was happening. It was the luckiest break he'd had in his forty-two years for he didn't experience even a moment of fear. It took no more than ten seconds from the moment the younger man made his move until his victim lay on the basement floor; his throat ripped open. It took another few seconds for his heart to stop beating in the futile attempt to pump blood through a system that had already been sucked dry.

The young man stood up, flush with the energy that had come from the much-needed feast.

"You lied to me," the young man said to the corpse. "Your associates at the Home Depot were sharing a joint. The taste is unmistakable."

He gently dabbed a drop of blood from his lower lip, took a deep satisfied breath then walked back to his comfortable chair and sat down, satiated.

"Done!" he called out.

~~~~

"Eat," Kira said to her father as she placed another pancake on the tall stack she'd already put in front of him. "You're losing too much weight."

Carter Breem was a proud dad. His wife had passed when Kira was only six years old, and it had been just the two of them since. He had to be both Mom and Dad to the young girl and by all accounts, had done a stellar job. Though Carter had the final say in all matters, he listened to Kira's opinions and more often than not gave in to whatever whim she had gotten into her head if only because she always presented a well-thought-out argument. And besides, he hated saying no to his one and only child.
~~~~

Rather than raising a spoiled, entitled kid, he somehow managed to help guide her into becoming a self-sufficient, confident, and creative young woman. His wife would have been pleased, mostly because Kira was a mini version of her. She even had his wife's long, auburn hair and fair skin. On that morning she wore her mother's *Ghost In The Machine* sweatshirt, which made the uncanny similarity complete. The one difference was that unlike his wife, Kira swam in the oversized sweatshirt, making her appear much younger than fourteen.

"Yes ma'am," Carter said with a chuckle and tucked into the stack. He didn't have much of an appetite but didn't want to disappoint Kira after she'd gone through the trouble of cooking.

"How are you feeling today?" Carter asked.

Kira gave a non-committal shrug and sat down next to him while chomping on a piece of bacon.

"Same," she said. "Little tired. I've got a check-up after school."

Carter's expression fell.

"I didn't know," he said with alarm. "I'm booked with patients all day."

"Dad, it's okay. I'll take the bus."

This made Carter smile, and also gave him a touch of sadness. His daughter was becoming more self-sufficient by the second.

"Of course," he said. "Take notes."

"Nah, I never ask the right questions. You can talk to him after." She popped to her feet, kissed her father on the top of his head and said, "Gotta get ready for school. You can clean up."

With that, she bounded out of the room.

"Thanks for breakfast," Carter called after her.

Her response was a casual, over the shoulder wave. Carter watched her scamper off, in awe of her boundless energy. Once she had disappeared up the stairs, he quickly dumped the pancakes into the garbage disposal and buzzed the evidence.

He truly wasn't hungry.

~~~~
~~~~

"Just a slight pinch," Carter said as he expertly inserted the needle into the vein of his patient. "Followed by a slight burn. It won't last long."

The elderly woman closed her eyes and took a deep breath. She hated needles.

Doctor Carter Breem was a General Practitioner with an old-school practice that he ran out of a wing he had specially built onto his house. It was as modern and well-equipped as any that could be found in a professional medical building. His patients appreciated the homey, old-school vibe. He'd built the office shortly after his wife got sick so he could be close-by when needed. He continued to see patients there long after his wife passed in order to be around for Kira. He hated the idea of a hired caregiver raising his daughter for he wanted to be a strong presence in her life. He limited the number of patients he would see in a day, which allowed him to make her lunch, play with her in the back yard and attend school functions. In many ways he was the ideal father, and the community recognized it. He had the support of every other parent in school. In a pinch he could call on any of them for help. Though he rarely needed it.

He was an old-looking fifty, with not-so-prematurely gray hair and a slight build that would have benefitted from some exercise. The past decade had been tough on him. His face bore the deep lines of sadness and fatigue. His one joy was Kira. She kept him going.

"All good?" Carter asked his patient.

The woman smiled with relief.

"Hardly felt it," she declared triumphantly. "You've got a good touch."

Carter's practice wasn't a taxing one. He dealt with common colds, yearly physicals, and the occasional injury. Mostly he served as the trusted referral resource for patients who needed more specialized care.

The woman sitting in his exam room wasn't one of his regular patients. He had discovered her that morning sleeping in a grimy tent under a highway overpass near the center of the city.

"Take a deep breath," Carter instructed gently. "How do you feel?"

"Same as before you jabbed me," the woman said with a wheezy cackle.

She was dressed in filthy jeans and a stretched-out sweater that was once royal blue. Or maybe it was forest green. The layers of grime made it difficult to tell. On her feet she wore an ancient pair of black high-top Chuck Taylors with soles that barely clung to the canvas uppers. The clothes seemed more fitting for a teenager, though the woman had to have been in her sixties. Her long gray hair was matted and most probably hadn't been brushed out since Obama was in the White House. The pungent aroma she gave off was not a pleasant one.

"When do I get paid?" the woman asked.

"Right away," Carter answered. "But I want you to relax here for a few minutes. This is a new vaccine. I want to make sure there are no harsh side effects."

"Better not be," the woman snapped. "Fifty bucks ain't worth getting sick for."

"It's worth the risk," Carter said with a chuckle. "You might never be sick again and you'll be fifty bucks richer to boot."

"So you say," the woman said. "What's supposed to happen now?"

"Hard to know exactly," Carter answered. "That's why it's called an experiment. You might not feel a thing, or you might have a slight allergic reaction. The real test will be over time. I'm going to have to check up on you every week or so and—"

"For fifty bucks a pop," the woman said sharply.

"Correct. I'll pay you fifty dollars every time I bring you here for an exam and to take a blood sample to see if—"

The woman suddenly sat bolt upright. Her face went blank and her back stiffened. It was such a dramatic change that Carter pushed back in his seat in surprise.

"What?" he asked.

"I…I…don't know," the woman said. "I'm suddenly feeling all hot inside, like I got a fever."

"What else?" Carter asked, his excitement growing.

The woman's eyes glazed over, and she lost focus. Her attention was completely on her body and the alien feelings she was experiencing. She made two fists, clenching and unclenching while taking deep breaths as if each intake of air brought on a wave of newfound strength.

And she laughed.

"I feel, strong," she said with a grin. "Like when I was a kid."

Carter deflated. That wasn't what he wanted to hear.

Her eyes blazed with excitement. Though she spoke of feeling intensely hot, her skin had gone porcelain white.

Carter slowly pushed his rolling chair away from her and stood up. While continuing to face her, he backed toward the door of the exam room.

"I like this, Doc," she said, breathless. "I really like this. I'm suddenly feeling kind of…horny. Haven't felt that in a while. Can't say I ever felt it quite like this. It's like I want something. Bad. Not sure if it's sex, though."

Carter's back hit the wall next to the door where there was a row of electric switches. He knew what he had to do. He'd done it before, but it never got any easier. He felt sorry for the woman, and for himself because this meant he had failed once again. He had no idea how far away he was from success, or if he'd ever achieve it. All he knew for sure was that it wasn't then.

"Doc?" the woman asked in a voice that was more like the hungry purr of a predator than that of an elderly homeless woman who lived under a freeway bridge. "I know where this is going."

Carter saw the look in her eyes. He'd seen it before. The whites had a slight red tint. Her pupils had dilated. Her gaze was locked on him. Her prey. He too knew where this was going, but it wasn't where the woman expected.

She stood up in an oddly sensuous manner. If there was anything that surprised Carter it was that it had happened so quickly. That was different. Did that mean he was getting closer to cracking the code? Or chasing an elusive shadow down an endless dark alleyway toward yet another dead end?

The woman walked slowly toward him. Moving with confidence. Stalking. She knew what she wanted to do. What she had to do. She had changed, and with the change came centuries of learned behavior.

"I need this," she said.

"I know," Carter said, and flipped one of the switches on the wall. "I'm sorry."

The louvres covering an overhead skylight snapped open. Bright, noonday sunlight streamed down on them. The woman looked up, stunned, as though she had been splashed with a wave of muriatic acid. She let out an unearthly howl of surprise and pain. Her last conscious effort was to look at Carter with pleading eyes.

"What is happening to me?"

It made Carter's heart ache. If there was any solace to take it was that her pain would be short lived. But she would never know just how much her death would help Carter to perfect his serum.

"Thank you," was the most he could offer.

The woman's head cocked to the side like a curious dog as if to ask; "Why?" because she could no longer form words. With one last gruesome spasm, she convulsed and fell to the floor. By the time her body hit, it was nothing but ash. Her terrified scream echoed, outliving her physical self.

Carter stared at the pile of gray ash for a long moment, said a quick prayer, then went to the closet to retrieve the broom and dustpan he had used far too many times.

~~~~

"It was yet another soul-crushing failure, I assume."

The man's voice came from an intercom speaker that was set in the wall next to a heavy, wooden door in the basement beneath the medical wing of Carter's house.
~~~~

Carter stood with his hand on the wall for support. He hadn't fully recovered his composure after having lived through the horror of having to destroy the homeless woman whose ashes he had just dumped into the outdoor garbage bin normally used for grass clippings. As if that experience wasn't bad enough, he now had to deal with the smug criticism from his guest on the other side of the door.

"May I ask?" the voice said. "Was death instantaneous? Or was there first a turn?"

"She turned," Carter said, though it pained him to say so. He wasn't sure why he answered. It wasn't as though his guest was trying to help him.

"I pity you, Doctor," the man said with a sigh. "Truly. Your attempts to apply science to a decidedly un-scientific situation is a fool's errand. I can't count how many times I've told you that. How many more failures must you endure before you accept the truth?"

"I'm not here for a lecture, Hoagland," Carter said.

"I know why you're here," the man, Hoagland, replied. "I'm inclined to deny your request."

Carter hadn't expected that. Hoagland had been his "guest" for nearly a year and not once had he refused Carter's requests. Carter tried not to show panic. He kept his voice calm and reasonable.

"And why is that?" he asked.

"Because I don't appreciate you making me a party to murder."

Carter hadn't expected that either.

"Seriously?" he said with a laugh. "That's an odd sentiment coming from a monster."

"I beg to differ," Hoagland said with indignation. "I have no say in the matter. You, on the other hand, have choices."

"I don't see that I have a choice," Carter said.

"Ahh, and that brings us back to your fool's errand. You're a learned man, Doctor Breem. I respect that. And clever. But your passion has clouded your thinking. You assuage your guilt by convincing yourself that your victims have no value. They are the wretched whose wasted lives are filled with filth and misery. That's how you see them, no? You may have gone so far as to believing you're actually doing them a favor by ending their suffering; and their sacrifice is warranted because it may lead to a greater good. But you are wrong, on all counts. When I kill, there is a practical purpose. It is no different than slaughtering a cow. If I could survive without the killing, I would. But you? Your white whale doesn't exist. Your quest is doomed to fail which means the killings are for naught. So, tell me, who is the monster in this scenario?"

Nothing that Hoagland said was new to Carter. He was all too aware of the dilemma, and it consumed him. The guilt was enormous. But it wasn't enough to stop him.

"Release me," Hoagland said. "Perhaps there is something I can do to help you."

"The moment I release you, I'm a dead man," Carter said.

"Believe me, Doctor," Hoagland said with a dismissive laugh. "I bear you no ill will. My stay here will ultimately be for no more than a blip of time. Once I move on I will think back on this sojourn as having been nothing more than a tragic diversion. If I were considering revenge, allowing you to continue living with your pain would be a far harsher sentence than if I put an end to your torment. Death would offer merciful relief."

"Unless I succeed," Carter said.

"You will not," Hoagland shot back. "I implore you, for your own sanity, accept reality and release me."

A sane man would understand that Hoagland's reasoning was sound.

Carter could no longer be considered a sane man.

"Are you going to refuse my request?" Carter asked.

Hoagland took a deep, tired breath for he realized his words were having no impact.

"It's done and waiting for you, as usual," Hoagland said. "Along with a housekeeping chore you need to attend to."

Carter felt as though a weight had been lifted. There was still hope. He checked the two small lights that were above the intercom speaker. Red lights indicated locked doors. Both were red. He reached for the keypad imbedded in the wooden door and entered a four-digit code. One of the two red lights turned green.

He opened the door and stepped inside…

…without realizing that for the last few minutes he was being watched.

Kira was peeking around the corner at the bottom of the stairs that led up to his exam room. She had come to the office to ask her father what she should cook for dinner and was drawn to the sound of his voice coming from the basement. Normally she would have announced her arrival, but when she hit the bottom of the stairs, the sound of the second man's voice coming through the intercom stopped her. Who was he? Why was he in the basement behind a locked door? Kira hadn't heard the entire conversation, but it was enough for her to understand that her father was keeping a secret from her. When he disappeared through the door, Kira headed back up the stairs, her mind racing, wondering what she had just heard and how she'd ask her father about it.

Leaving when she did would prove to be a wise move. It prevented her from witnessing what then happened.

Beyond the door Carter had stepped through was a four-foot square anteroom. On the far side was a second locked door, hence the second red light. It was the same door that was closed and locked behind the man who Carter had recruited from Home Depot with the promise of work. It was the same man whose bloodless body now lay at Carter's feet. It didn't shock or repulse him. He had become numb to the process. It was a necessary evil. Hoagland had to feed. If not, he would no longer be able to provide Carter with what he needed.

The old man lay face down. which was a slight relief. Carter hated seeing the bloodless faces. Resting on the man's back was a plastic medical bag filled with blood. Hoagland's blood. The sight of the nearly black blood gave Carter a surge of relief and hope. With each new bag he received he was hit with a boost of renewed confidence that he would find the answers he so desperately sought. He felt certain that he would eventually crack the code. Science would prevail. In spite of what Hoagland thought, he knew there was a white whale out there, ready to be harpooned. Perhaps it would happen with this next pint of precious blood.

But first there were housekeeping chores. He had to bag the victim and eventually transport his body to the crematorium where he would pay an exorbitant sum for its disposal, and the discretion of the owner of the facility. While the homeless man would not be missed, the discovery of a bloodless corpse wouldn't bode well for the future of his work.

If Kira had stuck around a few minutes longer she would have made that discovery for she would have witnessed the grisly sight of her father dragging an already rotting corpse out of their basement.

~~~~

Kira knew better than to disturb her father when he was in his office with a patient or during the times he was focused on his research. Though his office was technically at home, when he was there he was at work and Carter implored her to respect that. That was fine with Kira, though lately she took note that he was spending far more time doing research than seeing patients. But she didn't think much about it. Why should she? Her father's research didn't interest her in the slightest. Fourteen-year-olds had far more important things on their minds.

That changed when she heard the conversation in the basement.

She had never challenged her father, about anything. Now she had questions, and she wasn't entirely sure how to ask them.

"Dad?" Kira said tentatively as she peeked her nose into his office.

Carter was sitting at the high counter in his exam room, surrounded by the accessories common to scientific research: a microscope, slides, a calculator, a centrifuge, bottles of liquids, and racks holding test tubes that were filled by what looked like dark blood. There were pads of paper filled with data that appeared as gibberish to civilians.

"Dad?" Kira called again.
~~~~

Carter jolted upright, as if shocked from deep thought.

"Kira!" he snapped. "What do you want?"

Kira took an involuntary step back. For that one instant, her father seemed like a stranger. His eyes were bloodshot and watery, his perfectly combed hair looked anything but, as if he'd been pulling at it.

It took a second for Carter to focus and register the frightened look on Kira's face. He instantly softened and Kira saw her father return.

"I'm sorry sweetheart. You know how I get when I'm concentrating."

"Yeah, I know," Kira said.

The initial shock of seeing her Dad pull a Hyde-to-Jekyll had worn off, but she was still left with disturbing questions.

"I'm worried about you, Dad," Kira began. "You've been acting kinda weird."

"Weird?" Carter asked with genuine curiosity. Or perhaps it was genuine obliviousness. "How so?"

"Well, you're here, but you're not. Not really. It's like your mind goes far away. Even when we talk, I get the feeling that I'm keeping you from doing something else. And you've been angry a lot. At little things that don't really matter. And you've been losing weight. Are you sick, Dad?"

The idea that Kira was worried about his health when she'd already lost her mother made Carter's heart ache.

"No, honey. I'm not sick. I promise."

"So, what's going on?"

Kira's questions had to do with far more than why he'd been acting strangely, but she figured she'd open the door and give him a chance to tell the truth without coming right out and asking: "Why is there a man locked in our basement?"

"I'm working on an important project," he said with sincerity. "And it hasn't been going well. It's fair to say that it's stressing me out. I'm sorry that it's affecting my behavior. The last thing I want to do is upset you."

Kira felt a slight bit of relief. Her Dad was opening up and being honest, just like always.

"What's the project?"

"Nothing you'd be interested in," he said, blowing off the question. "It's for a paper I'm writing on hematology and genetic coding."

"Tell me about it," Kira said.

"You wouldn't understand," was his sharp answer, closing the door that Kira had cautiously opened.

And just like that, her fear was confirmed. He was definitely hiding something, not the least of which was the man in the basement.

"I might," she said, pressing. "Does it involve humans?"

Carter's face fell.

Kira tensed up again. She'd hit a nerve.

"Why do you ask?"

"You've got a lot of blood samples. Are they from people?"

Carter relaxed and chuckled.

"They are. I've gotten samples from patients who volunteered to be part of the experiment. So yes, I guess you could say it involves humans."

"That's it?" Kira asked. "That's all you want to say about it?"

Carter stood up and gave her a hug. Kira wanted to hug back the way she'd done a few thousand times before, but this time felt different. Her arms stayed at her sides.

"I'll say this," Carter said. "If the results come back the way I think they will, it'll make a lot of people very happy. Including you and me."

That only confused Kira more, but she didn't question further. It was obvious that her father was dancing around her questions. If she wanted to find out the whole story, there was only one person she could ask.

She had to talk to the man in the basement.

~~~~
~~~~

Kira waited until her father was asleep, which wasn't easy since her father rarely went to bed before midnight. It was adrenaline that kept her awake until she finally heard him in his bathroom brushing his teeth. A few minutes later, his light went out.

She would have preferred to go on her adventure during the day, but the door that led down to the basement was in her father's office. There was no way she would be able to get there without him knowing, and given how secretive he was being, she had no doubt that he would stop her. She didn't want to confront him about what she'd heard until she had a better idea of what was going on. Talking to the man behind the locked door seemed like the best way, the only way, to find out.

After waiting a few extra minutes to insure he was asleep, she got out of bed, threw on sweats, and made her way downstairs. She didn't risk turning on lights for fear it would alert her father in case he was still awake. She would have to travel by memory and hope that she wouldn't knock anything over or smash a toe into a chair leg.

Kira had lived her entire life in that house and knew every inch. She made it downstairs and into the kitchen with no problem and went straight to the counter that her father used as a work area to do his bookkeeping. She was hunting for something specific. In the top drawer was a metal ring of keys. She knew that one was the key to the front door and figured the others would be to the locks in her father's office. She had no idea if she'd need them but took them just in case.

Getting to the kitchen was the easy part of her journey. It was the office and by extension, the basement below the office that were less familiar. Once she passed through the corridor that connected the house to the office wing, she found herself in pitch blackness. The rest of the house had been dark, but not like this. When she was in the main part of the house, light coming through windows from streetlights and the stars gave her enough ambient light to navigate. The office was a different matter.

She literally could not see her hand in front of her face. She hadn't thought about it before, but as she stepped into the inky darkness she realized there were no windows in the office wing. Not a one. She dismissed it as something to do with medical hygiene or patient privacy and shuffled on, trying to piece together the layout from memory. She banged her knees a few times and had to keep from screaming out in surprise and pain. That would have shattered the quiet and brought her father running.

Finally, after using her hands to feel along the wall, she came to the door that led down to the basement. She could finally breathe again, but the feeling of relief didn't last. Up until that moment her entire focus was on getting to that door. Now the mission would change. She was going to meet the mysterious man.

She tried the door and discovered that, as expected, it was locked. It took only a few tries to locate the right key from the ring. She unlocked the door and opened it slowly to prevent it from squeaking. After swinging it just wide enough to squeeze through, she slipped inside, closed it gently, and flipped on the light. Earlier that day she had gone there out of curiosity. Now, staring down the stairs that led to the subterranean basement, she had to deal with fear.

Fear of what she might find.

She steeled herself and descended quickly for fear she'd change her mind and flee back to her bedroom. At the bottom of the stairs, she turned left to see the long corridor that ran the length of the basement. She'd only been down there a few times and didn't think twice about why the basement had been sectioned off into rooms with doors. All of her friend's basements were wide open spaces taking up the footprint of the house. They used the space for storage, or for doing laundry or as a game room complete with a pool table and a TV. But not hers. This basement had a stark, narrow corridor made of cinder blocks with three doors along the inside wall. It was at the far door where she heard her father speaking to the man through an intercom.

Kira summoned her courage and walked slowly toward it. Her ears were tuned for any sound that would indicate a sign of life. When she arrived at the door, she looked up at the intercom speaker. There was a single button beneath it which she figured would activate it. Above it were two red lights.

It was past two o'clock in the morning. Until that moment Kira hadn't considered that whoever was beyond that door would most likely be asleep. She tried to convince herself that it would be wrong to disturb the man but knew this was the only way to talk to him without her father knowing.

She reached up to the intercom. Her finger hovered next to the power button. She hesitated because she felt certain that once she pressed it, life would change.

"Hello young one," came a man's voice through the intercom.

Kira let out a surprised yelp and jumped back.

"You're up quite late," he added.

The man sounded pleasant enough. Friendly even. Those few words gave Kira the impression that he was an educated person.

"It is you, Kira, isn't it?"

Hearing her name was another shock. Kira's throat closed up, making it difficult to speak.

"You know me?" she asked hesitantly.

"I know *of* you," the man said. "But we haven't been introduced. My name is Hoagland. It is a pleasure to finally make your acquaintance."

"Who…who are you?" Kira asked.

"I've been a guest of your father's for quite some time now," Hoagland replied. "We've been working on a project together. Or more to the point, he has been working on a project and he has enlisted my help."

"What kind of project?" Kira asked.

"That is a question that would be more appropriately answered by your father."

"But he's not being honest with me," Kira cried out. Once she started talking she couldn't stop. "I heard him talking to you over the intercom, that's how I knew about you. Why didn't he tell me somebody was living down here? Now I'm wondering what else he's not telling me. It's like I can't trust him. I don't even know you, but I think I'd believe you more than him right now so please, tell me why you're locked down here."

Kira heard the man sigh as if wrestling with how best to answer.

"You are locked up, aren't you?" Kira added.

"I am."

"Why?"

"I'll tell you," Hoagland said. "But first you have to open the door."

Kira took a step back from the door as if afraid of it.

"It's simple," Hoagland continued. "There's a four-digit code to open the first door, then another for the inner door. Find those codes, unlock the doors and I'll tell you exactly why I'm here."

"I...I don't want to do that," Kira said, hesitantly.

"Why not?"

"Because my father's not a bad man. He's not being honest with me, but if he wants you locked up, maybe you should be locked up."

"Your father loves you very much," Hoagland said, soothingly. "I've known him long enough to understand that. There's nothing he wouldn't do for you, remember that. But he's also done some things that aren't right. Locking me in here is the least of them. He may not be a bad man, but he has done some very bad things. I'm sorry to have to tell you that, but it's the truth. If you let me out, there's a very good chance that we can make things right."

"I don't believe you," Kira said sternly. "You just want me to let you out."

"I hesitate to do this," Hoagland said. "But if I can prove to you that your father needs our help, will you release me?"

Kira's mind raced. She thought about how her father's personality had changed over the past year. He didn't exactly seem sick, but he kept to himself and snapped at every minor thing that went wrong. That wasn't like him, even when her mother was so sick. She tried to ignore it, but it was becoming more difficult. Was it because of the bad things this Hoagland guy said he was up to? She didn't want to know, but she had to know.

"Maybe," Kira said. "How can you prove it?"

"You're a strong young woman, Kira, but I'm not entirely sure you'll be able to deal with this. It would be difficult for anyone."

"I'm only fourteen," Kira said. "But I've had to deal with a lot. I can handle whatever it is you have to say."

"Don't be so sure of that," Hoagland cautioned.

"If you're telling me that what my father is doing something really bad, then I'm going to have to deal with it sooner or later. I can't pretend like it isn't happening. So just tell me."

"I can't tell you because you won't believe me," Hoagland said. "But I can show you."

"I'm not letting you out!" Kira snapped.

"You won't have to. Go outside. To the back of your property. Your father parked a vehicle there. Have you seen it?"

"Yeah. It's a camper. He said we'd take it on a vacation one day."

"Look in the rear compartment. It's probably locked so you'll need a key.

"I've got his keys," Kira said.

Hoagland chuckled. "You are quite the resourceful young woman."

"Yes I am," Kira said with confidence.

"You'll need that confidence, and strength," Hoagland said. "I take no pleasure in directing you to that truck. What you find inside you will not like but be strong. Once you've seen, come back here. What I will then tell you won't be a comfort, but you'll believe me."

"That's it?" Kira asked.

"It's enough."

"All right," Kira said. "I'll be right back."

"And I'll be right here."

Kira felt as though she was in a dream. Dreams can't be controlled, and this was no different. As much as she wanted to go back to bed and pretend like none of this was happening, that wasn't an option. She'd had to deal with some very bad news in her young life and always felt that it made her stronger. But she feared this time would be different. The idea that her father was guilty of anything might put her over the edge. He was her rock. He was always there for her. The thought of having that taken away was too horrible to imagine.

But she had hope. Hope that this Hoagland person was lying just so she'd set him free. That would be the best-case scenario. She wanted to believe that whatever was in that camper would be explained away and her father would still be the good guy. Hoagland would turn out to be the villain and that was why her father had him locked up. They'd call the police to come get Hoagland and that would be that. That hope gave her the strength to go out to the yard.

The vehicle was parked on the far edge of their property, behind a stand of thick pine trees. It couldn't be seen from the house. When they first got it, Carter gave Kira a tour, after which he warned her not to go inside, or even to play nearby. He had several burglar alarms installed for security and triggering them would bring the police. Kira did what she was told. She never went back to the camper and didn't expect to see the inside again until they left on their grand adventure.

That was about to change.

Kira had grabbed a flashlight from the kitchen but didn't turn it on until she was past the curtain of pine trees. The camper was a large vehicle. She remembered thinking it was like a small house on wheels, complete with a kitchen, a bathroom a living room and two small bedrooms. She was thrilled to think that she and her dad would take it on a road trip to exciting parts unknown. She looked forward to getting back inside.

Now she didn't want to be anywhere near it.

She went to the side door and turned on the flashlight to search through the ring of keys. She saw that among the keys was a small plastic tag that showed two sets of four numbers. She'd seen it before but didn't know what it was. Now she had an idea. They could be the codes to unlock the doors of Hoagland's cell. She had no intention of using them, so she flipped past the tag to get to the keys. As she tried each in turn, she sensed a sound that was out of place. It was a slight hum that seemed to be coming from the camper. She put the palm of her hand on the outer wall and felt a slight vibration.

She pulled her hand back quickly, as if she had touched something that was alive. Of course, it wasn't. Something inside was running, probably powered by a generator or a battery. The camper had been there for months. Why was it powered up? Could it have to do with the security system? She had the brief, sick thought that when she opened the door alarms would sound, her father would come running, followed close behind by the police. As nervous as that made her, she also felt that maybe it would be the best thing to happen. Having a responsible policeperson around would make getting to the truth that much easier. So, she plunged ahead, trying keys.

She found the right one in no time and with one quick turn the lock dis-engaged. Kira was on the threshold of another life-changing moment. She couldn't even speculate as to what she might find inside which made the next step that much more frightening. Though it was chilly, her palms were sweating, and her heart was thumping. She summoned every last ounce of will power she could muster, squeezed her eyes shut and opened the door, expecting alarms to blare.

They didn't. It was one more bit of proof that her father wasn't being honest with her. His warning about alarms was to make sure she wouldn't snoop around. Whatever was in that camper, he did not want Kira finding it.

But she was about to.

She wiped her eyes to dry the sweat and the tears, took a deep breath, and stepped up into the camper. Her first reaction was that it was cold inside. That explained the humming. There was an air-conditioner pumping out cold air. And not just cold air, freezing cold air. The camper was frigid. She shone the flashlight around to see that most of the camping amenities had been removed. Gone was the kitchen and the built-in couches. The interior had been stripped bare. What was once a homey-looking house on wheels now looked like a freight truck. A heavy plastic curtain hung just inside the door, blocking her view of the back half of the vehicle. Whatever Hoagland wanted her to see had to be beyond that curtain.

Kira took a step inside, reached out, and pulled the curtain aside. She immediately saw that the rest of the camper had also been stripped of the camping accessories. It was an empty shell…that wasn't entirely empty. Stacked against both sides were long, black bags that looked to be made of rubber. There were six in all, three on each side stacked on top of one another. Each looked to be around six feet long. This is what Hoagland wanted her to see, but nothing about it made her believe that her father was up to no good.

She approached one of the stacks to see that the bags were zipped shut. She knelt down, held the flashlight in her teeth, and zipped the top bag open. She was immediately hit by a smell that made her gag. She stayed focused, trying not to wretch, pulled apart the opening in the bag, and came face to face with the corpse of an old man. His eyes were open, staring straight at Kira. She would have screamed if she hadn't been holding the flashlight in her teeth. She fell back onto her butt as the corpse-head flopped out of the opening and hung there.

Now the freezing cold made sense. These were body bags. Occupied body bags. There were at least six dead bodies in the camper that was no longer a camper, but a makeshift morgue.

Kira couldn't get out fast enough. She fought panic and tears as she crawled on her hands and knees to the door and tumbled out of the camper onto the grass. She was breathing so hard she came close to hyperventilating and passing out, but she had the wherewithal to jump back to her feet, slam the door closed and lock it.

She fell to her knees, sobbing.

What had her father done?

~~~~

"I am genuinely sorry you had to see that," Hoagland said through the intercom.
~~~~

Kira sat on the floor with her back against the door, sobbing.

"I'm afraid it's partially my fault," Hoagland said.

Kira sat up straight. Suddenly a ray of hope.

"Did you kill those people?" she asked.

"I did."

Kira sighed with relief. Her father wasn't a murderer.

"I had no choice," Hoagland added. "Your father is keeping me here and if I don't feed, I'll perish."

Kira heard the words, she understood what he said, but it made no sense.

"You eat dead people?" she asked, incredulous.

"No," Hoagland said flatly. "I'm an immortal. I feed on their blood."

Kira struggled to her feet, her head spinning.

"You're a vampire?"

"That's a term used in literature and entertainment. The truth is more nuanced than that. But if that's how you can understand it then yes, I am a vampire."

"I don't believe you," she said. "There's no such thing."

"I beg to differ," Hoagland said. "We are very real, and none of us live in a dark castle in Eastern Europe. At least none that I'm aware of. We walk among you, living relatively normal lives. You've probably met one or another of us, but you wouldn't have known because there's nothing unusual about us, other than we've been cursed."

"And you kill people," Kira said.

"To survive," Hoagland countered. "None of us chose the immortal path. But once on it, the instinct for self-preservation is overwhelming."

Kira had so many questions, but one mattered far more than the others.

"Why are you in our basement?"

"Your father is a brilliant man. He sought me out. When we met he talked of his search for a cure that would rid me of this curse. But that wasn't his true goal. It wasn't until he lured me down here, and confined me, that I discovered his true intent."

"And what's that?"

"He needs my blood for his research."

Kira thought to the vials of the nearly black blood her father had lined up at his lab table.

"What kind of research?"

"He's trying to unlock the secrets of immortality. He's convinced that the answer lies in our blood, but he's only partially correct. He could bring all of his knowledge of hematology to bear and break down the genetic code of an immortal's blood, he might even duplicate it synthetically, but that won't change the inevitable. Immortality comes with a price, and that price is the need to feed on the blood of the living in order to regenerate our cells. Your father is trying to create an equation where that need can be purged, but he has failed. He will continue to fail. But he is doggedly continuing with this obsession."

None of what Kira was hearing lined up with how she thought the natural world worked. Or her father worked, which was just as disturbing.

"Why is he so obsessed with immortality?" she asked.

Hoagland didn't answer.

"Did you hear me?" Kira cried out. "Does he want to live forever?"

"He does not," Hoagland said softly.

"But you said--"

"I said he's trying to unlock the secret of immortality, not that he wants to be immortal."

"Then what does he want?"

"He wants to cure you, Kira." Hoagland said.

Kira felt as though the walls were closing in on her. Until that moment, everything she had seen and heard had nothing to do with her. She was an observer. An innocent. Now she faced the reality that she was in the dead center of it all.

"Your father is in pain," Hoagland added. "The loss of your mother devastated him, and the fact that medical science couldn't save her cloyed at him. You've been diagnosed with the same illness. The idea of losing you has pushed him over the edge. I'm not saying I condone what he is attempting, but I understand it. He wants to save you, Kira. But he is doomed to fail. At least this course of action is doomed to fail. The only question is how many more people he will lure to their deaths before he realizes it?"

Kira was stunned numb.

"How many?" she asked, barely above a whisper. "How many have died?"

"He brought those six people whose bodies you saw in the camper to me, to sustain me," Hoagland said. "I don't know how many others he used as test subjects. Perhaps another six? Maybe more."

Kira winced.

"Twelve people have died because my father is trying to keep me alive," she said, though barely believing the enormity of the concept.

Her father was indeed a murderer.

"Now you know the truth," Hoagland said. "Let me out. I would never harm your father, or you, but this insanity must end. My leaving will end it."

Kira looked up at the two red lights over the intercom. The lights that indicated both doors into the cell were locked. She glanced at the plastic tag on the key ring that held the codes to unlock the doors. She looked to the four-digit lock on the door.

"Kira?"

Kira turned her back to the door and shuffled away, as if in a trance.

"Kira!" Hoagland called out. "Please! Help me end this!"

Kira ignored his pleas. She climbed the stairs back to her father's office, turned out the lights, and went back to bed.

~~~~
~~~~

Carter had had a restless night of sleep. That had become the norm. He was haunted by dreams, none of which he could remember, but they kept him from the healing of deep, continuous sleep. When he finally dragged himself out of bed he made his usual first stop to Kira's room to get her up for school.

She wasn't in her bed. That was strange for he usually had to blast her awake. A quick check on the time showed him that it was an hour later than usual. He had gotten more sleep than he thought. Kira was already up and out to school.

Carter took an extra-long shower. He was in no hurry to start the day. He hadn't scheduled any patient appointments for he had other plans. After a round of gene-editing with Hoagland's latest blood sample, he was prepared for another test. It was an arduous, trial-and-error process to identify and isolate the genomes that drove the cell-regenerating blood-lust of immortals. He felt he was getting closer but there was only one way to be certain. He needed to test it on humans. For that, he needed subjects. He wouldn't allow himself to call them victims, though ultimately that's what they were. He trolled the city's homeless encampments for suitable subjects. His definition of "suitable" was someone who, by his estimation, had nothing to live for. No family, questionable health, and horrible long-term prospects. He even justified his actions by telling himself that if successful, he'd be giving them a new and better life.

So far, that hadn't happened.

Once dressed he went downstairs to fix himself breakfast and was surprised to see that the kitchen was immaculate, just as he had left it the night before. Kira was a good cook, but not the greatest at cleaning up afterward. He was at least expecting to find a few Pop-Tart wrappers on the counter and a glass she'd used for orange juice. But there was no sign that Kira had eaten anything. His biggest concern was that she had been late getting up and left without eating. She needed to keep her strength up.

The rest of his day was spent in futility. He trolled the known areas where the homeless gathered. The cardboard and tent cities. It was a depressing but necessary exercise. He engaged a few people but in each case found that they had more ties to a normal life and family than fit his criteria. Others simply weren't interested, even with the promise of making an easy fifty dollars. He had come up empty in the past. But he was feeling particularly frustrated because he genuinely felt that he was on the verge of a breakthrough. His "project" had been going on for more than a year and it was taking a toll on him. Impatience was the least of his troubles. He was far more concerned with how quickly Kira's disease was progressing, and at what point it would become irreversible.

And of course, there were the killings. He wasn't exactly a doctor who embraced the sacred code: "first do no harm". Whether directly or indirectly, he was responsible for multiple deaths. But he was too far gone to care. There was no way to know for certain, but he felt as though time was running out on Kira's chances. And his.

He finally gave up his hunt once the shadows started getting longer ahead of sundown. He didn't feel safe driving his BMW through such sketchy areas once it got dark. Besides, he had to make dinner for Kira.

When he returned home, Kira wasn't there. He couldn't call her for she didn't have a cell phone. He made a mental note that it may be time to break down and get her an iPhone, but that didn't solve the problem at hand. Where could she be? A quick search of the house to see if she may be napping somewhere, which was often the case, was for naught. The only place he didn't check was the office wing. But she never went there. Almost never.

Carter was hit with a growing sense of dread. This wasn't a simple case of a fourteen-year-old girl losing track of time and being late for dinner. Not with a dangerous predator lurking in the basement. He picked up the pace and by the time he'd gotten to the end of the hallway leading to his office, he was on a dead run. He burst into his office and scanned about. Kira wasn't there. He hurried to the basement door and found that it was locked.

He could breathe again.

His relief didn't last long.

He went to his lab table to discover items had been moved. He was fastidious about where his materials were placed, and things weren't as he had left them. It wasn't in disarray, but someone had definitely been moving things about. He immediately turned his attention to the small refrigerator where he kept his blood samples. At first glance inside everything seemed to be in order. He was about to close the door when he noticed something that made his stomach drop.

He had loaded two hypodermic syringes with the modified blood he intended to inject into his next test subject. They had been placed side-by-side on a sterile gauze pad.

One was missing.

"Hi Dad," Kira said.

Carter spun to see Kira standing on the far side of the room. For a brief moment she appeared to be the little girl of six who had just lost her mother. She seemed so young and vulnerable, standing there wearing the same sweats she had worn to bed the night before. But this wasn't that little girl. This was a fourteen-year-old young woman who was mature beyond her years.

"Thank God," Carter said as he let out a relieved breath. "I've been looking all over for you. I had no idea where—"

"I've been here all day," Kira said flatly.

"You didn't go to school?" Carter asked.

"No."

"Why not?"

"It didn't seem all that important anymore."

Carter felt a quick sting of concern. Something had changed.

"Why do you say that?" he asked cautiously.

"I don't know," Kira said with a touch of sarcasm. "It may have something to do with finding out that my father is a serial killer."

Carter had been living with the fear of Kira learning the truth for a very long time. It played on him nearly as much as the guilt over the killings. Now the worst had happened. How much did she truly know? Or understand? There was something in her tone of voice, and body language, which gave him even deeper concern. She didn't sound like a frightened, disillusioned little girl. That would have made sense. Instead, her attitude seemed oddly knowing. Perhaps even accepting. She stood there, stock still, staring at him. Her dispassionate gaze unwavering.

It was chilling.

"There is a purpose," was all he could think to say.

"Right," Kira said. "You're trying to save my life. I suppose I should be grateful but I'm not sure the tradeoff is something I could live with…assuming I'm around long enough to try."

"How?" was all he managed to say in that horrifying moment.

"You mean how do I know?" Kira asked. "Isn't that obvious? I met your houseguest."

There it was. Kira knew it all, and that knowledge had somehow changed her. Was it shock? Disbelief? Was her cool appearance a defense mechanism against the horrors of the truth? Or was she in shock? Whatever the reason, she no longer looked at him as the infallible parent she could always rely on. That may have been the hardest truth for him to accept. He had lost his little girl, long before the disease could take her.

Kira slowly walked toward her father; her eyes locked on his.

"I don't want to die," she said. "But I can't live with this."

"I didn't want you to know," Carter said, feebly.

"And you think that me not knowing made it all right?"

"No. The chance to save you made it all right."

"And you're failing. Yet you keep going. People keep dying. For what? One life?"

All the excuses Carter had been using to justify the horror were crumbling in the face of the harsh, disillusioned glare of his daughter.

"Not just one life," Carter said with passion. "Your life."

"I love you, Dad," Kira said. "But all you managed to do was curse us both."

That's when Carter saw it. It was in her eyes. The whites had gone subtly red. Her pupils were dilated. Her change in personality now made sense. Once Carter understood, he wanted to scream out in agony.

"What did you do?" he demanded, though in his heart, he already knew.

"I ended your experiment," she said with smug confidence. "I figured that however it turned out; whether I ended up dead, turned or cured, the experiment would be over, and the killings would stop."

Carter glanced back to the open refrigerator where only one of the two syringes he had loaded with the serum remained. The crushing truth hit, severing his last tenuous connection with sanity. He not only failed to save his daughter; he had sentenced his innocent little girl to a monstrous eternity.

"And now we know," Kira said. "You haven't perfected your serum, have you? Now I'm the one who'll be doing the killing. Kind of ironic."

As she drew closer, Carter slid along the desk and continued moving with his back against the wall to keep her at a distance.

"I can keep working on it," he said, sounding more desperate than reassuring. "We don't need Hoagland. Now I can use your blood. I was so very close to finding a cure, not just for you but for the immortal curse. I can reverse it."

"No, you can't," Kira said. "Hoagland is right. There is more to this than science can unravel."

"That's not true!" Carter exclaimed. "It's in the DNA. I found it. It's only a matter of identifying and duplicating the proper genome."

Carter kept moving, slowly, headed for the door and the row of switches that would open the overhead louvres. The truth was, Carter no longer believed in his theory. There had been too many failures to think he was simply missing something. He had come close to accepting that his work was a failure and that his daughter's life would be a short one. It was a hard reality to swallow, but that now seemed trivial compared to the fact that his work had condemned her to a lifetime of murder. Of feeding. He couldn't allow that to happen. He wouldn't allow that to happen.

All he had to do was spring open the overhead louvres.

"Is that what you want Dad?" she asked. "Do you want to keep finding victims to experiment on while I'm out hunting for blood? Is that the plan now?"

If Kira would agree to that plan, Carter would have gladly accepted it. But he knew she wouldn't. His whole life had been focused on saving the life of his daughter. Now he was faced with the horrible reality that he had to end it.

"I love you, Kira," he said as he reached for the switch. "I want that to be the last thing you think about."

He threw the switch. The louvres snapped open. Kira looked skyward with confusion. It took only a moment for her to realize what her father had done and when she did, she laughed.

"That must have been a tough thing to do," she said. "Ironic that this is the moment you developed a conscience."

Carter looked up to see a night sky through the glass ceiling. The sun had gone down. There was no light to snuff out the life of an immortal.

It drove him to tears.

"I'm sorry, sweetheart," he said, weeping. "I didn't want you to endure such a horrible existence."

"Horrible existence?" Hoagland said, incredulous. He was standing in the open doorway that led to the rest of the house. "I beg to differ. We are imbued with the cumulative wisdom of the ages. There isn't a one of us who hasn't flourished and lived the kind of life that mortals can only dream of. You should be happy, Doctor Carter. You've given your daughter a most wonderful gift. One that is far more valuable than the extension of a pedestrian mortal life."

"But it's…wrong," Carter snarled.

Hoagland stepped into the office and stood next to Kira.

"Who is to say what is wrong or right?" he said. "People die every day. World leaders all have blood on their hands. Death is a fact of life. Would I prefer not to have to kill to survive? Of course. But I try to make the tradeoff worthwhile. I have created multiple business entities throughout time that have benefitted mankind. One has even been quite successful in developing vaccines to control viruses that have squashed pandemics. This may be difficult to accept, but in the long run, I'm responsible for having saved thousands more lives than I've taken. You have no right to call my existence horrible. Certainly not when you were responsible for killing so many in order to save only one life. As I asked you before, which one of us is the monster?"

Carter slumped against the wall, crushed.

"I'm going with Hoagland," Kira said. "He'll help to get me adjusted."

"It's the least I can do," Hoagland said. "After all, it was my blood that turned her."

Carter winced as the full implication of what he had done was becoming clear. He had brought the beast into his house, and how he's leaving with his daughter.

"You probably won't see me again," Kira added. "I think it will be better that way."

That was the final gut-punch. Carter slid to the floor.

"Please stay," he said, barely above a whisper.

"I love you, Dad," Kira said. "Good-bye."

She turned and headed for the door.

Carter dropped his eyes. He couldn't bear to watch her go.

"As I've told you," Hoagland said. "I'll look back on the short time I've spent here as nothing more than a unique and tragic diversion. In time, so will she. Good-bye doctor. Good luck."

Hoagland spun on his heel to follow Kira out of the door and away from what was now her former life.

Carter was left alone on the floor, broken. Though all that had happened was of his doing, and had been coming for a long time, the sudden and irreversible ending was crushing. He had failed in every way. He had lost the one person in the world he loved. His theories proved to be false. And he was, to use Kira's term, a serial killer. As he sat on the floor, facing a future that would surely be more horrible than what he feared was awaiting Kira, he couldn't think of a reason why he should want to continue living.

He pulled himself to his feet, not sure of what to do. He stood on shaky legs, unable to find a thought that would give him hope. Or purpose. Or direction.

He shuffled to his lab table as if in a dream, with a growing urge to break something. His anger and frustration were boiling to the surface, and he was ready to take every last blood sample from the refrigerator and smash them onto the floor. He threw open the door, reached in, and swept a dozen vials of black blood out of the cooler. The glass containers smashed to the floor, creating a slick layer of immortal blood. It was strangely cathartic. Carter reached to the top shelf, ready to continue the destruction, when he spotted the second syringe filled with his latest serum. He stared at the innocent looking device, its twin being the vehicle that took his daughter from him.

But it wasn't the fault of the blood in the syringe. It was all his doing. No amount of justification could change that. Because of his selfishness, he would never see his daughter again. His life was as good as over.

He took out the syringe and stared at the dark liquid. Perhaps there was another way. It was an idea that only a few minutes before would have seemed preposterous. Unholy. A crime against humanity.

But things had changed.

He might not have lost his daughter after all.

With that in mind, he popped the cap off of the needle.

<u>THE END</u>

FRESHLY SQUEEZED

Jon Gottlieb didn't believe in ghosts.

He wasn't that kind of guy. He was more of a "life is orderly, life makes sense, life is predictable" kind of guy. He worked hard, maybe too hard, to provide a comfortable living for him and his wife. He was a one-man-band of a tax accountant with a stable of wealthy clients in Darien, Connecticut which was home to many well-to-do captains of industry and finance who would never even think to do anything as pedestrian as filling out their own income tax returns. That was fine by Jon, he was more than happy to provide that service and collect the healthy fees.

And then there were the ghosts.

It was a Sunday morning in mid-March. Jon's plan for the day was to grab a quick coffee at home, skim the Sunday paper, then head to the office for a few hours of work. It was tax season, crunch time when he worked seven-day weeks and piled on hours. He probably should have hired another accountant to lighten his load but wasn't comfortable trusting his client's precious assets to anyone else. That was Jon. Conscientious and controlling.

Being Sunday, John put on the weekend uniform of all middle-aged men in Darien…khaki chinos, and a V-neck sweater over a button-down shirt. As he started down the stairs of the well-appointed Colonial-style house that he and his wife Lyn had gutted and re-designed to authentic (with all the modern conveniences) late 1800's style, he was surprised by the aroma of brewing coffee along with something else that vaguely tickled his memory. Could it be? Bacon? Nah. Pancakes? Maybe. Both? Impossible. Yet his house had the unmistakable aroma of a breakfast-hour diner.

"About time you got up!" Lyn chirped merrily.

Jon stepped into his kitchen and went into brain lock. Lyn hadn't made him breakfast in years and here he was staring at a sumptuous kitchen scene that could have been staged by the Food Network. Lyn had even dressed for the occasion, passing on her normal Sunday sweats for a smart sweater (that Jon had given her for Christmas) and a jean skirt. My God, was she wearing make-up? Jon was stunned by the lengths to which Lyn had gone.

Truth was he and Lyn hadn't done anything remotely this thoughtful for each other in quite some time. They were married right out of college and had no children. Fast forward twenty-five years and the two had grown in opposite directions. Jon had steadily and conservatively built his local accounting practice, while Lyn commuted into the city where she taught art classes at The New School. She travelled in the world of academia and the arts while Jon dealt with entitled captains of industry and the IRS. They lived the majority of their lives in different worlds and in many respects, lived different lives.

Neither felt the divide growing until their common interests had dwindled to a scant few. Worse, in recent weeks Jon feared that Lyn might be having an affair. There were too many late nights in the city, too many calls to announce that she'd missed the last train home and would be staying with friends (who he never met), too many unanswered cell phone calls, and too little physical affection. Both had become increasingly quick to anger and silently harbored resentment toward the other over the disintegration of their relationship. It made for ever-more frequent arguments and uncomfortable nights where Jon ended up sleeping in the guest bedroom.

"Have a seat!" Lyn exclaimed. "I haven't cooked like this in ages."

Jon thought, *Yeah, no shit,* but chose not to voice that particular opinion.

Lyn seemed to be her "old" self, truly enjoying the task of cooking bacon, frying eggs, slinging hash browns, and griddling blueberry pancakes. She had even produced a tall pitcher of orange juice.

"What's the occasion?" Jon asked, more than a little shell shocked.

"It's Sunday," she chirped. "We used to do this every Sunday."

Jon thought, *And we used to read the comics together too, but that hasn't happened in a few decades.* Again, he was savvy enough not to point that out.

Jon sat down at the only place at the table that was set.

"Aren't you eating?" he asked.

"I've been nibbling," she said. "I want you to enjoy this yourself. In peace. Here's the paper."

She handed him the weighty Sunday New York Times with a big smile.

Jon wanted to say: *Who are you and what have you done with my wife?* but continued to keep his more cynical thoughts to himself.

"Thanks," he said. "I don't know what to say."

"You just did," Lyn said as she placed the plate heaped with steaming hot breakfast treats before him. "Enjoy. The orange juice is freshly squeezed and icy cold."

For a fleeting second Jon thought he might actually be dreaming, but that made less sense than Lyn suddenly acting like some 50's-era doting sit-com housewife.

"You know I love all of this," he said as he eyed the plate with eager anticipation.

"I do. I hope the OJ isn't too tart."

"Let's see," Jon said and took a healthy gulp. "Perfect," he said sincerely and drained the glass.

"I'm glad," Lyn said as she re-filled his glass. "I'll leave you to it. Bon Appetit!"

"Lyn, this is great but, why? Seriously."

"Because things need to change. Is that okay?"

Jon sensed a touch of sarcasm, but in the spirit of détente, let it go.

"I appreciate it."

"It really was needed," Lyn said and left the kitchen.

Jon couldn't believe his luck. Did Lyn truly want a fresh start? Were things going to get better? He couldn't bring himself to believe that anyone could make such a drastic change, especially since the night before they had had another blow-out battle over her mysterious absences. But maybe that was the last straw. The turning point. It was certainly a promising start.

With that hopeful thought in mind and a five-star breakfast in front of him, Jon tucked in. At 49 and sporting an all-weather grade spare tire, he couldn't afford to eat like that very often. But it was all too perfect, and he felt that if he didn't enjoy it the way Lyn had intended, he would be putting the brakes on this new journey before it could begin. So, he downed his second glass of orange juice, poured a cup of hot coffee, and feasted. In between bites he dove deep into the Sunday paper, something he hadn't made time for in months. He didn't think for a second that he needed to hurry in order to get to the office. Perhaps that meant the changes Lyn wanted were already underway.

Halfway through the short stack of pancakes, Jon sensed a presence. He glanced over his shoulder to see Lyn watching him from the doorway, as if quietly spying to see if he was enjoying himself. He was about to say, "All's good!" but the look on her face made him hesitate.

Her expression seemed wistful. Maybe even sad. Was there a tear in her eye? It certainly didn't track with the cheery attitude she showed earlier. Was she lamenting over all the time they had wasted fighting? Was she remembering how wonderful and loving they used to be together? For that matter, did she still love him? He certainly loved her, and not because she had cooked him a nice breakfast.

Her expression conjured conflicting emotions in Jon. He couldn't find the adequate words to convey them, so he simply smiled at her.

Lyn didn't return the smile. With a sigh, she turned and walked away. It was an odd and unsettling moment. Perhaps it was part of her process as she worked to repair their relationship. Maybe it was a good thing.

Jon went back to the paper and lost track of time. He dared to entertain the thought of blowing off work, a reckless move in tax season. He thought maybe he and Lyn could go for a bike ride to the beach. They hadn't done that in…he couldn't remember how long. Did they still have bikes?

He may have stayed there for hours to savor the last of the orange juice and coffee if his eye hadn't caught something outside. He looked to the window over the sink and was startled to see a woman standing outside, staring in at him. It was such a surprise that he was jolted back and splashed coffee on his freshly laundered khakis. He could only see her from the shoulders up, but it was clearly a woman with straight black hair to her shoulders and deep brown eyes. She wore a powder blue top with an old-fashioned cameo pin at her neck.

Jon gathered his wits and hurried to open the door.

"Can I help you?" he asked.

He stepped outside and looked to the window where she was standing, but no one was there. He glanced around his yard but there was no sign of the woman. He reasoned that he must be mistaken. It was probably an odd reflection of light off of the window.

Feeling foolish, he chuckled then closed the door and headed out of the kitchen to hunt down Lyn and suggest the bike ride. They could even bring a picnic. Jon felt lighter than he had in ages, mostly because he had something to look forward to other than pouring over a pile of unartfully padded Schedule C's.

He walked through the downstairs hallway, headed for the stairs, passing the doorway to the living room. On the far wall of the room was a large mirror, the ornate golden frame of which Lyn had designed. Jon thought it was ostentatious, but it was Lyn's work, so it stayed. As he passed the doorway he sensed that there was something odd reflected in the mirror. Something out of place. It was as if someone was standing inside the living room and their image was reflected in the mirror. He hadn't looked directly at it but registered something blue.

Jon stopped and backed up a few steps to take a longer look.

He was mistaken. There was no odd reflection.

I must be on a food high, he thought dismissively.

He headed for the stairs and climbed up, knowing Lyn would be in their bedroom. As he got to the top, Lyn stepped out of the bedroom and met him face to face.

"I've got a great idea," Jon exclaimed.

Lyn screamed.

It was such a shock that Jon took a step back and nearly fell down the stairs.

Lyn's eyes were wide and wild.

"No," she cried and ran back into the bedroom.

"Lyn?" he called. "Are you okay?"

He followed her into the bedroom to find that she had gone through to the bathroom and closed the door.

"Sorry, I didn't mean to scare you," he said to the closed door, though he wasn't entirely sure why running into each other in the corridor was all that terrifying. Or why he should be the one to shoulder the blame.

"Go away!" Lyn shouted. She sounded desperate. Even panicked.

"What's the matter?" Jon asked.

"Go!" she screamed. "You have to go! Now!"

What had happened? Only a short while before she was acting the part of a loving wife, now she had flipped back into full-on I-hate-everything-Jon mode. It actually made more sense than the Martha Stewart act, but the sudden one-eighty didn't. Was the veneer of her "loving" persona so thin that it only took a minor jolt of surprise to shatter it?

So much for the bike ride and picnic at the beach.

"Sorry I surprised you," he said. "My fault. Thank you for breakfast. It was great. I'm going to the office for a few hours. Leave everything. I'll clean up when I get back."

She didn't reply but he could hear her breathing heavily. Was she crying?

"Lyn?"

He tried the doorknob. Locked.

"Go away!" she screamed.

Her outburst was so ferocious it made Jon involuntarily take a step backward.

"Okay, okay. I'm going," he called out.

Jon headed back down the stairs, holding on to the banister for support. What had just happened? Did Lyn have a psychotic break? He made a quick memory-scan of the last twenty years, searching for any hint of burgeoning mental illness that he hadn't picked up on; or was too busy to have noticed. He decided it would be best to leave her alone and hope that by the time he returned she'd have calmed down enough to talk about it rationally.

Jon often walked to his office. It was less than a mile and one of the simple pleasures he enjoyed about where they lived. Though it was a brisk March day, he didn't feel the need for a jacket, so he went without and began the pleasant stroll through a neighborhood of manicured lawns and colonial style homes.

Sunday mornings were always quiet and other than the occasional dog-walker, Jon rarely saw another soul. Strangely, on this morning he encountered a man on horseback who came up from behind and trotted past him in the middle of the street.

"G'day," the man said with a tip of his brimmed, woolen cap.

"Mornin'," Jon replied.

The guy wore a long, dark coat that came to the top of his high, scuffed leather boots. Darien was an affluent community with lots of wooded space that was used by equestrians. The riders normally kept to trails in the less developed parts of town, or to the rings at their tony riding clubs. Seeing a rider this close to town was unique. And kind of fun, Jon thought. The rider made a quick turn onto the driveway of a home and disappeared into the thicket of trees beyond.

The rhythmic clip-clopping of hooves gave way to the sound of kids playing on a ballfield a block further ahead. It was the joyful soundtrack of youth filled with laughter, taunts, and cheering. For a brief moment Jon was reminded of a time when his biggest worry in life was if he could round up enough friends to make two teams for touch football.

He passed the heavy oak tree that anchored the corner of the park and looked to the field to see...

...no one was there. The sounds of play drifted off with the wind.

Jon looked around with confusion. How could the kids have run off that quickly? It was an unnerving moment, but ultimately he knew there had to be an explanation. Still, it was oddly unsettling. He quickened his pace and turned onto Main Street.

The busy Boston Post Road narrowed as it passed through Darien to create a half-mile stretch of businesses that were housed in quaint, two-story brick buildings that hadn't changed much since before World War II. The ground floors held retail stores and restaurants; the second floors were occupied by small businesses. Jon's accounting firm was above a Baskin Robbins, which didn't help him with the battle of his spare tire.

Many of the shops went old-school and didn't open until past noon on Sundays once most people had fulfilled their church obligations. Without the normal hubbub of activity, it felt like a mythical, sleepy small-town of days gone by. Jon knew it was an illusion, but on those quiet Sunday mornings he liked to pretend it was real. It was a blissful moment of serenity...

...that ended abruptly when he saw the woman in blue standing on the sidewalk a half block ahead.

The sight of her stopped him cold. She was wearing an ankle-length powder blue woolen coat with blue leather boots to match. Her straight black hair fell to her shoulders. Her blue-gloved hands were clasped together below her waist. He guessed she was around his age but without a single gray hair. There was nothing unusual about her, other than the fact that she stood stock-still, staring at him.

"Hey, don't move!" Jon yelled once he'd gathered his wits.

He hurried toward her, but the woman turned and walked slowly toward the alley between buildings.

"Stop!" Jon yelled.

He accelerated into a run. When he got to the spot where she had been and looked into the alley, she was nowhere to be seen. Jon was out of breath, both from the run (he wasn't used to running) and from the shot of adrenalin that hit hard when he saw her.

"Who are you?" Jon screamed, his voice echoing off of the brick buildings.

No answer. He didn't yell again for fear he might disturb a shopkeeper who had arrived early for work. He didn't want anyone to think he was crazy, but in that moment, he felt crazy. He stepped into the narrow alley, looking for a doorway that the mysterious woman might have ducked into. There wasn't one, but even if there was it wouldn't explain why she had been at his house. He was now convinced that she had been there. It was no trick of light.

Not knowing what else to do, he took a deep breath to calm himself and left the alley, headed for his office.

Gottlieb Accounting was on the second floor of a small brick walk-up. Jon bounded up the stairs, took a left at the top and unlocked his door. Stepping inside, he immediately sensed that something was wrong.

The reception area had a small fireplace that had never been lit. Across from it was a desk where an assistant might sit if he had an assistant. A small office to his right was where a second accountant might work if he had a second accountant. At the end of the short hallway was his personal office. No one should have been there, yet he heard a voice coming from behind the closed door. A man was angrily yelling about something, the words too muffled to make out.

Jon wasn't frightened or confused. He was angry. How dare someone defile the privacy of his office? This was the one place where life made sense and he was not about to let anyone take that away. He grabbed the brass fireplace poker and strode down the hallway. He couldn't imagine actually striking someone with the metal rod but hoped he could fool someone into thinking he would. He stopped at the office door, raised the poker, yanked the door open and leapt inside.

"Who are you?" he shouted.

No one was there.

Though it looked as though someone had been. Jon's leather desk chair was pushed back, the phone was out of the cradle and the window was open…three things Jon would never have left that way. The phone being out of the cradle explained why he had heard only one voice. It was an argument over the phone. But it didn't explain where the screaming guy had gone. Jon kept the poker up high, walked cautiously toward his desk and peeked to the floor behind it.

No one was hiding there. Jon glanced to the open window. Could the guy have gotten out that way? It seemed unlikely, but it was the only thing that made sense. If the intruder had gone that way, he most likely would have pulled a John Wilkes Booth and broken his leg. Jon went to the window and looked down to see if a man was crumpled on the pavement.

There wasn't.

There was someone else.

The woman in blue.

She was looking up, directly at Jon, as if she had been standing there waiting for him to look out. Jon wanted to scream at her, but before he could open his mouth she dropped her gaze and walked slowly toward the building.

She's coming in!.

A moment later he was jolted by a knock on the outer door to his office.

How did she get up here that fast? he wondered with growing panic.

Another knock. The sharp sound yanked Jon out of his stupor.

"Enough," he said to no one.

With new-found conviction he stormed out of his office, still clutching the poker, headed for the front door.

"Who are you?" he yelled. "What do you want?"

He raised the poker and yanked the door open.

"Whoa! Easy there, Ebenezer!" the man standing outside said. "I didn't come to your counting house looking for money!"

"Rick?" Jon said with dismay.

"Not exactly the warm greeting I was expecting," Rick said with a laugh.

Rick Banca and Jon had been friends since childhood. They had remained close, thanks mostly to social media since Jon lived in Connecticut and Rick had moved to Maine. They only laid eyes on one another every few years thanks to the occasional boy's trip reunion.

"I can't tell you how glad I am to see you," Jon said with genuine relief.

"Then how about lowering the poker, John Wick."

Jon laughed and lowered it.

"Come in!" Jon exclaimed. "What are you doing here? Why didn't you tell me you were coming?"

"I did, " Rick said. "Remember? The Route One Ramble?"

Rick motioned to his clothing. He was wearing bright red biking gear.

"That's right!" Jon exclaimed. "The bike trip. The length of Route One."

"Maine to Key West," Rick said proudly. "Two thousand three hundred and sixty-nine miles of ass-burning, nut-numbing fun."

"That's insane," Jon said with a laugh.

"A little," Rick said. "Okay, a lot."

The two laughed as Jon hugged his best friend then led him down the hallway to his private office.

"Sit," Jon said, motioning to a couch. "Or is your butt already tired of sitting?"

"No, soft is good," Rick said and plopped down with a satisfied sigh.

Jon moved to sit in his desk chair, but thought twice, knowing that a stranger had recently been in it. He chose instead to sit on the other side of the couch from his buddy.

"How's the ride going?" Jon asked.

"It's going," Rick said. "Let's talk about you. How's Lyn?"

"Good, she's good," Jon lied, a little too quickly.

"Really?" Rick asked skeptically. "Let's go see her."

"Not a good idea," Jon said. "Wait, did you go to the house first? Is that why you came here? Did she tell you to come?"

"No, I figured you'd be at work on a Sunday morning because that's what you do. Let's go there now."

"Things are a little weird," Jon said. "We had a fight last night that carried into this morning."

"Sounds gruesome."

"You could say that. I think she's having an affair," Jon blurted out. "I didn't accuse her of anything, but she must know that I know. Truth is I can't say that I blame her. I've been so preoccupied with things here and we just don't talk anymore, and she's got her own thing going on in the city and nothing about that interests me and--"

"Whoa, TMI buddy," Rick said. "There's plenty of time for that. Let's head on back to the house and try to settle things."

"That won't be easy," Jon said.

"Probably not, but let's give it a shot," Rick said and stood up.

Jon couldn't think of a reason to refuse, so he went along. He knew from experience that when Jon had his mind set on doing something, it got done. But he didn't mind. Rick was a good friend. Even Lyn liked him. Maybe having him as a buffer would help to calm her down. They left the office and went straight to retrieve Rick's bike that was parked outside of the Baskin Robbins, unlocked.

"You're lucky nobody snatched it," Jon said.

"I wasn't worried."

"True. Not a lot of bike thieves trolling around Darien on a Sunday morning."

"Right, something like that," Rick said.

The two friends walked back along the same route Jon had taken earlier. Rick listened while Jon laid out the litany of problems he was having with Lyn and to his credit, she was having with him. By the time they arrived at the house, he had pretty much covered every issue they'd been dealing with over the last twenty years.

"Thanks man," Jon said.

"For what?"

"For letting me spew. I don't have anybody to talk to, or at least anybody who would listen for more than a few seconds before losing interest."

"People suck," Rick said.

"Maybe I do too. I haven't asked about you."

"There's plenty of time for that," Rick said. "Right now, it's about you."

Jon had taken his friendship with Rick for granted. One doesn't make many truly great friends in life, and for Jon, Rick was the best. In that brief moment he made a promise to himself to be in touch more.

They stepped up to Jon's front door and while Rick parked his bike, Jon took a second to look around.

"Problem?" Rick asked.

Jon wasn't about to tell him that he was being haunted by a strange woman wearing a long blue vintage coat.

"No," Jon said, too casually. "It's just that…nothing."

"If you say so," Rick said. "Onward."

Jon opened the door and had to brace himself for fear Lyn was still upset.

"Maybe this wasn't such a good idea," he said nervously.

"It's the exact right idea," Rick countered with confidence. "Where is she?"

"When I left she had locked herself in our bathroom."

"Upstairs?" Rick asked.

"Yeah."

With a quick smile and a wink, Rick bounded up the stairs. Jon was taken back by such a bold move but didn't say anything for Rick was always one to take charge. He followed him up the stairs but stopped halfway. He had an odd feeling that made the hair go up on the back of his neck. He slowly turned around and looked back down to the closed front door. There were narrow windows to either side of it. Standing outside, looking in at him, was the woman in blue.

Jon's knees went weak. He tried to call out to Rick but his throat had seized, and he couldn't get the words out. He held eye contact with the woman for a few seconds then forced himself to hurry after Rick.

"This your room?" Rick asked once Jon joined him in the hallway. Jon nodded. Without asking permission, Rick strode boldly into the room as if he belonged. He went directly to the closed bathroom door and motioned for Jon to step up and say something.

Jon looked to Rick for encouragement. Rick gave him a wink.

"Lyn?" Jon said meekly. "How're you doing?"

"No!" Lyn screamed.

Not well. Jon realized this couldn't still be about her being startled at the top of the stairs. She was sobbing and it made his heart ache. Jon looked to Rick, helpless and confused. Rick pointed to himself as if to say: "Tell her I'm here."

Jon wasn't so sure it was a good idea, but Rick gave him a nod of encouragement.

"Lyn?" Jon said softly. "I'm not alone. Rick's here. Rick Banca. He stopped by for a visit. He's worried about you too. How about if you try to come out so we can all talk?"

There was a long pause and Jon wondered if Lyn had heard what he said.

Finally, in a soft, pained voice that he barely recognized, Lyn said, "Rick is here? Now?"

"Right here Lyn," Rick said, flatly.

Lyn's crying had seemingly stopped.

"Lyn? Sweetheart?" Jon said gently. "Open the door, okay?"

"Go downstairs Jon," Lyn said, suddenly calm. "Both of you."

It was another pendulum-like mood swing.

"Come with us," he said. "Please."

"I need a few minutes," Lyn replied, now sounding in control.

Jon looked to Rick and shrugged. Rick motioned that they should leave.

"Okay, we'll wait for you in the living room," Jon said. "Take your time."

Lyn didn't respond.

Jon led Rick downstairs and glanced at the window to see that the woman in blue was no longer there. He thought about telling Rick but figured there was enough drama going on without adding his own crazy into the mix.

"I don't get it," Jon said as he fell down into his favorite easy chair. "If she were on meds I'd say they were throwing her off, but she isn't. At least as far as I know."

"That's not the problem," Rick said with authority. "She's confused. I don't blame her. But she brought it on herself."

"I wouldn't say that exactly," Jon countered. "We're both guilty."

"Guilty of letting your marriage fall apart? I wouldn't know about that. I don't know enough about what's been going on between you two to have an opinion one way or the other."

"So then how can you say she brought this on herself?"

"A lot of things go sideways in life," Rick said. "When shit happens, the strong find solutions, but not everyone has that kind of strength. How do those people handle rough seas? Ride it out? Roll over? Fight to stay afloat? Or do they lay blame and lash out? Depending on what you do to try and fix things, you could be creating a world of hurt that's far worse than whatever problems you're facing."

"That's getting way too philosophical for me."

"All I'm saying is that there are lots of ways to handle a tough situation and not all of 'em are good."

"She's clearly hurting," Jon said.

"Yeah she is," Rick shot back. "But not for the reason you think."

Jon was growing uncomfortable with the way the conversation was going.

"How would you know that?" he asked.

Rick gave a non-committal shrug.

"Maybe you should take off," Jon added. "I can talk to her by myself."

"If that's what you want," Rick said. "But I want to help you."

"I appreciate that, but this is between Lyn and me."

"It's bigger than you realize, Jon. You're gonna need me."

Jon had heard enough. He stood up and said, "If we're going to work this out it's best we do it on our own and—"

"Rick!" Lyn gushed as she hurried into the living room. "What a great surprise!"

She gave Rick a big hug. Rick looked uncharacteristically uncomfortable, which only added to Jon's confusion.

Minutes before Lyn sounded like a wounded animal. Now she was back to being her best and brightest self. Her hair and make-up were perfect, her clothes were sharp and stylish. Jon couldn't comprehend how she could have been huddled in the bathroom, sobbing, only minutes before. Which was the act? Or were both personas real because his wife had gone bipolar?

"Tell Jon what you did, Lyn," Rick said, dead serious.

That threw Jon for another loop. Rick was an outgoing guy, even when he was spewing deeply philosophical theories about life. Now, suddenly, he had turned dark.

"What do you mean?" Lyn inquired with confusion.

Jon's attention was drawn to the living room window. Someone was outside, looking in. It wasn't the woman in blue. It was a man he'd never seen before.

Who was dressed in a powder blue suit.

"Look!" Jon yelled.

Rick and Lyn looked to the window.

"Oh shit," Rick exclaimed.

"You see him?" Jon asked. "I'm not crazy, right?"

"Yeah I see him," Rick said and took off running from the living room.

Jon hoped he was going for the front door to confront the man in the blue suit, but instead Rick turned the other way and ran up the stairs.

"Where are you going?" Jon yelled after him.

"Who is that outside, Jon?" Lyn asked with genuine confusion.

Jon was more concerned about Rick's behavior than about the mysterious visitor. Knowing that others saw the man outside was actually a relief, so he ran after his friend.

"Jon?" Lyn called sweetly. "Should I let that man in?"

Jon took the stairs two at a time. He reached the top, bounded down the hall and was stopped by Rick who stepped out of the bedroom looking dour.

"Rick, what the hell?"

"Let's go back downstairs."

He gently took Jon's arm to lead him back to the stairs, but Jon pulled it away.

"No!" he exclaimed. "What's going on?"

"Look Jon, there's a reason I'm here--."

"What the hell does that mean?" Jon said. "You're freaking me out."

"I know I'm sorry. That's exactly what I didn't want to happen. But I didn't see this coming."

"See what coming?"

"This is going to be tough, Jonny, but trust me, you're going to be okay."

"Would you please just tell me," Jon pled.

Rick gave his friend a reassuring squeeze on the shoulder, then stepped aside in a clear gesture that he wanted Jon to enter the bedroom.

Jon hesitated. As confusing as everything had been since he woke up that morning, there was one thing he felt certain of given Rick's doleful attitude: whatever was in the bedroom wouldn't be good.

Jon stepped in to see that the bathroom door was cracked open, and the light was out. Jon shot Rick a questioning look. Rick gave him a nod that encouraged him to keep going.

Jon walked the few steps across the bedroom with leaden feet, the product of an overwhelming sense of dread. He stopped at the bathroom door, gingerly pushed it open, flipped on the light, and fell to his knees.

Lyn was there, lying in a tub full of water that had turned red. Her eyes were closed. Her arms were crossed on her chest, ready for the coffin. She was no longer bleeding from the slits in her wrists. Once the heart stops beating, blood is no longer pumped.

The gruesome reality of the situation was obvious, but Jon was still Jon. He summoned what little shred of sanity he had left and hurried to his wife to fix the problem.

"Call nine one one!" he shouted to Rick as he felt Lyn's neck for a pulse.

"She's gone, Jon," Rick said calmly.

"You don't know that!" Jon screamed as the tears began to flow.

He lifted her arm, splashing wet blood that soaked into his freshly dry-cleaned sweater.

"Jon," Rick said. "Look over here."

Rick stepped aside to reveal that Lyn was standing in the doorway to the bedroom, staring in at the scene with wide eyes.

Jon stood up straight and backed away as Lyn slowly entered the bathroom, staring at the lifeless body in the tub.

Her body.

"I couldn't go on living like we were," she said in a daze.

She was clearly in shock. Seeing your own corpse will do that.

"But that's not why you killed yourself," Rick said. "Is it?"

"I'm so sorry, Jon," she said. "I have no excuse. I...I...just wanted out."

"So, you killed yourself?" Jon asked, horrified. "Our problems didn't justify this."

Lyn stared down at her bloody self as if the body was a museum curiosity and not the precious vessel she once lived in.

"That's not why," she said. "I couldn't live with the guilt."

"Over an affair?" Jon asked, incredulous. "I would have forgiven you. I do forgive you."

"I don't deserve forgiveness," Lyn said. "For anything."

"Lyn?" came a new voice.

Everyone turned to see the man in the powder blue suit standing in the bedroom doorway. He raised his hand toward Lyn, beckoning her.

Lyn looked between Jon and Rick as if they might know who this man was and why he was in their house.

"Go with him," Rick said.

"I don't understand," Jon said, mostly to himself.

Lyn relaxed, as if accepting the reality of the situation.

"I loved you, Jon," she said. "You may not believe that after what I've done. I still do."

"I love you too," Jon said. "I never stopped."

Jon made a move toward her as if to hug her, but Lyn held her hand up to stop him.

Jon stopped. It crushed him, but he stopped.

Lyn walked to the man in blue. He stepped aside to allow her to leave first. She left the room without a look back. The man in blue gave a quick look to Jon, offered a sympathetic smile, and followed Lyn.

"I've been seeing a woman dressed in blue," Jon said as if in a trance. "Was I supposed to follow her like that?"

"Not yet, Jonny."

"I'm not liking any of this."

"That's why I'm here for you," Rick said. "Take your time. I'll be downstairs."

Rick left Jon alone to spend a few final moments with the body of his wife. In those brief seconds, Jon's memory flashed back to the life they had shared. Most of it was good. He wanted to hold on to that, rather than to dwell on what their life had become.

He left the bedroom, headed down the stairs and went straight for the kitchen as if he knew it was where he needed to be.

Rick was there waiting for him by the door.

"Do I have to do this?" Jon asked.

"Afraid so," Rick replied.

Jon steeled himself and stepped into the kitchen to see exactly what he feared.

Sitting in the same seat where he had enjoyed his last meal, was Jon. He was slumped forward with his head on the table.

"My guess is she put the poison in the orange juice," Rick said.

Jon shook his head. He couldn't take his eyes off of his lifeless self.

"She said we needed a change," Jon said. "Didn't see this coming."

"She said she couldn't go on living like you were," Rick said. "But in the end she couldn't live with herself for what she'd done to you."

"How do you know all this?"

Rick went to the table and picked up the Sunday paper that Jon had been reading when his heart stopped.

"It might not be here," Rick said. "Printed newspapers are like reading yesterday's news tomorrow. Or it might not have been newsworthy enough to…ah, here we go. Guess you missed it."

He folded the paper to reveal an article and handed it to Jon. Jon read the account of how five riders who started out on the Route One Ramble in Fort Kent, Maine, were killed in a tragic accident when a big rig lost control, hydro-planed across the rain-slicked road and plowed into the entire group.

"My God," Jon said.

"Yeah, we just started out. How much does that suck?"

"I'm so sorry."

"I never saw it coming, so there's that. I wasn't even sure of what happened until this guy showed up in a blue suit looking like he was in a throwback Motown group. I guess you'd call them after-life guides. Mine didn't bring me to any pearly gates though. He brought me to you. I think whatever the thing is we call our soul doesn't necessarily leave right away. Some stick around to tie up loose ends."

"Loose ends?" Jon asked.

Jon thought back to the strange events he had witnessed that day. He hadn't seen a single other person in town, which was odd even for a quiet Sunday morning. But he did see a man on horseback and heard phantom kids playing football. Then there was the man having an argument over the phone in his office. Were they all spirits who hadn't yet left? Who didn't have a guide in blue to show them the way?

"Yup. Seems like my loose end, was you," Rick said. "You didn't know Lyn poisoned you. I'm here to show you the truth so you can get closure before heading out."

"Maybe it would be better if I didn't know the truth," Jon said.

"No, you need to know. We all do. But Lyn killing herself, I didn't expect that. Hell of a thing."

"Rick?"

Another spirit had entered the room. It was a tall, thin man wearing the now familiar powder blue suit.

"That's my guy," Rick said to Jon. "Motown, am I right?"

Jon walked up to the new arrival and said, "Okay, Smokey. I guess we're out of here."

The man in blue headed for the door with Rick following.

"Rick?" Jon called out.

Rick turned back.

"Where we're going, are we going to see each other?"

"I think so. Maybe we'll get some guys together for touch football. We'll have plenty of time for that, right?"

"Right. Plenty of time." Jon said.

Rick turned to the man in blue and said, "After you, chief."

The two left the kitchen and once again Jon was alone with mortal remains. His own. He picked up the empty glass of orange juice and sniffed it. Did it smell off?

"Jon?" came a woman's voice.

Jon didn't have to look to know who it was. He kept his eyes on his own corpse.

"Why didn't you ask me go with you right away?" he asked.

"You first had to understand what had happened to you."

"I guess," Jon said with a sigh. "Rick was a good friend."

"He still is."

"Can you give me a heads-up as to what's next? I'm a little nervous."

"I understand," the woman said. "I promise you won't be disappointed."

"I never believed in ghosts," Jon said.

"And now?"

"Now I'm excited to learn about all sorts of things I never believed in."

He turned to his guide, who stood in the doorway of the kitchen.

"That's the spirit," the woman in blue said with a warm smile.

It made Jon feel as if everything was going to be okay.

"Plenty of time," he said.

THE END

TIME TRIALS, UNLIMITED

Time.

It's an abstract concept created by ancient Egyptians to bring about an orderliness that not even the yearly changes to Earth's orbit around the sun can alter.

The march of time.

What time is it?

The nick of time.

It can't be seen, touched, or heard. It certainly can't be manipulated. Yet it is always there and factored into most every decision made, both large and small.

Time to go.

Not your time.

The time of your life.

It can be used to one's advantage or feared for its unrelenting certainty, but it cannot be ignored.

Time's up.

Time for a change.

Running out of time.

It does not play favorites. It is more powerful than love, ambition, animosity, religion, insanity, and even disease.

Time after time.

Father Time.

No time like the present.

Time is nothing less than the organizational bedrock upon which a complicated world-order was built. Without time there would be chaos.

Or would there?

Jamie Coogan didn't think so.

His time had come.

The typical reaction most people have when they glance at their bedside alarm clock to learn that they'd overslept is to launch into an adrenalin-fueled frenzy to get up, dressed, and out to whatever appointment they are certain to be late for.

Not Jamie. He didn't have a bedside clock. Or any clock for that matter. Or a watch. He did have a cell phone, but he never checked it for the time. It wasn't that Jamie was deliberately being irresponsible or uncaring, though he was both. He truly believed that being a slave to time was counterproductive.

"There is no true or lasting benefit from being on time." Was his mantra." It may be polite, and arguably respectful to other people's priorities, but the stress of living your life ruled by the incessant ticking of a sixty second minute is no tradeoff for the freedom of functioning untethered to an unbending timetable. Without the ever-present guillotine of a second-hand hanging above your neck, one is free to think and create and allow the kinds of ideas that change the world to take root and grow."

Of course, Jamie's friends thought he was crazy. Or lazy. Most thought his high-minded theories were just a cover for the fact that he couldn't be bothered to arrive on time for a dinner date or a movie or work. It was rude. It was maddening. It lost him more than a few jobs and several casual friendships. His long-time friends accepted his eccentricity and made allowances. Nobody expected Jamie to arrive on time, which didn't necessarily mean he was always late. He was notorious for showing up to parties an hour or two early, bottle of wine in hand since he was ready for the festivities to begin, even if no one else was.

"Ideas come from inspiration, not perspiration," was one of his credos. "I've spent days focused on trying to find the solution to a problem only to come up empty. Yet I could be on a run in the park and with no warning the answer I'd desperately been searching for would come to me like a gift from heaven. When you waste valuable brain time fretting over structure and schedules, you're blocking the possibility for true inspiration."

It helped that Jamie's current job was project-based. He developed apps for a company called *Apperture* that ranged in function from exercise tracking to meditation to turning selfies into silly alien creatures. No one at *Apperture* punched a time clock. as long as the work was completed, management didn't care when or where it got done. While that fit nicely into Jamie's style, it didn't mean he could slack. He often worked tirelessly to bring projects across the finish line. His friends argued that he couldn't work that way in any other job. His comeback was that he wouldn't want a job where he couldn't work that way.

One person who rarely gave him grief about his theories on time was his girlfriend, Ariel McCarron. He wouldn't refer to her as his fiancé because to him that implied there was a specific period of time between acknowledging they were going to be married, and a wedding. His attitude was, "We'll get married when it's right."

Ariel was the polar opposite of Jamie. She was buttoned up, organized, and kept a detailed calendar. She knew exactly when they were going to be married and had started planning for it. She didn't ask for Jamie's opinion on any kind of schedule, only on the details of the event. In many ways the two were perfect for each other. Her penchant for organization allowed Jamie to be his freewheeling self. She picked up the pieces and filled in the gaps. Friends accused her of being an enabler, but for Ariel it was the perfect scenario. She was able to organize their world in whatever way she saw fit because ninety-nine times out of a hundred Jamie would go along with whatever plans she had put in place. Sure, he would often be late and occasionally push back on her insistence that he be respectful of other people's schedules, but in large part it was a perfectly symbiotic relationship.

And they truly loved each other. It could be argued that they were made for each other.

"Hey Jamie, did you schedule a three o'clock appointment?" asked Izzy, the young, front-desk assistant du jour for *Apperture*.

Jamie looked at him over the top of his glasses, and Izzy burst out laughing.

"Yeah, I know," he said. "Stupid question. But there's a lady out front who said she'd like to speak with you."

"Who is she?"

"Says she's from a company called Time Trials, Unlimited. They want to develop an app. She asked for you specifically. No idea why."

Jamie too off his headphones and said, "Because I'm the best."

"Yeah," Izzy said. "Or because she couldn't get an appointment with anybody else here. I'll send her to the conference room."

"Thanks, Iz," Jamie said with a chuckle as he closed his laptop.

Jamie preferred working at the company's office rather than at home. He thrived on the atmosphere where so many creative programmers were dreaming up new ways to tie people to their electronics. He loved to spitball ideas. For most, development was a solitary endeavor. Jamie saw it as a team sport, and it was hard to argue with him for he was the most productive developer on the *Apperture* staff. It also gave credibility to his disdain for time management.

He pulled off his hoodie, for even he realized that it was more the uniform of a high school gamer, not a professional in his late 20's. He quickly ran his fingers through his longish, and prematurely graying hair to add another touch of professionalism, swept up his laptop, and headed for the community conference room.

Waiting for him, seated at the far end of the silly-long table, was the visitor from *Time Trials, Unlimited*. When Jamie entered, she stood and confidently held her hand out to shake.

"Thank you for seeing me, Mr. Coogan. My name is Mercy Parr. Call me Mercy."

They shook hands and Jamie noticed that her grip was a heck of a lot stronger than his.

"Call me Jamie."

"Lovely. I will," she said and handed him her business card.

It read: "*Mercy Parr – Outreach- Time Trials, Unlimited.*"

Jamie's first impression of her was "corporate power player". Her perfectly tailored black suit and three-inch heels looked expensive which meant that whatever *Time Trials, Unlimited* was, she wasn't a low-level employee. Her dark hair was pixie-cut, her make-up understated, and her jewelry tasteful. In a word, she was beautiful. Jamie appreciated beautiful women. As he often said to his friends: "I love Ariel, but I'm not dead." He didn't share that particular sentiment with Ariel, but he also never cheated on her. He just so happened to appreciate the feminine aesthetic.

"What can I do for you, Mercy?"

The two sat and Jamie opened his laptop, poised to take notes.

"We're in the market for a new app that will extend the reach of our product to a wider audience," Mercy said.

"And what product is that?"

"We offer time management services," she said. "We feel that everyone can benefit from an organized—"

Jamie gently closed his laptop.

"—have I come to the wrong place?" Mercy asked.

Jamie chuckled and said, "Right place, wrong person."

"Aren't you the lead developer here?"

"Yah, I guess," Jamie replied. "But I'm also someone who needs to have an affinity for the projects I take on. There are several other developers here who would be more than happy to—"

"You're saying you don't see the value in time management?"

"It's not as simple as that. I believe that the more rigidly we conduct our lives, the less forward thinking we become."

"So, it *is* as simple as that," Mercy said with a sly smile.

"I suppose so," Jamie said as he stood up. "Let me see if someone else is available who'd be more appropriate for your project."

"I think you would be perfect."

"But my thinking is diametrically opposed to the service you're offering."

"Maybe. Let me try and understand that thinking. You believe that structure limits productivity."

"Not productivity per se, but certainly creativity. I believe that most breakthroughs in any field are the result of happy accidents. Success can't be manufactured or wrestled into existence by persistence. At least not in its initial stages. Our minds need to wander and imagine. The more restrictions we put on our thinking; the less inventive our thinking becomes."

"It sounds as though you value chaos."

"That's a little dramatic," Jamie said. "But I believe more options create more chances for success."

"Options," Mercy said as if weighing the value of the word. "Did you ever consider how many options an individual is presented with each day? I'm not talking about obvious life and death decisions; I mean the hundreds of simple choices that are made without much thought. Do I wear the black shoes or the brown? Is it cereal for breakfast, or eggs? Which route should I drive to work? Which parking space should I take? Do I ask my co-worker how their evening was; or simply give them a passing nod? Uber or Lyft? These are the kinds of mundane, trivial decisions we are constantly making, with no thought as to whether they will have little effect on the rest of our day or trigger a series of events that will lead to the destruction of civilization."

"I thought you weren't talking about life and death decisions."

"Every decision has the potential to be about life or death," Mercy shot back. "But since no one can see into the future, the best we can do is decide what is right in that moment."

"What's any of that got to do with time management?"

"You contend that existing as a free-floating entity, not bound by societal structure will lead to more successful choices. While that may be a possibility in isolated cases, I believe that the more control we have over our lives, the better the chances are for success. Call it time management, call it hedging one's bet or simply being organized. Minimizing the chances for random outcomes is the only way to avoid starting a butterfly effect that could lead to chaos."

"But you can't predict that," Jamie said.

"No, there are no guarantees," Mercy said with a smile. "That's life."

"Interesting" Jamie said, and he meant it. He'd never met anyone who had given as much thought to the benefits, or dangers of time management as he had.

"I'd love to debate this, but it won't change my mind about taking on your project. Let me find someone else to—"

Mercy stood up quickly. "Don't bother. I too need to have an affinity for the projects I take on, and for the people I work with. I can't imagine there is anyone else in your company who has given as much thought to the subject of random versus calculated choice as you have. It's either you, or no one."

"And you've just made one of those choices," Jamie said.

"We both have."

Mercy held out her hand to shake and added, "It was lovely to meet you, Jamie. If you change your mind, my number is on the card. And good luck with the rest of your day."

With one last quick smile she skirted around Jamie and left.

Jamie stood there feeling slightly shaken. It wasn't so much that he had just blown the chance at scoring a new client for *Apperture*, it was about Mercy's choice of words.

"And good luck with the rest of your day," he said to himself.

It felt vaguely like a warning.

The rest of Jamie's workday was uneventful as he struggled to de-bug a string of code that was causing one of *Apperture'*s premiere apps, a file-sharing service, to crash. It was mind numbing work and he had to struggle to keep his eyes open. No amount of coffee helped, and he nodded off more than once.

He was awakened by his cell phone, and the custom ringtone he had programmed for Ariel. It was the guitar riff from the Beatle's song *Blackbird*.

"Hi," he said brightly, trying to sound as though he hadn't been asleep three seconds before.

"Were you asleep?" Ariel asked playfully.

"How do you know these things?" he replied. "Are you a witch?"

"Yes I am, and I need you to wake up and focus."

The connection was a poor one. Ariel kept breaking up and Jamie only caught every other word.

"Are you in a dead zone?" he asked.

"No, it's my phone. I dropped it and now it's like I'm calling from Mars. I'm dropping it off at Rocky's right now. I should put that guy on retainer."

"Or get a new phone," Jamie said.

"What did you say?" Ariel said with frustration. She was having trouble hearing Jamie as well.

"Forget it," Jamie said, louder, as if that would somehow overcome the electronic glitch.

"The concert starts at eight," Ariel said "We have six-thirty dinner reservations at Augie's. I know this information has little meaning for you, but I don't want to be standing outside of the restaurant waiting for you. It's cold."

"I understand," Jamie said. "You will see me precisely at six-twenty-nine."

"Right," Ariel said with a chuckle. "And I'm going to win the Powerball lottery. But just to guilt you into making the effort, I'm not going to go inside and sit alone until you get there. Imagine a freezing witch standing on a street corner looking pathetic and cold."

"And pretty, don't forget pretty."

"That too. And since I'm dropping off my phone you won't be able to text me to say you're going to be late. Did you hear all of that?"

"Barely, but no worries, I got it," Jamie said with authority. "I'll be there at six-twenty-nine. Don't keep me waiting."

'No chance. I love you. See you then."

"Yes you will, I love you too."

Jamie punched out of the call as Izzy walked by his desk.

"Iz, what time is it?"

Izzy stopped abruptly and stared down at him.

"You want to know the time?" he asked in mock horror. "Who are you? What have you done with Jamie?"

"You're hysterical."

Izzy looked at his watch and said, "Big hand's on the six and little hand's on the five. You can figure it out from there. Or can you?"

"Sass is totally underrated," Jamie said.

"I always thought so," Issy said and continued walking.

Jamie shut down his laptop, ready to pack it in for the night. But he wasn't quite ready to leave. He glanced around his cubicle as if looking for something else he might get done before heading out. He drummed his fingers on his desk, got an idea, and jumped up. He headed straight for the cubicle of his friend Danni, a graphic designer.

"Hey," Jamie said as he peered over the top of her cubicle. "What's up with the fantasy football app?"

Danni looked frazzled.

"You have arrived at the exact right time," she said. "I'm tapped. Everything I come up with is a variation on something I've seen a thousand times. There are no new ideas."

"Not true," Jamie said as he entered the cubicle. "Do you know there are only twelve musical notes??"

"I didn't before you told me about a hundred times," Danni replied.

"Think of the variations," Jamie said with passion. "Even subtle differences can create dramatic changes."

"Easy for you to say, Beethoven."

Jamie pulled up a chair and said, "Show me what you've got."

The two instantly became immersed in the task of chasing those elusive, subtle design variations that would make an app stand out among the many others that did essentially the same thing. With Jamie's new perspective, fresh ideas were unlocked for Danni and soon she was playing with a color palette she hadn't considered before and found hope that she might actually deliver a relatively unique design.

"This is great," she said with genuine enthusiasm. "Imagine what we could do if there were thirteen musical notes?"

"Nah, that would make it too easy," Jamie said.

"Thanks Jamie, I got this. Go home to Ariel."

"I'm meeting her for dinner. What time is it?"

Danni checked her computer. "Six o'clock."

"Hey, try monkeying with the background texture," Jamie said as if he hadn't registered her answer. Or didn't care to. "Maybe try the leather-look. Might make an interesting contrast with the modern text font."

Danni went right back to work as Jamie watched with interest, and the clock kept moving. Soon Danni went down a creative rabbit hole that continued to vastly improve the look of the app, which fascinated Jamie.

"Nice," he exclaimed.

"Yeah. It is. Now go! I don't want your girlfriend blaming me for you being late."

"She won't. She always assumes it's my fault, even when it isn't."

"You mean there are times that it isn't your fault?"

"See you tomorrow."

Jamie headed back to his desk while peeking into other's cubicles to see what they were working on. Nothing grabbed his interest, so he took his coat and headed for the elevator.

Apperture was on the twelfth floor of an 80's era steel and glass office building in midtown Manhattan. Grabbing an elevator at the end of the day was always a challenge since everyone seemed to leave work at the same time, which of course Jamie would point to as yet another example of schedules being a hindrance. But he always took it as an opportunity to chat with whomever he was waiting with.

"Mekhi, hi!" Jamie said.

Mekhi was one of the two partners who started *Apperture* and lured Jamie away from his previous job.

"How's my superstar?" Mekhi asked.

"Which one?" Jamie asked. "Check out what Danni's got going with that fantasy football app. She's killing it."

An elevator door opened and closed.

"Is she as good as I think she is?" Mekhi asked.

"I don't know what you think, but please keep her happy because she's making us all look good."

Another elevator opened. Mekhi made a move for it, but Jamie stopped him. The door closed.

"I have to apologize," Jamie said. "Somebody came in today looking to develop an app. I didn't think I was right for it and tried to bring somebody else in, but she wouldn't go for it. I'm sorry. I blew it."

"Did you get her name?" Mekhi asked.

"Yeah, I got her card. It's on my desk. Hang on, I'll get it."

Jamie hurried off as a third elevator door opened.

"Give it to me tomorrow!"

"But it's right here," Jamie called back. "Wait!"

"It's okay, nothing gonna happen tonight."

"I'll be right back. Don't move!

Jamie took off while Mekhi hurried into the elevator. He was not going to miss a third one.

"Tomorrow Jamie!' He called out as the door closed.

Jamie was already out of earshot. He retrieved the card and hurried back to the lobby to see that Mekhi was gone. With a shrug he jammed it into his pocket and took the next elevator down.

Augie's was a restaurant across from the southernmost end of Union Square park, a short subway ride from Jamie's office. He left his building and headed straight for the station at 60th and Lexington Avenue. If you had asked him what time it was, the best he might have come up with was "rush hour" based on the dense, after-work crowd. Jamie descended the steps into the ancient station and used his MetroCard to pass through the turnstile.

He stepped onto the platform just as a #4 train pulled in. Jamie would have taken it, but his eye caught sight of a bold, back-page New York Post headline at the news vendor's kiosk. *"GONE!"* it screamed in three-inch letters. He couldn't pass that up, so he grabbed a paper and elbowed his way through the crowd to pay for it.

The train filled, the doors closed, and it slid out of the station without Jamie.

Jamie had no real love for the New York Post, other than for its sports coverage. He found an unoccupied spot against the wall where he could get away from the crush of humanity to read. The headline teased an announcement by the New York Jets, the team he'd been a fan of since forever.

"Unbelievable," he uttered as he read about how they had yet again traded away an All-Pro who was tired of playing for a perennial loser.

As he read, another train arrived, spewed passengers, sucked in new ones, and continued on its way.

Jamie finished the article and tossed the paper into the trash. "I gotta stop caring about that joke of a team," he thought as he boarded the next train, along with dozens of other passengers.

The #4 train was an express that made only one stop before Jamie's destination. The trip took only a few minutes and he soon got off at 14th street/Union Square. By complete accident his eye caught a grimy clock on the dingy wall of the station.

It was 6:40. Rather than thinking he was going to catch hell for being late, he congratulated himself for it being only by ten minutes. For him, that was a victory. Still, it was past the time he'd promised to be there. Instead of picking up the pace, he stopped at a vendor at the top of the station's stairs. He wanted to buy a small bouquet of spring flowers to present to Ariel. Certainly, that would compensate for his slight tardiness. It took him a few more minutes to examine every last bouquet before deciding on the perfect arrangement.

Feeling proud of himself, he clutched the flowers and made his way along 14th street, headed for Broadway and a date with his girl.

New York City is a vibrant place filled with sound and energy, especially during rush hour when the sidewalks are jammed with people hurrying to be somewhere else. Jamie strained to look above the crowd to see if Ariel was standing outside of Augie's as she promised. Or threatened. The restaurant was across the wide avenue that was Broadway. Jamie walked to the curb, looked across the street and saw Ariel standing behind the crowd waiting to cross in his direction. From that distance he couldn't tell if she was pissed off, but he felt certain the bouquet of flowers would defuse any hostility.

He heard the siren before he saw the flashing lights. As he waited for the pedestrian crossing signal, he looked back to see what might be coming. A fire truck? An ambulance?

It was neither, at least at first. He saw a non-descript dark sedan speeding west on 14th street. Further back a cop car was in pursuit with its siren wailing. Still further back was a second cop car with its lights flashing. Traffic was at a standstill. The sedan weaved through the cars and nearly ran down a pedestrian crossing 14th. It was a miracle that the sedan hadn't hit the innocent man, or any of the other cars that were frozen in place. It reached the intersection of Broadway several car-lengths ahead of the first cop car that was moving with more caution as it struggled to catch up.

When the sedan reached Broadway, it made a sharp left turn south, directly in front of Jamie. The driver accelerated into the turn and Jamie heard its wheels squeal as it slid across the pavement. The wet pavement. It had been raining all day and the road was slick. The sedan lost control. Like a stunt car doing an intentional "drift", it side-slipped to its right, headed for the far curb.

Exactly where Ariel stood waiting for Jamie, who was fifteen minutes late.

The people in front of Ariel saw what was coming and fled. It was like a curtain of people had been pulled to either side to reveal her standing there. She saw the out-of-control car coming, too late. It hit the curb and flipped onto the sidewalk. Ariel was either in disbelief, or too shocked to react. Whatever the reason, she didn't move, and the careening car hit her.

Jamie saw the entire event unfold as if in slow motion. He saw Ariel, he saw the careening car, he saw the split second of terror on Ariel's face as she took one inconsequential step backward, and then she was gone. He ran across the street to get to her, dropping the bouquet along the way. One quick look into the flipped wreck showed him that the driver was not going to make it.

Another look ahead told him that Ariel wasn't going to make it either.

Her time was up.

The funeral was a surreal affair, as is usually the case when someone meets a tragic and sudden end. Especially when that someone was so young. The service and internment took place at a cemetery in Westchester County where Ariel had grown up, and her parents still lived. Jamie floated through the day, zombie like.

Ariel's parents never fully took to him. The idea that someone as flighty as Jamie could be their son-in-law went against their protective and rigid nature. But he was dutiful toward them at the service and said all the right things. They were grateful for his heartfelt condolences and appreciated that he too had lost someone who meant the world to him. Jamie had minimal contact with anyone else. His friends sensed that he needed space and left him alone.

Losing his best friend was difficult enough. Jamie also had to contend with the fact that he felt somewhat responsible. The harsh reality was that if he had been on time as promised, he and Ariel would have witnessed the event from the safety of the restaurant and Ariel would be spending today with him on their couch watching Netflix rather than sitting in an urn that would soon go into a wall that would be sealed with a marble slab engraved with her name, date of birth, and date of death.

The service was a blur. Jamie was there in body only. His spirit was still on the corner of Broadway and 14th street, replaying the horror. After the internment and a few gracious good-byes, Jamie got an Uber and rode back to the apartment in Manhattan that was no longer "their" apartment.

While in the car he took out his phone to scroll through pictures of Ariel. It wasn't a comforting experience. He opened up her contact card and saw her picture, along with the details of how to get in touch with her: Her email, address, cell number, and home number.

All the important details of someone's life that no longer had value. Still, he couldn't bring himself to delete them. He wanted to hear her voice, so he dialed her cell to hear her recorded greeting. He knew it would be gut wrenching, but maybe that was the point. It was a form of punishment. He pressed the number. It rang and he braced himself to hear her voice.

He didn't.

Someone answered the phone.

"You lookin' for Ariel McCarron?" a man said, sounding more than a little put out.

Jamie sat up straight.

"Who is this?" he asked.

"Look, I've been trying to get hold of her for a week," the man replied. "I'm tired of answering her calls."

Jamie's mind was spinning. What was happening?

"This is Ariel's boyfriend," he said with more than a touch of indignant anger. "Who are you?"

"It's Rocky the phone repair guy. She was supposed to pick it up days ago and I can't even call her to come pick it up because I've got the freaking phone!"

Now Jamie remembered. Ariel had dropped her phone off to get repaired the day of the accident.

"I can pick it up," Jamie said.

"Uh, I ain't supposed to let nobody pick up a phone but the owner."

"You will if you want to get paid. Ariel's dead. You probably saw the accident."

There was a long silence.

"She was the one who got hit outside Augie's?"

Jamie didn't feel the need to explain and punched out of the call. An hour later the Uber driver dropped him off in front of Rocky's Electronics, which was a few doors away from Augie's. Jamie kept his head down while striding for the shop. He couldn't bring himself to take in the scene of Ariel's death.

Rocky didn't need to ask Jamie who he was. The moment he saw him walk into his shop; he knew. He handed the phone over, no questions asked.

"What do I owe you?" Jamie asked.

"You don't," Rocky replied. "It was just minor water damage. I cleaned it up and it's as—" he stopped himself. "I guess that don't really matter now. I'm sorry, man. She was a sweet girl."

Jamie gave him a quick nod of thanks, jammed the phone into his pocket and hurried out, headed for home with a treasure that felt somehow illicit. He was carrying a piece of Ariel. Like everyone else, a big part of her life was bundled into her cell phone.

When he got to the apartment he placed the phone on the low table in front of their couch and got himself a Heineken. He sat down on the couch, the same couch where he and Ariel watched hours of TV, ate many a meal, had countless conversations, and often made love. Now all he had of her was a cell phone that sat on the table, dark and mute. At least it no longer had water damage.

So many details of a person's life are contained in their phone. It's like a diary. But a diary is private. Would he be violating a trust if he explored it? Did it matter anymore?

He decided that his need to hang on to Ariel for a while longer justified his actions, so he powered up the phone. He knew her password, so he quickly got to her home screen. The first thing he did was open her picture folder. Unlike the photos on his own phone, most of the pictures were of him. Made sense. He took pictures of her with his phone and visa-versa. There were also several selfies of the two of them, some of which he'd never seen, and it made his heart ache. He wanted to be that guy again but knew he never would. And he had nobody to blame but himself.

"I'm sorry, Ari," he said while holding back tears.

He closed the photo app and realized there wasn't much more on the phone he felt the need to explore. There was no point in going through her contacts, or her calendar. If anything, swiping through the icons of her various apps gave him a much better snapshot of the person she was. She had TikTok and a banking app, which pretty much represented both sides of her personality. She had a yoga workout app and an app dedicated to meditation. That was a surprise. He didn't know that she mediated. There were the standard Twitter, HuffPost and Instagram apps.

He eventually came upon an app he didn't recognize. It was a stylized logo showing two intertwined T's. Being someone who developed apps for a living, he thought he knew them all. But not this one. Without hesitation, he touched it and the app opened.

The log-in page read: *Welcome to Time Trials, Unlimited.*

Time Trials? Where had he heard that name before?

He didn't know Ariel's username and password and wasn't about to start making random guesses. The app seemed fairly bland anyway. There was nothing about its name that gave a clue as to what it offered. Bad branding.

He was about to close it out and shut down the phone when it hit him.

Mercy Parr.

Time Trials.

This was the app that the confidant woman who came into *Apperture* wanted to re-do. Ariel had downloaded it. Coincidence? What exactly was *Time Trials, Unlimited*? Had Ariel opened an account? He remembered that it was something to do with time management. That's when he shut down the conversation with Mercy Parr. Now he wished he hadn't.

He ran into the bedroom, dug through the hamper of dirty laundry, and found the pants he'd worn that day. In the back pocket was Mercy Parr's business card, right where he tucked it away after he went back to his desk to get it for Mekhi. That was only a week ago. It felt like a lifetime.

Mercy Parr – Outreach – Time Trials, Unlimited.

Ariel hadn't mentioned anything about it.

Jamie's curiosity went into overdrive. He wanted to call the number right then and there. Though it was past business hours he didn't hesitate for a second. It was the way he rolled. He dialed the number. After one ring, the call was answered by a familiar voice.

"I don't understand," was how Mercy Parr opened the conversation.

Jamie was momentarily thrown by the odd salutation but pressed on.

"This is Jamie Coogan. From *Apperture*. You gave me your business card."

There were a few seconds of silence, which Jamie took as the time Mercy needed to process the information.

"It's ten o'clock at night," she said coldly. "Though I suppose this is in keeping with your disdain for the accepted norms of daily organization."

"This isn't a business call," Jamie said. "It's about my girlfriend."

"Ariel. Of course. I heard of the accident and was surprised to see that a call was coming in from her number. It now makes sense. I am sorry for your loss, Jamie."

"Thank you. Did Ariel have an account with Time Trials?"

"She did."

"Did you know she was my girlfriend when you came in that day?"

"I did."

"Why didn't you tell me?"

"We don't discuss clients, not even with their partners."

"Clients," Jamie repeated thoughtfully. "What exactly is it that you do again?"

"As I began to explain to you, we help people with time management issues. The service varies depending on the individual and their needs."

"And Ariel signed up?"

"She did register, yes."

"That's bullshit because she was the most organized person I'd ever met. She had no time management issues."

"That's not true, she had one very big issue."

"And what was that?"

"You."

That rocked Jamie. There was no question that Ariel was sometimes frustrated with his loose association with the clock, but she never made it an issue because it wasn't an issue…

…until it led to her death.

"Is that why you came to my office?" Jamie asked, shaken. "To see her so-called issue firsthand?"

"It was. Though I do believe we would benefit from a re-branding. I looked at it as killing two birds with one stone, but since you shut me down I only ended up killing one of those birds. I got a very good sense of your feelings about being a slave to time."

"And how was that supposed to help Ariel?"

"We'll never know," Mercy replied. "She signed up for our program but hadn't activated it."

"What would have happened if she did?" Jamie asked. "Is this some kind of self-help class?"

"In a matter of speaking. As we discussed in your office, our program deals with the randomness of life and with the small choices that could lead to dramatic outcomes."

"So that means you really can predict the future," Jamie said sarcastically.

"Let me offer a suggestion. Rather than have me continue to explain, try it for yourself. Ariel paid the fee. You could take her place."

"And do what?" Jamie asked, more adamantly.

"You can play out the program that she was so enthused about. Think of it as fulfilling a wish in her memory. It's kind of poetic, actually. If you're not interested I'd be happy to issue a refund to you, or to her family."

"Can I ask what the fee was?"

"Ten thousand dollars."

Jamie's knees went weak.

"Ten thousand! What the hell kind of time management program costs ten grand?"

"Ours," was Mercy's unapologetic answer. "We're quite effective."

"I don't care what your so-called program is. Don't think for a second that it would change anything about the way I live my life, no matter how much it costs."

"Of course not," Mercy said. "But you might learn something. After all, it's what Ariel wanted."

That stung Jamie. He was feeling vaguely manipulated. The idea of this woman playing on his sympathy to get him to commit to something ridiculous, and expensive, wasn't exactly ethical.

"Just so you know," Mercy added. "If you aren't satisfied with the results we will issue a refund, less five percent for our miscellaneous expenses. You really don't have much to lose."

The idea intrigued Jamie, if only for the fact it would give him a chance to demonstrate how ineffective and ultimately wasteful the whole concept of strict time management was.

And it was what Ariel wanted.

"Ten thousand dollars is a very expensive lesson," Jamie said.

"We're good at what we do."

This intrigued Jamie even more. What service could this outfit provide that didn't turn out to be a scam?

"All right," he said. "I'll give it a shot."

"Lovely. On the app go to the sign-up page and fill out the brief questionnaire. We already have the payment from Ariel so once you're registered I'll credit that to your account. Once the transfer is made a link will appear that simply says engage."

"Then what happens?"

"Nothing. At first. We'll need to do some prep work though it won't take long since most of what we were preparing for Ariel applies to you."

"Right," Jamie said with a snicker. "Because I was the issue."

"Something like that," Mercy said. "After you engage, we'll be in contact. Do you have any other questions?"

"I have a load of questions, but I'll assume they'll be answered once I start the program."

"They will."

"All right, you're on. I'll fill out the form right now."

"Lovely," Mercy said. "Thank you for using Time Trials."

The phone went dead.

"Uh, did you hang up?" Jamie asked.

No response.

"I guess that's an example of your efficient use of time," he said, scoffing. "Don't want to waste valuable seconds with niceties."

Jamie immediately went to the app's sign-up page and filled out the form that asked for his name and date of birth. He hit "enter" and was immediately taken to a screen where he had to select a password. His choice: "Ariel". Once that was accepted he was taken to the next screen that said: *PAID IN FULL.* Mercy worked fast, almost as if she had been prepared to make the transfer all along. He hit the button marked *NEXT* which brought him to a lengthy disclaimer page that Jamie assumed would absolve *Time Trials, Unlimited* from any liability should something go wrong. He wouldn't know for sure because like most everyone else who are faced with pages of daunting legalize and disclaimers, he immediately scrolled through without reading and quickly hit *ACCEPT.*

The next page showed a large green button with white lettering that said: *ENGAGE.*

"This is just dumb," he said and hit the button.

The screen went black, then a single line of copy appeared: *Good luck with the rest of your day.*

"Scam," he said with disgust. He powered Ariel's phone down and placed it on the table in front of the couch.

"I hope we get your money's worth, Ari," he said to the phone. "But I doubt it."

It had been a brutally long day and Jamie was physically and mentally exhausted. He took a quick, hot shower and went right to bed. He hadn't yet decided if he was going to go into the office the next day. He was inclined not to, if only to prove that no app could guide him into living his life with the kind of structure most people surrendered to. It would be a small act of defiance, but a meaningful one. The bonus would come when he got Ariel's money back from the smug Mercy Parr...less 5%

He didn't set the alarm.

Then again, he never set the alarm.

Jamie was awoken by the familiar notes of the Beatles' song, *Blackbird*. He always loved that song, mostly because it was one of Ariel's favorites. It gave him a warm, nostalgic feeling...that lasted a solid three seconds before he remembered that Ariel was dead.

He opened one eye to see he wasn't in bed. He was sitting at his desk at *Apperture*, and his phone was ringing, with Ariel's ringtone. It took a few more seconds for him to shake away the fog of sleep. He looked at his phone and sure enough, a picture of Ariel's smiling face was on the screen. He was getting a call from her. Or at least from her phone. But her phone was in their apartment. Which is exactly where he thought he should be. He had no memory of getting up and going to work.

Who was calling?

He snatched the phone and answered.

"Who is this?" he demanded.

"Were you asleep?" came the reply.

The connection was a bad one. The voice crackled and broke up, but it was definitely her. It was Ariel.

Jamie went numb.

"Jamie?' I need you to wake up and focus."

"Who is this?" he yelled into the phone.

"It's me. Who else would it be? My phone is messed up. I'm dropping it off at Rocky's before dinner."

"Ariel? How--?"

"I can barely hear you. I hope you're hearing me. The concert starts at eight. We have a six-thirty reservation at Augie's. I'll be standing outside waiting for you. Please don't be late, it's cold."

Jamie could make out every fourth word, but he knew exactly what she was saying because he'd heard it before. He started to shake as tears welled up.

"I'm dreaming," was all he managed to say.

"I know you know all this, but I won't have my phone so if you're late you won't be able to tell me."

"Ariel?" he said weakly.

"You're not getting any of this, are you? I love you. See you at six thirty. Or earlier would be good but…never mind."

She hung up, leaving Jamie holding the phone to his ear, unable to move.

Izzy walked by the desk, glanced at him, and stopped.

"I never thought I'd say this to anybody, but you look like you've just seen a ghost."

Jamie shot a look to him that was so vicious it actually made Izzy take a step back.

"That's just cruel," Jamie snarled.

"Really? Then you don't know true cruel," Izzy said, nonplussed, and hurried off.

Jamie was in a daze. There was only one explanation for what was happening. It was a dream. It had to be. An incredibly vivid dream that tore his heart out. He stood up and glanced around the office. Nothing seemed remotely dream-like or out of the ordinary. People were in their cubicles, diligently working away. He stepped out of his space and walked slowly past the rows of desks, glancing down at his co-workers, looking for any sign that this was some elaborate, cruel prank.

When he arrived at Danni's cubicle, he watched her work for a few moments to see she was still wrestling with the design for the fantasy football app.

"Hey," he said weakly.

Danni spun her chair around and looked visibly relieved when she saw him.

"You came at the exact right time," she said. "I'm stumped. Everything I've come up with for this fantasy app is like, been done. Can I pick your brain?"

"What time is it?" Jamie asked.

Danni glanced at her computer screen and said, "Five fifteen. Since when did you care about time?"

"What day is it? I mean the date?"

"The eleventh," she replied. "You want to know what year it is too?"

"Is this a dream?" Jamie asked.

Danni stared at him, not sure of what to make of his odd behavior.

"If it is, we're both having it," she said. "But that technology's a little beyond my skill set. Have you been working on a dream-sharing app?"

Jamie turned and ran back to his cubicle. He fell down into his seat, breathing hard, his heart racing. There was nothing about what was happening that made this feel like a dream, other than everything. He checked his computer to verify that it was indeed the eleventh. The day that Ariel was killed.

He grabbed his phone and dialed Ariel's number, only to get her voice mail. He threw the phone onto his desk and tried to concentrate, wracking his brain for a shred of information that would explain what was happening. He was fully awake, of that he felt certain. Was it possible that everything that had happened over the past week was the dream and this was reality? He was living in a moment of time he'd already lived through. When would that have started? The morning of the eleventh? It had to have been before Ariel called to remind him about their dinner. That was the first duplicate event.

Time was overlapping.

Time.

Time Trials.

He dug through the papers on his desk and located the business card of Mercy Parr that he hadn't yet put into his pocket. He quickly dialed her number using his cell phone. After one ring there was an answer, but not one that made sense. It was Mercy, but her voice was recorded.

"Hello. There will be no contact between clients and Time Trials personnel during an active trial. I will return your call upon its completion."

The call disconnected.

Jamie was reeling. Though his hand was shaking on his mouse, he managed to Google *"Time Trials, Unlimited".* The familiar sign-in page came up asking for his name and password. He entered his name, the password "Ariel" and hit *ENTER.* The screen immediately flipped to a page with the double "T" logo and the message: *"There will be no contact between clients and Time Trials during an active trial. Please visit once your trial is complete."*

Jamie wanted to scream. He had signed up for Time Trials, that much was certain. Was it the night before? He paid for it with the fee Ariel had given them for her own trial. Ten thousand freaking bucks. He remembered it all. He also remembered that it had happened a week after Ariel died.

That meant what had happened before was not a dream. Nor was what was happening in that moment. The only other explanation was the most incredible one: He was re-living events from a week ago. Whether it was some kind of hypnotic spell, or artificial intelligence, or virtual reality he had no clue. But Time Trials had sent him back a week. Back to the day that Ariel died. In that moment, in that reality, Ariel was still alive.

"Izzy!' Jamie shouted.

The assistant appeared quickly and looked down into Jamie's cubicle.

"What" he asked petulantly. "Is it your turn to be cruel?"

"What time is it?" Jamie asked.

"Seriously?"

"What time is it!" Jamie demanded.

"Fine, all right!"

Izzy looked at his watch and said, "Big hand's on the six and the little hand's on the five. You can figure it out from there. Or can you?"

Izzy waited for a response but got none.

"Whatever," he said with a shrug and moved on.

"This is the trial," Jamie said to himself. "I'm getting a second chance."

It was 5:30. The accident happened at 6:45. There was plenty of time for him to get to Union Square and make sure that Ariel was nowhere near the spot where the car would flip onto the sidewalk.

He actually relaxed for now he had a mission. Trying to understand how Time Trials could make this happen was a task better saved for later. He didn't want to waste valuable brain time on anything but saving Ariel. But he couldn't keep his mind from spinning out the possibilities. Once he saved her would the spell be broken? Would reality come flooding back? What would the point be in that? Was it about Time Trials teaching him a lesson on the value of time management? Was that worth ten thousand dollars? Especially since Ariel would still be dead and the whole exercise exposed as cruel fiction.

Jamie could see a lawsuit in Time Trials' future. He opened up a new document on his laptop and took down notes as they came to him. Who could he hire to press the case? What litigators did he know? Could he find other disgruntled and manipulated clients to file a class-action suit? Was there criminal negligence here? What was in the release he had signed, and would it take away any culpability from Time Trials?

As he sat in his office debating with himself and taking thorough notes, he realize that he was doing the exact same thing that got him here in the first place. He was wasting time. He slammed his laptop shut, grabbed his coat, and hurried out of his cubicle, only to be headed off by Danni.

"You gotta see this," she said with excitement. "I think I cracked it."

"I can't now," Jamie said. "I've gotta go—"

"It'll only take a second. You're gonna love it."

Jamie couldn't resist. When people got excited about their work, it excited him as well. He had plenty of time, so why not?"

"Okay, show me. Quick."

Danni brought Jamie to her cubicle and proudly showed him the new direction she'd hit upon for the design of the fantasy football app. She hadn't been exaggerating. It was bold and fresh and for something that had been done a hundred times before, it somehow seemed new. It was even better than the version with the leather-textured backgrounds that the two of them had come up with the first time they had gone through this exercise.

The first time. The week before. That was somehow being repeated today. That realization brought Jamie back to the moment.

"It's great. I gotta go," he said abruptly then ran off, leaving Danni not sure of what had just happened.

As he hurried toward the elevators, Jamie passed the large office of Mekhi, who was packing up, ready to head home.

"Jamie!" Mekhi called to him. "How's my superstar?"

"Good," Jamie called back. "Sorry, can't stop. I'm late."

Jamie ran on, leaving Mekhi confused. Izzy stepped up to Mekhi's door as he watched Jamie run down the hallway.

"Late?" Mekhi said to Izzy. "When did he ever care about being late?"

"Aww, our boy has finally learned how to tell time," Izzy said with an exaggerated sigh. "They grow up so fast."

Jamie ran for the elevator lobby just as an elevator door was closing.

"Hold it!" he yelled.

Nobody did. The doors closed and the elevator was gone.

"Thanks!" Jamie yelled angrily.

He hit the down button and paced. And paced. He never gave much thought to how long it took for the elevators to show up during rush hour. Now every second felt like an eternity. Finally, mercifully, an elevator door opened. It was jam-packed. Jamie didn't care. He pushed his way in, much to the annoyance of everyone else who was being pressed together.

A harsh buzzer sounded. The doors wouldn't close.

"It's overloaded!" an angry old gent yelled from the back where he was being crushed against the wall.

Jamie was not about to get out, but the others made the decision for him and firmly nudged him back out of the door.

"Please, I gotta get down to—"

The doors closed as one passenger gave Jamie a smug "buh bye" wave.

Jamie kicked at the door in frustration and almost didn't see that another elevator had opened behind him. The doors were already starting to close by the time he realized it.

"Wait!" he screamed and dove for it, making it aboard the second before the doors slid shut.

He spent the next few minutes avoiding the stares of the other passengers who wanted nothing to do with the sweaty man with the crazed look in his eyes. The elevator stopped multiple times on the way down. Each time it did, Jamie's gut twisted. Would the other elevator have made fewer stops? He still had plenty of time, but he was never so aware of how minutes, even seconds might count. When the elevator doors opened in the lobby, he bounded from the car and sprinted out of the building.

New Yorkers are used to pretty much everything. Seeing a man sprinting through busy foot traffic at rush hour wasn't at all unusual. People simply parted to make way before continuing on their own journeys. Jamie ran straight for the subway station at 60th street, dodging pedestrians like a halfback. He made it down the stairs and through the turnstile while angering more than a dozen others.

He hit the crowded platform and had the wherewithal to look to the newspaper kiosk and the stack of New York Post newspapers, hoping to see a story on the back page about the All-Pro New York Jet who had been traded that day.

GONE! the headline screamed in typical New York Post overly dramatic fashion. Seeing the story was a relief for it proved that what was happening wasn't a drama performed solely by the people at *Apperture*. If this was theater, then all of New York City was part of the performance, which made no sense. Ten thousand dollars wouldn't buy that. Sorting out how this could be happening would have to wait for another time. Another day. Another reality. In that moment, all Jamie cared about was getting to Ariel.

A train rolled into the station. It was the #6. The Lexington Avenue Local. Jamie had to make a quick calculation. It took him a few seconds to locate a clock on the wall. It was 5:50. There was still plenty of time, but his margin for error was tightening. The #4 train was an express that made only one stop before 14th street. The local train made five. But it was the first train into the station. Was he better off hopping on that train to keep moving? Or wait for the much busier express train and risk that it be so packed that he couldn't get on? He decided that moving was better, so he pushed to the front of the crowd, annoying everyone who was in his way, and boarded the #6.

He did a quick calculation and figured he'd hit 14th street with plenty of time to spare. He actually allowed himself to relax but had to make a conscious effort to keep his thoughts from going to the puzzle of how this could be happening. He knew the dangers there. He'd get so caught up with speculation that he could easily see himself missing his stop.

The train made its regular stops at 51st, 42nd, and 33rd. He was going to make it. His thoughts shot ahead to how best to get Ariel away from the danger zone. He envisioned his actions from the moment he'd step off the train to the route he'd take to get to the scene. It dawned on him that Ariel wouldn't be the only one in danger. Other pedestrians would be there. Saving Ariel might turn out to be one of those choices that Mercy Parr spoke of. You never knew what small decision might kick off a butterfly effect of events that leads to chaos. Could injecting himself into the action to save Ariel cause other people to get hurt?

He needed to add to his plan. How could he convince a group of people to clear the sidewalk in anticipation of an accident that was yet to happen? People ranting wasn't a unique sight to New Yorkers. They'd ignore him. How could he convince them to move?

In the long run, none of that truly mattered. He had to have singular focus, and that was to save Ariel. He couldn't help but smile.

Perhaps Time Trials knew what they were doing. However this played out, he had newfound appreciation for the importance of making the most of his time. Would this carry over to the rest of his life? All it took was a visit from three ghosts to completely turn Ebeneezer Scrooge around, which Jamie never quite bought. There was no way to tell if he was going to be a changed man. Only one thing was certain, he was not going to waste another second in getting to Ariel.

These thoughts consumed his last few minutes on the #6 train. He was so lost in the possibilities that he hadn't realized the train wasn't moving. That wasn't unusual. There were always delays. Sometimes the train ahead was a bit late pulling out of the station. Or they might have been ahead of schedule and had to stop in order to keep the whole line on time.

But this was different. A short delay usually lasted only a few moments. When Jamie finally registered what was happening, or not happening, it had been several minutes.

"Why are we stopped?" he asked a man in a rumpled business suit who was standing next to him.

"Do I look like a conductor?" the man snarled.

Jamie turned to a young woman with a nose ring and blue hair who could have been on her way to Pratt.

"How long have we been stopped?" he asked.

"Couple of minutes," she said with a shrug.

"Have they made an announcement?" Jamie asked.

The man in the suit said, "Did you hear one?"

"No."

"Then why do you think anybody else did?"

Jamie ignored the obnoxious guy. He was more concerned about the slow but definite sense of panic that was tickling the back of his brain. How long would they be stuck there? As his pulse quickened, the train rumbled and rocked on its wheels. Were they back underway?

No. It was a #4 express train that had caught up with them and sped by on the inside track. It was the train that Jamie would have been on if he had made the decision to wait for it back at 60th street. That train would be pulling into 14th street in a minute. There was no telling how long he'd be stuck on the local, not moving.

He looked to the student again and asked, "What time is it?"

She glanced at her phone. "Six fifteen."

"Relax fella," annoying suit-man said. "We all got someplace to be."

Jamie wanted to punch him. He was now sweating. There was still plenty of time, but only if the train moved. Soon.

"Attention passengers,' came a voice from an antiquated speaker. "We've got a switching delay at 28th. Some problem with the lights. As soon as it's cleared up we'll be rolling. Thank you for your patience."

Jamie wanted to scream. He shoved his way to the front of the car and to the small room where the conductor sat when the train was between stops. He knocked on the window. A heavyset conductor with mutton-chop sideburns gave him a sour look, rolled his eyes, and cracked the door open.

"How long?" Jamie asked, sounding somewhere between worried and desperate.

"When I know I'll tell ya," the conductor said and pulled the door shut.

Jamie began to hyperventilate. He considered forcing the train doors open and jumping out but there was no guarantee he wouldn't kill himself on a third rail which of course would end any chance he had of saving Ariel. And living to realize his mistake. All he could do was wait and sweat. He was absolutely helpless.

Was this all part of the Time Trials scenario? Were they dragging him over the coals, throwing up obstacles, to make this as gut-wrenching as possible?

"I got it!" Jamie yelled out to nobody. "You made your point!"

A few people gave him sideways looks, but nobody said a word. People have screamed out worse on the subway.

"What time is it?" Jamie asked a tired looking guy wearing a trench coat.

The guy looked at his ancient Timex and said, "Six twenty-five."

Jamie was ramping up to full-on panic mode. The idea of being stuck on a train to nowhere while Ariel was standing alone, oblivious to the fact that the Grim Reaper was rolling her way, sent him over the edge into irrationality. He made a move toward the door at the end of the car, ready to force it open and jump out. He got as far as wrapping his fingers around the edge of the door when the train lurched and started rolling.

He could breathe again.

The train was moving, but maddeningly slow. Clearly things were not back to normal on the #6 line. It took a painfully long time for it to pull into the 28th street station. The doors slid open, and Jamie was faced with yet another choice. Did he stay on the train and hope that service would be back to normal? Or did he bail and get to 14th street on foot? There was no doubt that the train would be faster, but that's only if it was moving and at full speed.

He stared at the open door, tortured over what to do. All those disembarking were gone, and new passengers were boarding.

Ultimately, he wanted fate to be in his hands, not the Metropolitan Transit Authority's so he bolted for the door, fighting against the crush of people who were boarding.

"I gotta get out!" he shouted. "Let me out!"

Some people got out of his way while others not-so-gently elbowed him for daring to go against the flow. He took his lumps, squeezed out of the door and onto the platform. He was now back in control of his own destiny, and Ariel's. He started for the stairs leading up and out of the station, as the train doors closed, and the train rolled on.

Once again he had made the wrong choice. He couldn't dwell on it. He had to keep moving.

He bounded up the stairs and out into the evening. It had been raining all day and smell of fresh, clean air re-invigorate him. That was a good thing because it was time to run. Fourteen blocks. 28th street to 14th. How long would that take? The challenge wasn't so much about the distance, it was having to navigate through the rush-hour crush of people and cars. Dodging pedestrians made the journey even longer. The real challenge came at every intersection. He timed a few lights so that he hit the curb the moment traffic stopped, and he didn't have to break stride. Other times he wasn't as lucky, but that didn't stop him. He charged straight into traffic again and again causing more than one "ole'" moment as he was nearly hit by several speeding cabs. He was blasted at by several car horns and had multiple f-bombs hurled his way but none of that deterred him.

Sitting at a computer for days on end didn't exactly keep him in top shape. His legs hurt, his breathing was labored, and he had a nasty stitch in his side, but the constant flow of adrenaline kept him moving.

He got a boost when he finally hit 17th street which was the north end of Union Square Park. There were three more blocks to go, and it was through a park with no car traffic to contend with. He was like a marathoner who finally caught sight of the finish line. He sprinted along the winding paths, not sure of how much time he had left. He listened for the sound of police sirens, knowing that once he heard those, he would only have a few seconds left. But he heard nothing. The intersection of Broadway and 14th was in sight.

He quickly approached the dramatic statue of George Washington on horseback. Next to it was another man on a horse, a mounted policeman.

"Excuse me" Jamie said, gasping for air. "What time is it?"

"You okay pal?" the cop asked. "You're not gonna keel over, are ya?"

"I'm fine, just the time please," Jamie said.

The cop checked his watch. "Six thirty-five."

Jamie laughed with relief. He'd made it.

"You sure you're okay?" the cop asked.

"Couldn't be better, thanks," Jamie said.

"Take it easy, you'll live longer," the cop said.

With a slight kick to his horse, they trotted away.

The pressure was off, but Jamie couldn't relax. Not until Ariel was safe. Walking quickly, he made it to 14th street, a block from

Broadway. He went straight to the subway entrance where the vendor was selling small bouquets of flowers. Jamie thought it would be poetic to complete what he had begun the first time he'd made this journey. He gave a listen for the police siren. Hearing nothing, he went to the vendor to get flowers for his girl. This time he didn't linger to look for the exact right bunch. He grabbed the first one he saw, paid for it, and hurried off.

As he drew closer to the crosswalk that spanned Broadway he was hit with a strange surge of emotions. Was this really happening? Would Ariel be on the other side of the street? Could he save her? Or was he operating in some kind of virtual-reality mind-control fantasy that Time Trials put him into? In that moment, he didn't care. He wanted to see Ariel, the girl he'd loved and lost. For the past week he had been tortured by the guilt of knowing his negligence had caused her death. If this was a virtual reality simulation, he didn't want it to end.

He made a conscious effort to stop speculating and stay focused on the moment. He wanted his girl back, whether it turned out to be real or not. All those thoughts and emotions rolled over him as he stood on that curb, impatiently waiting for the light to change. At any moment he'd get the signal to walk, and he'd be back with her. He was happy…

…and then the sound of the siren jarred him back to the danger of the moment. This wasn't over. Not yet. Jamie's adrenaline spiked. He had expected to hear it coming from a long way off. He'd forgotten that the cop didn't hit the siren until he was nearly at the intersection. What time was it? Had he lost too many precious seconds talking to the cop and buying flowers? He looked to his right to see the flashing lights of the cop car were a long black way. The second cop car was a block behind it. The sedan would be closer. Much closer.

He didn't wait for the light to change and sprinted across the intersection, dodging cars. He had cut it too close. As had happened so many times before, time had slipped away from him. But it wasn't too late. As he ran through the crosswalk, he glanced back and to his right to see the dark shape of the fleeing sedan snaking through traffic, headed his way. Headed toward Ariel. It would be close, but he was going to make it.

"Move!" he shouted to the crowd that was gathered on the far curb. "Get out of the way! There's a car coming. It's gonna crash right here!"

He knew this made no sense to them, his only hope was that the sight of a madman waving his arms and demanding that they scatter would force them to leave, whether they believed they were in danger or not. Better, they might think that the only danger was from him. That would be okay too.

"It's gonna crash right here!" Jamie screamed. "Get outta here!"

He dropped the bouquet of flowers in the street and waved his arms frantically.

The siren grew louder. He was running out of time.

From the middle of the street, he kept waving his arms while approaching the curb. Finally, the people decided they wanted nothing to do with this crazy person so the split up, going left and right. It was working. Jamie was going to save them all. Most importantly, when they parted, they revealed Ariel standing a few feet back, her arms wrapped around herself to keep warm.

Jamie's heart melted. She was alive. He wanted to keep her that way.

"Ariel!" he shouted. "You gotta move!"

"Jamie?" Ariel replied with confusion. "What're you doing?"

She stood frozen, not understanding what was happening. Getting her to safety would be up to him. As he ran toward her, he heard what he knew was the squeal of the sedan's tires as it made the turn too fast and started its skid toward the spot where Ariel stood. He didn't waste the second it would have taken to look back. His focus was on Ariel. He jumped over the curb onto the sidewalk, took the few steps to get to her, wrapped his arms around her, then lifted her up and physically carried her away from the spot where she had died.

Jamie heard a few people scream in surprise and fear. He hadn't remembered that from before but then again, he was laser focused on Ariel back then too. But this time she was in his arms. He moved her the few feet away that would mean the difference between life and death.

The sound of the car's wheels hitting the curb was unmistakable. Jamie didn't bother to look back at what was happening. He'd already seen it. The car flipped onto its side but kept moving, scraping across the sidewalk to the spot where Ariel had stood. Where she was no longer. With one last shriek of tearing metal, the car came to a stop.

And Ariel was alive.

Jamie finally put her down and looked back to confirm what he knew he would see. The wreck of the car was there. The driver was just as dead. But Ariel was in his arms.

"Sorry," he said.

Ariel looked up at him with wide, frightened eyes.

"For what?" she asked with tears in her eyes. "You saved my life."

"Yeah but I was fifteen minutes late. I promise I'll never be late for anything ever again."

Ariel pulled him into a tight hug. He could feel her shaking. That was okay. A near-death experience can be unnerving. But he also felt her warmth. She was alive. This had to be real.

"You really did save my life," she said.

"I hope so," was Jamie's honest reply.

She looked up at him through tears and said, "I love you."

"I love you too. Oh, almost forgot. I brought you something."

Jamie let her go and jogged back to the street as the first cop car arrived. It screamed up to the curb and skid to a stop. Two hyped-up cops jumped out and headed straight for the wreck of the sedan.

Jamie thought, "Relax, he's not going anywhere."

He scanned the road until he saw what he was looking for: the bouquet of flowers he'd dropped. He jogged to it, picked it up, and raised it high into the air.

"I brought you flowers!" he exclaimed.

Ariel laughed, but her joy was cut short as the second cop car came screaming up.

"Look out!" she shouted.

Too late. The car hit Jamie at full speed, sending him airborne for a few horrifying seconds until he hit the pavement and lay there, still, his hand clutching the flowers.

Ariel screamed.

Jamie's time had come.

The funeral was an intimate gathering. A short memorial service was held in the cemetery's chapel. Prayers were said and a few mourners came forward to share memories. This was no celebration of life. It's difficult to celebrate a life that was cut short so young and so tragically.

Ariel's parents were there, along with some of Jamie's distant cousins. Of course, there were the requisite friends and co-workers. They all went through the paces in a numb state of denial.

Sitting alone to the rear of the chapel was a woman in a dark business suit. She made no attempt to interact with the mourners or console anyone. She sat silently. Stoically.

After the service, most of the group walked quietly to the adjacent mausoleum where Jamie's ashes where interred in a vault that would soon be sealed by a slab of marble engraved with his name and the dates of his birth and death.

The woman in black did not join this part of the service.

It was a short walk to the parking lot where mourners said their good-byes, hugged, offered final condolences, and went to their cars. The woman in the dark suit stood alone next to her black Porsche, observing.

"Give me a second," Ariel said to her parents.

"Take your time," her mother said.

Ariel approached the woman, who stepped forward to meet her. The two stood facing each other for a silent moment, as if neither knew what to say.

It was Ariel who finally broke the ice.

"Thank you for coming," she said.

"Of course," Mercy Parr replied. "I'm so very sorry for your loss."

"There's a huge irony here," Ariel said. "This was probably the first time in his life that he bowed down to time."

"And it saved your life," Mercy said. "I hope you take solace in that.'

"I suppose, but it's hard. It'll take time."

"It always takes time," Mercy said. "Time is an inevitable fact of life. As is death."

"He'd disagree with you on that."

"He might have, but it was his time."

"Yes it was," Ariel said. "Goody-bye, Mercy."

"Goodbye, Ariel."

The two separated, ending the trial.

And time rolled on.

As it always does.

As it always will.

THE END

THE SCOUT
(Redux)

If I knew then what I know now, would I have done the same thing?

Hard to say.

If I'd made different choices when I was a boy would that have made the last thirty years any easier for me? And at what cost? Could I have lived with myself? Most would like to believe that when faced with a moral dilemma the right choice is obvious. But what if making the correct moral decision means turning your back on all you had thought to be right, and guaranteed you a life fraught with turmoil and guilt? It's difficult to be noble when faced with such a dire sentence.

My choice wasn't quite as difficult as that for at the time I hadn't expected to live long enough to suffer any repercussions. It took an unforeseen twist of fate and stupidity to keep me alive.

I could argue that an early death would have been far easier.

Was taking what I believed to be the noble route worth a lifetime of anguish? It's a moot point because the past can't be changed. But it does beg the question: if I knew then what I know now, would I have done the same thing? I was a headstrong kid, but I might not have been so bold if I had seen the future.

In any event, what happened cannot be undone. I can only sit here, on the verge of yet another dramatic event, thinking back to what had happened to me so many years ago, and wonder if there might have been another way.

~~~~
~~~~

I was on my own.

That was my first mistake.

I was the kind of guy who didn't follow the rules, even at the tender age of fourteen, especially if I saw no good reason to. I wasn't a trouble-maker but unlike most of my friends who blindly bowed to authority, I made my decisions based on what common sense told me was right…even when I was the only one who felt that way.

My latest misadventure began innocently enough on an excursion with my Scout troop. The plan was to head out on foot from our base with a group of thirteen Scouts and two Leaders for a long hike through rocky, desert-terrain. It was all about honing survival skills. I didn't see the point other than to earn a badge I couldn't have cared less about. I knew what I was capable of. I didn't need to wear a sash to show off a sea of badges that proved I could swim a mile or treat wounds or repeatedly hit a bulls-eye.

The Scout Leaders didn't agree. They wanted their young charges to compete with one another, which was why I found myself trudging across the blazing hot desert with a light backpack along with twelve other sweaty Scouts who actually cared about adding to their badge collections. I wanted to be somewhere else, anywhere else, but with two Leaders keeping a watchful eye on us there was no way I could dodge what was sure to be a grueling, pointless couple of days.

It was hot. Torturous, nasty, heatstroke hot. That didn't stop the Leaders from driving us deep into the desert. Five miles, ten miles. We passed towering cliffs and crossed long-dried riverbeds. Rationing water was crucial. We each started off with a small bottle of water that had to last until we found resources in the desert. The Leaders instructed us to keep our mouths moist by sucking on small pebbles to activate our salivary glands. I was way ahead of them. I'd been working on a couple of pebbles long before the Leaders offered the tip. I wanted to point out that if this was a true survival situation we wouldn't be hiking, like fools, during the heat of the day. Instead we'd be resting in the shade to conserve energy and bodily fluids. But this wasn't my show, so I kept quiet and went along.

I made a point of veering into the shade whenever possible, even if it meant adding a few extra steps. And I didn't talk, unlike the others who were laughing and joking from the get-go. I wondered if the Leaders realized how much precious energy was being wasted. They were driving us hard and letting us make dumb mistakes. But why? Was it another test? Another competition? Or did they want to push us to the brink of dehydration and exhaustion for a little sadistic fun? It sure seemed that way. Or maybe the Leaders were just as clueless as the Scouts. Whatever the case, I wasn't about to do anything that would make the adventure any worse than it already was, so I kept my mouth shut and sucked on my pebbles.

Once we'd hiked further into the desert than I'd ever been before, the true point of the excursion was revealed. It was indeed a competition. The Leaders split the group in two. Each would take half the Scouts and move off in different directions. Whichever group fared better would be treated to an exceptional meal when they returned to base. The losers would be left to watch the gluttony with envy.

I had no idea who would be the judge and what the criteria for winning might be, and didn't care. What I saw was an opportunity to salvage this miserable experience.

When we split up there were seven in one group and six in the other. I made sure I was with the group of seven. The two teams hiked in opposite directions and after we'd gotten what I thought was a suitable distance away from the others, I approached our Leader and requested permission to head back and join the rival group. I explained that my good friend was in that group, and I was worried that he might be in over his head. I wanted to look out for him. The Leader actually complimented me on my leadership qualities and sent me on my way to catch up with the others.

Idiot.

I didn't have a close friend in the other group.

I had no intention of joining them.

What I wanted was to be on my own and with both Leaders thinking I was with the other, I got my wish.

Once certain that I couldn't be seen by either group, I pulled off my pack, found shade and got off my feet. I wasn't thrilled about having to spend two days in the desert by myself, but I knew I was far better off on my own than trudging along with a bunch of clueless rookies being prodded on my sadistic Leaders. My plan was to lay low for the entire time to conserve energy and water. I'd then march back into camp and announce I'd gotten lost when I tried to change groups but managed to survive with no help from anyone. Who knows? Maybe I'd be declared the winner of the dumb contest.

With that brilliant plan in place, I put my feet up and relaxed, comfortable for the first time in hours and with the confidence that this adventure in the desert was going to be far less torturous than it would have been if I had followed the rules.

But I couldn't rest for long. I still had to work to survive in the harsh environment. Digging through my pack I saw that the Scouts had equipped me with a few essential survival tools: A long length of light rope, a thin reflective blanket, a simple first aid kit, flint & steel to spark a fire, a small hunting knife, and an item that was only to be used in a dire emergency…a communication device. If we were truly in trouble we could use it to call for help. The Leaders may have wanted to push us to the limit, but they wanted everyone back alive. At least I thought they did.

Knowing that as soon as night fell the desert temperature would plunge from searing hot to bone-numbing cold, I erected a simple shelter using lengths of scrub that I propped against a wall of rust-colored rock. I gathered kindling and found enough dry wood to use as fuel. With a few quick flicks of metal on stone, I sparked up the tinder and in minutes had a crackling fire that would keep me warm during the long, desert night.

I was feeling quite proud of myself.

Sunset came quickly. It was stunning, complete with long streaks of orange and lavender clouds that hung above the nearby mountains. The breathtaking sight almost made the adventure worthwhile. Almost.

When the sun dropped below the mountain range the temperature dropped with it, but I was warm and secure with fire and shelter. My plan was to get up before sunrise to search for food and water before the cool morning hours gave way to oven-like temperatures. I wasn't stressed about finding either. If I came up empty I knew I'd still be okay. I'd been hungry before. Gutting it out for two days wouldn't be a problem.

I stretched out in the shelter with my head resting on my pack with only my thoughts to keep me company. With a completely clear mind, my thinking turned to a difficult decision I'd been weighing for months: I wanted to quit the Scouts. My parents had forced me to join, saying it was every guy's duty to serve. I signed-up to make them happy (and to stop the nagging) but never fully bought into the Scout culture. I loved being outdoors and made several good friends, but I didn't see any purpose to the regimentation and military-like training. It wasn't my style. But quitting would upset my parents while the Leaders would do their best to convince me to stay until the mission was complete.

The mission. It was the only reason I'd lasted as long as I had. As much as I was adverse to most everything the Scouts stood for, I did feel a sense of responsibility. Of duty. And if I was being honest, of adventure. Maybe I should list that first.

I lay back and gazed up at the night sky. It's a wonderful memory that I still cherish, if only because it was one of the last precious moments of what had been an innocent life. Being in the desert, away from the glow of civilization, I could see more stars than I had ever seen before. It was an endless canopy of lights that was so incredibly vivid I felt as though I could see through them to the other side of the universe. The immensity of it all was both staggering and humbling as I tried to comprehend how many different worlds I might be seeing. How many civilizations? How many people? How many lives were beginning and ending at that exact moment? I wondered which of the twinkling spots held life, and which were nothing more than gaseous masses that had burned out centuries before and their light was only now reaching me.

Equally staggering, how many people were out there staring back at me, wondering the exact same thing? The idea that I might be gazing at multiple, living worlds was a concept straight out of science fiction.

Or was it?

A single, shimmering "star" moved across the sky. At first I thought my eyes were playing tricks and it was the residual impression left by another bright star. I blinked, but it was still there moving steadily and quickly until it disappeared behind the distant ridge of mountains.

The experience rocked me. Speculating about the potential enormity of life on other worlds while gazing at a billion stars was one thing, seeing an actual sign of intelligent life speeding by was far more dramatic. What could it have been? A satellite? A space station orbiting the globe? Or was it a craft from another planet swinging by to take a peek at my home?

Seeing that tiny spec of light moving through the sky fired my imagination. There was life out there. I knew that. Everybody knew that. Reaching out to it was something I'd dreamed of since I was old enough to put my eye to a telescope. That ambition still burned. All it took was a simple light moving across the sky to remind me of that…and to question my desire to quit the Scouts. As much as I didn't appreciate their methods and rigid regulations, the Scouts offered me the best chance to touch the stars.

My thoughts were suddenly alive with possibilities. None of them had to do with something as trivial as desert survival. But that was okay. I liked thinking through challenges and there was no better time to do it than while alone under a sky full of stars. I lay back, let my mind float up to the heavens and soon fell asleep.

I might have slept well into the next day if it hadn't been for a loud explosion that shattered the tranquility of the desert. I was jolted awake and sat up quickly, bashing my head into the branches of the shelter. What was it? I hadn't dreamt it for I could still hear its echo drifting away. It was morning. The sun had barely crept over the mountains, so the temperature had yet to begin its inevitable climb. I shivered for the campfire had long since burned out and my thin Scout uniform did little to provide warmth.

That slight discomfort was the last thing on my mind. I scrambled out of the shelter and quickly climbed up onto the rock where I'd built the lean-to. I stood on top and scanned the desert, doing a slow three-sixty, looking for anything that might have created the boom. There was nothing to see but miles of scrub and sand and rock. I listened in case another explosion might follow, but heard only the wind and the far-off cries of birds in search of their morning meal.

I was about to jump down when my eye caught movement. Not on the ground, in the sky. A dark speck appeared that at first looked like a hovering bird. But birds didn't hover. I watched with curiosity and soon realized it wasn't hovering at all. It was growing closer. Fast. Whatever it was, it was falling. It didn't appear to have aerodynamic capability. Or power. It was freefalling…and headed for me.

The chance of getting hit by a falling meteor was less likely than getting struck by lightning but I wasn't taking any chances. Nor did I have time to do anything other than jump down and press myself against the rock for whatever protection it might offer.

The mysterious mass quickly grew larger. I felt certain that it was a meteor, and the explosion was the sonic boom it created when it tore through the atmosphere, faster than the speed of sound. But as it dropped closer to the ground, I could make out enough detail to prove that it was no meteor. Its shape was too consistent. It looked to be made up of several perfectly round spheres that were connected to form a mass that resembled a bunch of grapes. I had no doubt that it was man-made. The realization brought me back to the point of light I'd seen moving through the night sky. Was this the object I'd seen? The plummeting device could be a satellite that had fallen out of orbit and gravity was pulling it back home.

I soon realized that whatever it was, it was going to miss me by a few hundred yards. Confidant that I wasn't in danger, I climbed back up on to the rock to get the best view of the descent.

I briefly wondered if the other Scouts were watching…wherever they were. They had to have heard the boom.

The falling mass was seconds from crashing. I braced for a violent impact that would undoubtedly shatter the spheres and send pieces hurtling across the desert floor. I might not have been out of danger after all, so I tensed up, ready to dive out of the way in case debris came sailing my way.

There was a brief whistling sound, a moment of silence, and then it hit.

The object didn't break up. It bounced. The entire mass was launched back into the air, intact. The force of the impact sent the collection of spheres into a spasm of uncontrolled twisting and turning. It sailed impossibly high before gravity took hold once more and pulled it back to hit the ground only to bounce up again.

Now feeling safe, I jumped down from my observation platform and took off running toward it.

The object continued to bounce, each time hitting with less force and getting less height. It soon stopped bouncing altogether and tumbled wildly over the uneven desert floor. When it was finally close to settling, the object disappeared. My guess is that it had rolled into a gulley or a dry river bed…out of my sight.

With my heart thumping, I sprinted across the scrubby sand, leaping over small rocks, and dodging gnarled trees. I no longer cared about using too much energy or wasting precious body fluid. My curiosity had blasted those concerns straight out of my head. After running flat out for nearly five minutes I neared the edge of a deep culvert and peered over the edge to see the device had come to rest below me. The thought struck that if it was a spacecraft there might be toxic fumes or spilled fuel or any number of other dangerous substances I'd be wise to avoid. I'd learned about such things as part of my training. At this point, caution was key.

The craft, or whatever it was, lay jammed against the far edge of the deep, dry river bed. I didn't hear the hiss of escaping gas or the metallic ticks from a cooling engine. The device seemed decidedly low-tech and up close still reminded me of a massive bunch of grapes.

Each of the dark-gray spheres was roughly two feet in diameter making the overall size of the wreck close to that of a small truck. It had no markings or identifying numbers. Two of the spheres had been damaged during the crash and hung like deflated balloons. That spoke volumes. This device was designed to do exactly what it had done…bounce. The shredded spheres showed that they were fabricated out of something soft but durable. They dangled like limp rags from the rest of the bunch.

I had to get a closer look and slid down the near-vertical side of the culvert, dropping nearly twenty feet, until I was on the same level as the wreck. It appeared much larger and more daunting than when I was looking down on it from above, but that wasn't going to stop me from examining it. I made my way toward it slowly, cautiously. I wondered if there might be a living person inside, but dismissed the thought. Nobody could have survived such a violent, tumbling crash.

When I reached it, my focus was on the small space between the deflated spheres. I stopped a few feet away, knelt down on one knee, and peered into the void to see if anything was inside.

Black. That's all I registered. If anything was in there, I couldn't see it. I reached out and was about to touch one of the spheres when a single, green light flashed on inside. I started back in surprise, tripped, and landed on my butt. I quickly crawled away to escape from…what? A blast of noxious gas? I defensive laser? An alien creature with a scrambled brain who wanted to reach out and grab me?

A moment later I heard the muffled whine of a machine powering to life. This bulbous device wasn't as low-tech as I thought. I was torn between fear and curiosity. Both kept me from moving.

The whirring sound grew louder. Whatever was in there, it was powering-up.

There was a loud metallic clicking sound followed by the complete self-disassembly of the craft. It was like a latch had been released that had been holding the spheres together. The cluster of balls simultaneously fell away and tumbled across the dry riverbed, rolling, and bouncing every which way. One rolled toward me, and I instinctively jumped to my feet and kicked it away. They seemed harmless but I wasn't taking any chances. They bounced off of each other and rolled around like oversized toys until eventually coming to rest on their own, spread out everywhere.

What remained of the wreck was a rigid frame that seemed to be made of lightweight, black wire. At the base of this dark skeleton, resting on the ground, was a large toy.

Yes, a toy. Or it seemed like one. It was a miniature truck, but like nothing I'd ever seen before. It stood about two feet high and three feet long with six wire-wheels that looked as though they could handle most any terrain. Above the wheels was a flat, black, rectangular slab that was roughly eight inches thick. The top surface was black and shiny smooth. To either side of the body were silver tubes, stacked three high, running the length of each side. The green light glowed from beneath the body, above the array of wheels.

It was a miniature all-terrain-vehicle.

And it was activated.

Where had it come from? Was it a scientific experiment gone awry? Was it part of the Scout's survival training? Or was there something more incredible going on? Had this come from deep space? If so, why did it crash here? Was it intentional or a mistake?

The device didn't move. Neither did I. I had plenty of questions and not a single answer, but I knew how to start asking. I reached into the cargo pocket on the thigh of my pants and pulled out the communicator that was included in our survival gear. We'd been told to use it only in an emergency. I wasn't sure if this qualified and didn't care. I pressed the power button, waiting for the device to boot up. My thought was to report the crash to the Scout Leaders back at base and request that they send out a team to investigate. They could use the signal from the communicator to pinpoint my location.

As far as I was concerned, the survival exercise was over.

I looked to the communicator, expecting to see the display of icons that led to its various functions. What I saw instead, was static.

I shook it. Didn't help. There was power but no function which meant I had no way to communicate with the base.

I was about to turn it off and on again when the whirring sound of the little machine's engines grew louder. The wheels remained stationary as the body above them slowly rotated forty-five degrees, then stopped. The silver tubes that ran along the two sides pivoted away from the body until the three on one side were facing forward and the opposite three were facing back.

The three facing forward…were pointed straight toward me.

There was a short, sharp whine as if the machine was powering up.

Those few seconds saved my life.

I reacted more out of instinct than training. I dove to my right and landed flat on my belly as a focused blast of energy erupted from the device's front-facing tubes, sending out an invisible salvo that shot past me and blasted the wall of the culvert behind the spot where I'd been standing, creating an eruption of dirt and rock that blew high into the sky.

I lay there paralyzed with fear as dirt and debris rained down on me. The machine slowly rotated until the opposite set of tubes was aimed my way. It was followed by the sound of another energy-buildup. This time I made a conscious decision to move and rolled away quickly. The weapon fired. The powerful blast hit the spot I'd just vacated, creating a geyser of sand that left a gaping wound in the ground that might have been in me.

I didn't stop to analyze what was happening. Whatever this thing was, it clearly wasn't friendly. I scrambled to my feet and sprinted to my right, kicking loose spheres out of my way. I drilled one toward the weapon at the exact moment it fired again. The energy-salvo hit the sphere, bursting it.

There was no time to marvel at the machine's capabilities or wonder why it was attacking me. The training expedition had suddenly become about a much different fight for survival. I ran for the wall of the culvert, desperately scanning for a spot where I could climb out and quickly escape from this death machine.

I heard the sound of the machine powering up to fire again and instantly launched to my right as the truck let loose with another lethal blast of energy. It barely missed me because I felt its power tickle my skin as the charge flashed by on its way to blowing out another section of the culvert wall.

The few seconds the machine took to re-charge its weapon, and the sound it created, were helping to keep me alive. After each shot there was a short window of time to move. I sprinted for the side of the culvert, jumped onto a boulder, and leapt up to grab the edge.

Behind me, the weapon had powered up again. The window had closed. I let go of the edge and dropped back to the riverbed as the weapon unloaded and blew out a chunk of the wall where I'd been hanging seconds before. The deadly shots may have been telegraphed but they were on target.

I had a few seconds to act while the truck re-charged, so I jumped back on to the rock, launched myself up, grabbed the lip of the culvert and managed to pull myself out. It's remarkable what adrenaline can do. Figuring that another blast was on its way I quickly log-rolled away as sure enough, the next blast nailed the spot where I had climbed out, missing me by a few feet.

Since I was on higher ground than the machine, it no longer had a clear shot at me. I took a risk and crawled back to the edge on my belly to see what it would do now that I'd escaped. My hope was that I was targeted because the infernal truck perceived me as a threat and now that I was out of the culvert it would stop shooting at him.

I peered cautiously over the lip and saw that the device hadn't moved. I could breathe again. Cautiously, I reached for the communicator so I could try again to alert the Scout Leaders. I moved slowly so as not to put myself back into the sights of the mechanical monster. I slipped the communicator out of my pocket and saw that the screen was still showing static. How could that be? These communicators had never failed.

The machine's engine whined to life, but it was a different sound than when it was recharging its weapons. The device's wheels began to turn. It rolled slowly out of the skeletal frame and onto the sand.

Once clear, it lurched forward with surprising speed and rolled across the dry river bed…toward me.

How was that possible? Who was controlling it? My hope was that the machine had only been defending itself, but I was dead wrong.

It was on the attack.

The efficient all-terrain-vehicle sped along the dry riverbed, headed for the culvert wall beneath me. I was sure it would be a short journey. The wall was too steep. I relaxed, knowing that the mysterious weapon was trapped.

Again, I was wrong.

The rolling machine hit the wall. Its six wire-wheels dug into the sand and the truck effortlessly climbed the near-vertical rise. The machine couldn't be stopped, and it was coming after me. I didn't stick around to marvel at the device's climbing abilities or wonder about its motive. In seconds it would be back on my level and shooting again. All I could do was run. I took off, headed back toward the camp I'd made the night before. It was as good a direction as any and I needed my water and survival gear. Minutes before I had no intention of using any of it, now I feared my life would depend on having it all.

The sun grew higher, and the day got warmer. I didn't care. My entire focus was on putting distance between myself and the miniature ATV-weapon. I didn't even glance back to see if it had reached the top and was following me. I had to get my gear and find my way back to the Scout base. Surely the Leaders would know what the marauding machine was about.

I made it back to my camp, grabbed my pack and sat down to catch my breath and take a swig of water. It was going to be a long day. The last thing I wanted to do was pass out from exhaustion or dehydration. I took a single pull of water then pulled out my communicator. As before, the screen showed nothing but static. It defied logic for I had checked it before leaving the Scout base and it was working fine. Not only was I out of contact, I also couldn't use the geo-function to find my way back. Without that ability, I was lost. And both Scout groups thought I was with the other. I had out-smarted myself into being entirely on my own with a mechanical killer. I had to force himself to calm down, catch my breath and think.

BOOM!

The rock I was crouching behind exploded above my head. I jumped forward, flying through a storm of rubble that had blown out from the point of impact. I hit and rolled, then looked around quickly to see where the machine was.

It was nowhere to be seen, which was frightening for it meant it had long-range firing capability. I couldn't afford to underestimate the abilities of this demon because its intent was clear: It was hunting me.

I grabbed my pack and took off running while threading my arms through the straps. I needed another place to hide. A better place. I rounded a high mound of boulders and stopped to look back. The truck was several hundred yards behind me and closing. Its wheels spun quickly, kicking up dust in its wake as it moved impossibly fast over the desert floor, directly toward me.

I quickly took off in another direction. I was faster than the machine, but how long could I outrun it? Eventually I'd be out of gas and the hunter would catch its prey.

Boom! Boom!

Two explosions ripped the ground to my left. The mechanical demon had re-calculated my route and was lobbing salvos, forcing me to dodge back and forth to try and make a difficult target. I wouldn't be able to keep that up for long. I had to hope that whatever power source was driving the monster would run out before mine did.

Far ahead the desert gave way to wooded foothills that led to the towering mountains that ringed the desert floor. I ran that way, hoping the terrain would offer some protection and a place to hide and catch my breath.

The barrage ended, though I didn't think for a second that the machine had given up. I reasoned that I was either out of range or the monster was rationing its energy. It didn't matter either way. I kept running. There was at least a mile to cover before I'd hit the trees but as long as the machine didn't start shooting again, I'd make it. The endless sprints I'd done while training with the Scouts were paying off. Maybe they knew what they were doing after all. If I hadn't been so highly conditioned, I'd be dead.

As I neared the foothills I scanned ahead, looking for an escape route that offered some cover. I was about to reach trees and the uneven terrain that led to the mountains. My confidence grew. As fast and agile as the machine was, the varied terrain would force it to slow down. That gave me an advantage. I knew where I was going, the machine didn't. My hope for escape began to rise….

…and was immediately shot down when an explosion erupted directly in front of me that blew gravel into my eyes and knocked me to the ground. I was stunned and disoriented, but my survival instinct was intact. I rolled and popped up to continue running. That was the good news. Bad news was I'd been hurt. I'd fallen on my left shoulder and torn open a nasty gash on my upper arm that I could see through the ripped fabric of my Scout uniform. It was painful and bloody, but not life threatening. I would have to ignore it until I was somewhere safe.

I finally hit the trees and immediately started running an erratic course to try and confuse the machine. My plan was to lose the monster in the maze of boulders and trees and be long gone while it hunted in vain. As long as I didn't outsmart myself and choose a twisting course that led me back and directly across the path of the hunter, I'd have a chance.

The odds were in my favor, but I needed rest. Desperately. I'd been running constantly in the ever-increasing desert heat and was getting dangerously close to exhaustion. I threaded my way through the trees along the base of the foothills, looking for a place of refuge where I could catch my breath and plot my next move. I found the perfect spot in a stand of trees that surrounded a massive mound of boulders. I ducked behind one of the larger rocks, found a sliver of shade and dropped to my knees. I immediately yanked my pack off and grabbed my water bottle. It was two thirds full, but I could easily have downed twenty times that amount. Still, the water soothed my parched throat. I had to force myself not to drain it.

With the pressure off, I took stock. My arm was bleeding badly. Stitches were in my future. The agony came in waves as my heart sent a throbbing surge of pain down my arm with every beat. I dug through my pack for the first-aid kit and found a roll of gauze that I used to quickly wrap the wound and stem the blood flow. I didn't bother with the antiseptic gel, figuring that by the time infection became an issue I'd either be safe or dead. With the gash covered, I sat down with my back against the rock. My every sense was on alert, tuned to detect the sound of wheels creeping across sand or the whine of the weapon powering up for another attack.

There was nothing. I could relax, at least for a moment.

My mind raced ahead, calculating my next move, and trying to understand what was happening. I had been in the Scouts for over a year but had never encountered anything remotely like this. It was hard to believe it was part of the survival training but when it came to the Scouts, nothing surprised me. It was an organization that had become far more militaristic than when my father and mother belonged. Then again, life in general was very different from when my parents were young.

Poverty was widespread and growing daily. More people were going hungry than the government dared to admit. Cities had become impossibly crowded. Housing was a constant challenge. Homeless families, desperate for more space, moved to the country where filthy tent cities sprang up. The crime rate was off the charts. Disease was rampant.

And the planet was heating up. Climate change brought on by industrialization had brought drought conditions to areas that had once been green and fertile. Dire predictions of an upcoming famine had gone from theory to reality. The future did not look bright for our little planet.

The wealthy still lived in comfort, but they were a small fraction of the ever-growing population. Everyone else was left to fight for a sane and safe existence.

Joining the Scouts was a route that many took as a way to deal with the growing horror of poverty and hunger. The organization operated as an extension of the government and by association, the wealthy. The government provided food and housing for all Scouts and their families. In return the Scouts gave them blind allegiance.

Some Scout troops provided security for government buildings and big businesses. Others were used as escorts for wealthy industrialists who feared being harassed or kidnapped by the angry, struggling masses. I had even heard rumors about how some Scout troops were being used to keep peace in the tent cities by rousting "undesirables" who were never seen or heard from again.

I'd never been asked to do any of those things and hated to believe that the Scouts had become a violent tool of the government. If it were true, it might follow that they had created the killing machine that was chasing me. It could be a new weapon to be used in what the government called their "War on Poverty". That was the catchphrase they used but everyone knew it was really a war on the poverty-stricken.

But why was it after me? Was the so-called survival training a test of the weapon's efficiency? Had the thirteen Scouts been set up as guinea pigs? The thought stirred the kind of anger and disillusion that had been building inside me for a very long time. My only consolation was that I was enrolled in a specific Scout program that had nothing to do with security and didn't use violence. I was being prepared for something far more positive and exciting.

There was life out there, beyond our world. The Scouts were going to be used as good-will ambassadors. Our mission involved travelling off-planet to distant civilizations in the hopes of gathering knowledge and wisdom that might help us deal with the problems we faced at home. Several expeditions had already been launched. I was scheduled to leave on my own goodwill mission at the end of a two-year training program. It was a trip that held the promise of delivering all that I'd dreamed of as a child.

I was going to touch the stars.

But at the moment I wasn't even sure if I would get out of the desert.

I had to find my way back to base. Quickly. Before nightfall. I was fairly confident that I could dodge the machine for the rest of the day but once it got dark I'd be blind, and the mechanical monster would have me. I dug out the communicator in the hopes that whatever was wrong with it had magically fixed itself.

It hadn't. The screen still showed static. I was going to have to find my own way back.

I looked up to the mountains and tried to visualize seeing them from base. The desert was ringed by steep cliffs making it next to impossible to tell which way was which. There were no single, recognizable peaks or telltale valleys. It was all so frustratingly consistent. But sitting and fretting over it wasn't an option. I had to make a choice and hope it was the right one.

Now that I'd caught my breath and done a serviceable patch-job on my arm, I jammed the first aid kit back into my pack, hoisted it onto my un-damaged shoulder, turned for the trail and…

…saw the machine. It had been approaching slowly and silently like a predatory snake was now less than twenty feet away. How was this possible? Who was controlling this demon? Could it think and reason? That seemed impossible, yet there it was, blocking my way.

I threw the water bottle at it. It was a feeble gesture but all I could come up with in the moment. The silver tubes were locked on me, but no surge of energy erupted. Instead it moved forward slowly, drawing closer to make sure it wouldn't miss again. It proved that the machine was even more dangerous than I feared for by changing tactics, it revealed that it could think.

I wasn't about to stand still and be an easy target, so I sprinted around the mound of boulders and headed toward the mountains. I had to accept that losing the machine was impossible for each time I tried to shake it, the maniacal truck found me. Could it see? Was someone sitting behind a console at a command center watching my every move through the eyes of the demon robot?

Whatever the technology was, I no longer felt as though I could shake the killer. I had to outrun it and get to the safety of our base. Ignoring my aching shoulder and rapidly growing thirst, I ran deeper into the trees hoping they would shield me. All the while I scanned the foothills, desperate to find an escape route.

CRACK!

A towering tree was struck directly ahead of me. The mechanical beast wasn't far behind and was no longer holding out for a better shot. The force of the energy-missile blew out the base of the tree and sent it toppling back toward me. I changed course and ran toward the mountains, barely avoiding the tree as it crashed down, cutting off the path I'd been running along. I had to go-off trail and scramble up a massive rock that I hoped would at least slow the killer. When I reached the top I was faced with a sheer wall of granite that stretched high into the sky. Dead end. The only options were to run right or left. Neither provided any protection.

I turned left and sprinted along the base of the cliff, dodging boulders, and trees, until I spotted something that could be my lifeline. It was a cleft in the rock face; an opening that led to a slot canyon. I had studied satellite views of these mountains and knew they were laced with dozens of narrow canyons that snaked through the foothills, making several twists and turns before opening up on the far side. Running through one could provide protection from a missile fired from behind me.

Unfortunately, some of the canyons led to dead ends. There was no way to know which was which. The thought hit me that by knocking down that tree and cutting off the path, the diabolical machine might have been forcing me to head toward these canyons. Was it that smart? Could this be a trap? It didn't matter. I had to risk it and sprinted into the gap.

The canyon was narrow, which gave welcome relief from the relentless heat of the sun. I ran as fast as possible without slamming my wounded shoulder into a wall. The slot canyon wove through the rock, sometimes growing wide enough to sprint while other times narrowing down so that I had to slow to a walk and squeeze through sideways. There was no way of telling how long it would take to get to the far side, or if I was heading for a dead end.

As I ran I made another desperate attempt to use the communicator. I pulled it from my cargo pocket and stared at a static-filled screen. It was useless.

Or was it?

A realization hit me that made me want to scream with anger. The communicator was also a navigation device. It used satellite technology to direct me to any spot I chose. But it worked both ways. It not only received information, it also transmitted. If I was lost, the Scouts could zero in on the communicator's coordinates to find me.

Could a killer robot do the same?

I wanted to throw it to the ground and crush it under my boot because the truth was all too obvious. Back in the dry culvert the mechanical rover had focused on me at the exact moment I had activated the communicator. The monster always knew exactly where I was because it had locked onto the signal like a bloodhound following a scent. How could I have been so stupid?

I didn't waste time beating himself up. I powered down the communicator and continued my journey through the slot canyon. I knew I couldn't lose the killer in there, but felt as if I could get to the far side, I'd have a fighting chance to get away. As long as I kept the communicator off, the machine couldn't track me. All I had to do was get to the end. Confidence was high…

…until I rounded a sharp corner and hit a dead end.

The chasm was sealed off by an avalanche of rocks that had tumbled from the steep cliffs high above and filled the narrow crevice, blocking the way. I was doomed from the moment I ran into that canyon.

But I wasn't about to give up. The fallen rocks had actually created another possible escape route: The tumbled pile looked climbable. A quick look up showed that the rim of the narrow canyon was within reach. It was a long, steep climb on an unstable pile of rocks and gravel, but it was my only shot. Before I began to climb, another idea hit me. I took out the communicator and after a deep, nervous breath I powered it back up. Again, the screen showed static. I scanned both sides of the steep canyon until I saw a narrow crack in the wall opposite the rock pile. I ran to it and placed the communicator inside, deep enough to be out of sight. I then returned to the pile of rubble for what I felt was my last chance to survive, and began to climb.

It was easy going at first. The pile of rocks provided decent hand and foot holds. But the pile quickly grew steep which meant I had to slow down and use caution. I was totally exposed. An easy target. But it would have been a mistake to climb recklessly. One wrong move, one bad foot placement, and I'd tumble down the steep rock pile and land in front of the hunter, probably with a broken leg. I didn't look down for fear of seeing how high up I'd gotten. I wasn't good with heights. The last thing I needed was vertigo. I had to stay focused and climb, while listening for any sound that would announce the arrival of the truck below, or of its weapon powering up to shoot.

I was maybe ten feet from the top when I heard it...the unmistakable whine of the demon's engine. It was moving fast. Maybe it realized it was about to lose its prey. I risked a look down and saw it.

The little truck rounded a bend in the canyon, sped up to the base of the rock-slide, and stopped. My only hope was that my theory about the communicator was right, and it would start shooting at the cleft in the wall where I'd hidden it.

The machine didn't move. Or shoot. What was it doing? Was it intelligent enough to recognize that there was no way I could have squeezed through that narrow crack in the wall? The truck's body rotated until one set of its weapons was aimed at the cleft that held the hidden communicator.

I held my breath. This was it. As soon as the machine fired, no matter where it was aimed, I'd make my final move to reach the top.

But it didn't fire. Why? The waiting was torturous. I shifted my left foot slightly to get a more solid base to launch from, and kicked a rock loose. After all I'd been through, how could I have been so careless? It tumbled down, bouncing every which way until it landed two feet from the machine. I wanted to scream out in frustration. The weapon spun quickly; its gun barrels pointed directly at the fallen rock. I had no idea if this was a mindless machine that was simply firing at anything that moved, or if it took every bit of information that was presented in order to calculate a fully informed firing solution. There was no doubt that it had registered the fallen rock which meant that beyond being able to track the communicator, it could see or hear or both. I silently begged for the machine to unload on the rock, or swivel back and blast the hidden communicator. Either way I was poised and ready to scramble the last few feet to the top.

It was so deathly quiet I actually feared that the machine would hear my heartbeat. It stayed locked on the rock for a ten second lifetime, then slowly rotated back toward the cleft that held the communicator. I let out a relieved breath...

...as the weapon suddenly spun back and turned skyward.

It had found me.

Time to move. I made a final, desperate scramble to the top of the scree as the demon truck let loose. The first pulse of energy hit the wall of rocks several feet to my right. It may have sensed where I was, but without my communicator to lock onto, its aim wasn't precise. The pulse blew out a section of the rock wall, loosening the pile. I instantly felt the rocks destabilize beneath my feet. It was all going to come tumbling down and bring me along with it. If the fall didn't kill me the robot weapon would certainly finish the job when I landed in front of it.

I looked for a hand hold and saw a large boulder hanging above my right shoulder that had a fist-sized rock wedged beneath it. It was an opportunity, a long shot, but it was better than no shot. I reached for the smaller rock and yanked it out, releasing the larger boulder above. It fell fast. I had to dodge to my left to avoid being hit as it rumbled past me.

The machine fired. This time the entire wall collapsed. Rocks and boulders of all sizes tumbled down as I kept scrambling to my left to try and avoid the heaviest concentration of falling rocks. I no longer feared the robot since it was more likely that I'd be battered to death in the tumultuous avalanche. I grasped wildly to try and get a hand hold, forgetting the pain in my damaged shoulder.

The truck fired again. The energy bolt hit near me, sending out a spray of exploded rock that peppered me with a stinging wave of debris that tore at my uniform as well as my face and hands. I was able to grab onto the point of a stable rock but knew I wouldn't be able to hang there for long. The best I could hope for was to control my fall and hope that I wouldn't be hit by anything that was tumbling from above. I held onto the lifesaving rock, fueled by desperation, as the muscles in my forearm burned with the strain. I had a brief flash of hope that I could hold on until the avalanche settled…

…when the rock pulled out from the dirt. I half fell, half slid down, crashing through a storm of dirt and debris until my feet hit the solid, sandy floor of the canyon. I was so fueled by adrenalin and fear that I couldn't tell if I was hurt or not. I quickly pushed off to get away from the avalanche that continued to rain down around me. I stumbled backward and slammed against the far wall of the canyon, knocking the wind out of me. I may have been cut up and bleeding from more wounds than I cared to know about, but I was alive and didn't seem to have any broken bones.

But I wasn't safe.

I spun toward the center of the canyon, ready to dodge another blast and saw that my stalker had been flipped up on to its side. Next to it was the large boulder I had dislodged.

It had done its job.

The proof of that was the deep, black gash across the face of the rock…and the crushed side of the machine. The silver weapons were pointed skyward at nothing. There was no whine of an engine, no hint of a weapon powering up, no green light glowing beneath.

I didn't dare move as the dust settled around me and the tumbling rocks found their new resting place. I kept my eyes focused on the machine, ready for it to power back to life and train its weapons back on me.

It didn't.

I stood and took a few tentative steps toward it. I wanted a close look at the marauder that had been hunting me, and more important, I wanted to make sure it was dead. It seemed as though the boulder had delivered a crushing blow for the machine's body had been torn from the wheels and one half had been ripped open to reveal its mechanical and electronic guts.

It would not move or fire again.

As I knelt down to get a closer look at this mysterious machine, the shiny black top surface flickered with light.

I jumped back, ready to flee, but kept my eyes on the machine.

It didn't move, nor did its engines re-start. Though it was covered with dust, I could see that the damaged top surface was the only part of the device that showed life, lighting up as if it were a computer screen. Images appeared. Moving images. Moments later, sound came from the damaged machine. It was clearly a man's voice that was speaking a language I'd never heard before. The image of a man's face appeared on the glass. Was this the guy controlling the killer robot? Why would he be showing himself now? As frightened as I was, I needed to know.

I cautiously approached the crippled robot and looked down to see the man delivering what seemed to be a prepared speech. Was it a live transmission? Or a playback? His picture changed to a montage of images of burned out and damaged buildings. Some were photographs, others were active video. They were images of a city that had clearly been destroyed, but by what? An earthquake? A fire? A bombing? War? Whatever had happened, it was devastating.

The man's voice continued throughout as if he was narrating a documentary film.

I kicked the machine. It didn't respond. I was no longer in danger. But what were the images it was showing? On a hunch, I hurried to the crevice where I'd hidden the communicator. I pulled it out and inspected the face to see…icons. It was working normally. Coincidence? Or had the machine been jamming its signal? I scanned through the icons until I found the one I needed. It was the recording function. I activated it and held the communicator out toward the robot to record both picture and sound. I didn't know how long this strange show would continue and wanted to bring it back to the Scout Leaders as part of my report.

I watched the display as I recorded, and saw something new that made my stomach twist. There were images of people marching in formation through the rubble of the ruined city. People I recognized. They were Scouts, or at least they wore Scout uniforms.

And they carried weapons.

What was I looking at? What had happened while I was out in the desert? Had more of these killer robots landed in a city and gone on a rampage? Was I seeing images of what was left of my home? I didn't recognize any buildings or landmarks, but what was there to recognize about rubble? The only thing familiar about any of it were the Scouts.

Where were all the people who lived in this destroyed city? Who was the guy giving the speech? His image would appear every so often as he spoke. He was an old guy with short gray hair wearing a suit that seemed vaguely military, but like no uniform I'd seen before. He stood in front of a round, blue logo that I'd also never seen before, along with a colorful flag. The man looked tired, but he had a fierce determination in his eyes that made me believe he was somebody you didn't want to cross.

I had no idea what the guy was saying and wasn't sure I wanted to know because it couldn't be good. But it had to be important, so I continued to record it all in order to play it back for the Leaders.

After watching the carnage and the speech for several minutes, I realized that it was repeating. This was not a live transmission. It was a continuous loop that lasted several minutes before playing again from the beginning. I had captured it all, so I stopped recording. I needed to know what these images meant, and didn't want to wait until I'd gotten back to base, so I engaged the translation function on my communicator.

As it worked to translate the odd language into mine, I surveyed the rubble around me and realized how lucky I was to be alive. Now that the communicator was working, my new plan was to use the geo-tracking function to lead me home to the Scout base. Once there I'd turn the recording over to the Scout Leaders and let them deal with it. I was done. All I cared about was getting back to make sure my parents were okay.

A soft tone indicated that the translation was complete. I considered not listening to it until I got back, but couldn't fight my curiosity. I hit the icon which would play the translated recording and stood watching the same images I'd seen over and over again. Only this time, I understood their meaning.

I listened. And watched. Then watched it all again.

On the third time through, I cried.

The memory of that moment still brings me to tears. It was as if it had happened yesterday, not several decades ago.

I wanted to believe it was a hoax, but knew in my heart that it wasn't. What I was seeing, and hearing, was something I had suspected might be possible but never wanted to believe would actually happen. Other Scouts talked about the possibility but only in private and away from the Leaders' ears. My parents never thought events would come to this and convinced me that they wouldn't.

But they did. The proof was all there.

The question was, what would I do with the information?

I stopped the playback and activated the geo-tracking device. The powerful communicator quickly calculated my position and plotted a course to the Scout base, starting with a long walk back through the slot canyon. I hoisted my pack onto my good shoulder and limped away. My body may have been moving forward, but my mind was somewhere else. I wasn't concerned about thirst or my bleeding wounds or throbbing shoulder. Those were trivial problems.

Not like the images I saw on that destroyed robot.

I trudged out of the slot canyon, checked the tracking device, and followed the instructions that would bring me home. Part of me didn't want to make it back. I wanted the sun to knock me down and fry me so I wouldn't have to deal with what I'd discovered.

The harsh reality was that everything I'd been told by those I trusted, was a lie. That knowledge stings to this day. In some ways it hurts more than the lies themselves.

I trudged across the dry, sandy desert on leaden legs, relentlessly dragging one foot in front of the other. I hoped to come across the other Scouts so I could show them the images. I didn't want to be alone with the truth, but I never found them. The journey took most of the day. The sun was long past center and on its way to the horizon when I checked the communicator and estimated that if I didn't collapse I'd be back at the Scout base before nightfall. Once I felt certain that I'd make it, my mind went to what I'd do once I got there. Who would I tell? Who could I trust?

Boom!

The distinct sound of another explosion echoed over the desert floor. It was followed by another and then another. Many more followed. Too many to count, like the barrage of explosions that marked the finale of a fireworks display. But this was no show.

These were sonic booms.

I looked up with dread for I knew what I'd see. The sky was filled with black dots that hovered like birds. But birds didn't hover. Each of the dots would soon grow to the size of a massive bunch of what looked like grapes. When they hit the ground they would bounce across the desert before coming to rest so they could deposit their cargo. The sky was full of them, like a swarm of attacking bees. I stopped counting once I got to a hundred. They would land far behind me, further away from the base from where I stood. I was too close to home for them to stop me from getting there, as long as I kept going.

An hour more of zombie-like limping passed and I finally saw my destination in the distance. Waning sunlight reflected off of the multiple silver spires that stood like vigilant sentries in the desert. It had been my home for more than a year, the place where I had been training for the trip of a lifetime. It was a trip I was told would be about learning and adventure and the sharing of ideas.

But that wasn't the truth. I knew that now.

The badges. The competition. The mission.

All lies.

The Scouts were being groomed for a much different purpose.

When I reached the final rise before dropping down to the desert floor that held my base, I stopped to gaze at the impressive facility that was supposed to be my portal to the stars.

It now felt so very wrong.

I heard a sound. It was faint at first, but quickly grew. I knew what it was without seeing it, but I turned back to look anyway. There appeared to be a dust storm on the horizon, but it was no storm. The dust was being kicked up by something else entirely.

The high-pitched whining grew louder. It was familiar, yet not. When I'd heard it before it came from only one source. Now there were at least a hundred. The multiple sounds joined together to form a single, teeth-jarring, gut-rattling fanfare. Moving across the desert floor in a single line that stretched across the horizon were dozens of the killing machines. I figured they would be coming but the sight still made my knees weak. After all, I'd nearly been killed by one.

The first one.

The Scout.

The first truck was sent alone, maybe to clear the way of any threats before the rest arrived. If that was the case then it had failed. The Scout lay in a destroyed heap in a hidden canyon while the one threat it encountered had nearly made it back to his base. I stood my ground, clutching my communicator. It was still powered up. The icons still glowed. My training told me what I needed to do:

Eliminate the threat and alert my troops of imminent danger.

That was the moment. The moment where I had to make a choice. I had no doubt that whatever I decided to do, it would have a dramatic and lasting impact on me, the Scouts, and perhaps the entire planet. I didn't think that I had the power to prevent what was about to happen, but I could certainly communicate with my base to warn them. That's what I was trained to do. That was my duty.

The line of trucks grew closer. Soon they would be within firing distance. I listened for the telltale sound of their weapons charging to life. They were nearly on me. I didn't run. Where would I go? I scanned the long line from side to side. They were spaced ten yards apart and stretched out for as far as I could see. Their silver weapons were up and locked forward.

None were aimed at me for I wasn't the target. Not anymore. The line of small vehicles approached and rolled past me without any acknowledgement that I was there.

They were after larger game.

As they rolled past me I turned and watched them continue on, headed for the base. I lifted my communicator and found the icon that was a bright red triangle. It was the icon we had been instructed to use if the base came under attack. It was the alert. All I had to do was hit that icon three times and every last Scout and Scout Leader in the base would know that they would soon be under assault. Defensive forces would be activated instantly. Tactical weapons would emerge from underground. Steel walls would lift up from the desert floor to protect the silver spires. The base would become an impenetrable fortress. All would be safe so long as I hit the icon three times.

This was the moment I've relived thousands of times since.

I lifted the communicator, found the red icon…and dropped the device to the ground. There would be no warning.

The line of machines rolled toward the base, unopposed. Unexpected.

I sat down in the sand to watch, waiting for the moment the little demons would unleash their weapons the way the Scout had done on me. I didn't have to wait long. Moments after the wave of machines entered the base, the noise began. The explosions. The pointed attacks. I expected nothing less, based on the relentless pursuit I'd endured through the desert.

The machines knew what they were doing. One by one the tall silver spires were engulfed in flames and toppled. None were spared. They were the vehicles that were poised to take the next wave of Scouts to the stars. Not anymore. Within minutes they were toppled, and the base was ablaze.

Scouts ran about, desperately trying to put out the flames while fighting the marauders. It was wasted effort. The robots would not be denied. There would be no launch vehicles left, no way to lift off from the base, no way to travel to another world the way my predecessors had done.

Seeing the carnage gave me a moment of doubt. I could have prevented the destruction, or at least given the Scouts a fighting chance. Some were my friends who weren't guilty of anything. Yet. How many would survive the attack? Their deaths, and the destruction, would be on my conscience forever.

I had been told that I would touch the stars. That much was true. The lies were about what I would have been ordered to do once I got there.

I picked up the communicator, brushed off the dust, and played the video that had been a message from those who had sent the invading robots. With the determined voice of the speaker as narration, I once again watched images of destroyed cities, and marching Scouts.

"...if you are watching this, our mission has most likely succeeded. We are not a violent people by nature, but we will defend ourselves to the last. The images of destruction you see here have come at your hands. We offered you friendship. We understood and sympathized with your plight. We knew that your steadily warming atmosphere was making it difficult to sustain life. We had been through the same challenge and triumphed. We were willing to be your ally, your lifeline, yet you saw us as a world to be conquered.

We welcomed you and you attacked our cities in a brutal attempt to usurp and colonize. As you now know, we will not stand for either. You have brought a war to our doorstep. Now, we have sent it back to you. The attack that you have just sustained has destroyed your capability for interplanetary travel and aggression. If you attempt to construct more spacecraft, they too will be destroyed. You now know that we have the capability. Your forces have been defeated and are stranded here with us. They will be treated fairly. As for you…you are trapped on a dying world. We were prepared to be your friends, now we are your executioners. You have brought this upon yourselves, and I say this with all sincerity, in spite of your treachery we pray that some higher power will have mercy on your wretched souls. I deliver this message on this twenty-fourth day of May, 3003 A.D. in the name of the United Nations Security Council and as President of the United States of America on the planet Earth."

I turned off the communicator.

I'd made several mistakes that day, and in life, but in that moment I felt certain that this last decision was the right one. I wanted to touch the stars and in some small way, I had. The people who inhabited the light in the sky called Earth would never know my name, never know who I was, and never understand that a lowly Scout from a place they would never see had helped to save their lives, their civilization, and their planet.

My only regret was that they would never understand that not all of the people from my world would have supported such a war if they had only known the truth.

I wasn't one for following the rules. I may have been trapped on a dying world, but I had to hope that the end wasn't near. There was still time. If my people hoped to survive, they would have to find a new solution. A solution from within. We would have to save ourselves.

<p style="text-align:center">~~~~</p>

That was over thirty years ago. The projections for what would happen to our planet due to a steadily warming atmosphere were correct. If anything, they were conservative. Over the last several decades vast areas that once held fertile farmland grew dry and barren. Entire continents became draught-stricken, forcing mass migration and over-population that strained the steadily shrinking areas that were still habitable.

It led to un-checked violence as people fought to protect their homes from being overwhelmed by massive immigration. Millions died of starvation. Many more were killed during the migration wars. It was anarchy. Our planet was dying and its people along with it.

Could I have prevented that? No. Could I have prevented the death of millions of my kind by warning the Scout base of the attack? Only if I accepted that our survival trumped all else. If I had warned the Scout leaders of the attack from Earth and they had turned it back, it would have allowed our own invasion to continue as our forces overran another world. Either way I would have had the blood of millions on my hands.

After the attack on the Scout base, I felt certain that I would be captured and executed for my treasonous act. Perhaps it was selfish, but I took some measure of solace in knowing that I wouldn't have to live through the horror of what was to become of our planet.

I was wrong. I wasn't arrested. I was hailed as a hero for having survived alone in the desert and done battle with the first Earth-scout. It was an ironic twist of fate and stupidity. With so many of our Scouts having been killed during the invasion from Earth, I was eventually elevated to a position of authority. They made me an officer. A Leader. I had become one of the reprehensible types I had such disdain for. I had nothing to look forward to but the horror of seeing our planet die, while living with the guilt that I might have been able to save so much of our population.

I was faced with another choice. I could use whatever influence I had to rebuild and rally the Scouts with the goal of re-arming, strengthening our defenses, and re-building our ability to attack and conquer Earth. Or I could work to re-direct the mission of the Scouts to become a humanitarian one, doing what we could to aid and comfort those of our people who were the victims of dramatic climate change.

The latter choice seemed like it would be a losing battle, but it offered the slim possibility of hope.

As I sit here now, reflecting on the events that I'd set in motion by my inaction so long ago, I'm waiting to receive a delegation from Earth that will be our first direct contact with the people of that planet since they sent a mechanized army to save themselves from us.

Centuries before those events, Earth was faced with a similar dire situation brought about by climate change. The people of that time took the long view and altered their behavior in order to slow the degradation of their environment until the threat became manageable. They had saved their home.

We initially didn't have the foresight or the will to follow their lead, but we learned. In the time since the Earth-invasion, we completely de-militarized and focused the mission of the Scouts on preserving whatever quality of life we could salvage. We made no attempt to re-build our space fleet. We proved that we would no longer be a threat.

The people of Earth were watching. Time healed the wound. They eventually extended the hand of friendship once again. We negotiated a program where cautious, controlled migration would insure the continuation of our people. Thousands will be going to a planet where they will be welcomed and no longer have to live in fear of extinction. The thawing of hostilities with Earth also gave way to a dialog on climate change. We studied the steps taken by the Earth people and there is hope that we can follow their example and slow the man-made causes of our own climate catastrophe. We might even begin to heal. The results of that effort won't be felt until long after I'm gone, but I can take some measure of satisfaction in knowing that I helped get us on the right path.

The question remains: If I knew then what I know now, would I have done the same thing?

I honestly don't know. I've lived with the conflicting emotions of guilt and satisfaction for years. It's difficult to look back objectively and say with certainty that I wouldn't have taken the easier route and warned the Scout Leaders. Who knows how that story would have ended?

But I do know how this story will end, and there is no small measure of poetic justice. When the Earth delegation arrives, I will be on the committee to greet them, and begin final planning to determine how the immigration process will unfold. Part of the process will involve my travelling with the delegation back to Earth to oversee the preparations underway to receive our people.

I will become the Scout.

And finally, I will touch the stars.

<u>THE END</u>

THE WEEPER

lex was busy watching TV when he heard someone knocking on the front door. It was a gentle tapping, nothing out of the ordinary. Nothing urgent. But it made him jump as if he had been shocked by the sting of a cattle prod. He turned down the volume on "The Simpsons" and listened.

"Can Alex come out to play?"

It sounded like a sweet young girl. Nothing strange about that. It was three o'clock in the afternoon. On a school day. Nothing bad ever happens on days like that.

Then why was Alex's heart racing?

He ran to the window to see who was there, but his view of the front door was blocked by a thick hedge. He scanned his front yard, afraid that he would see the one thing he feared seeing.

The tree. He didn't want to see the tree.

Another knock.

"Come out to play, Alex."

Alex was tired of fearing something he didn't understand. It was time to put an end to it. He stormed to the door where he spotted his father's tool kit sitting open at the bottom of the stairs. Seeing it made him wish his parents were there. But they wouldn't be home for hours. He had to fix this himself.

He dug through the tools and found a hammer. He pulled it out, feeling its weight. He could do some damage with a weapon like that. He was feeling more confidant...

...until he heard the backdoor creak open.

Had he left it unlocked?

"Mom? Dad?" he called out weakly.

The door slammed. Whoever it was, was in the house. Alex didn't know which way to turn…as another knock came at the front door.

"Come on out, Alex. Let's play."

Alex grasped the hammer and strode for the door.

"Enough!" he shouted. "I don't want to play your game!"

He pulled the door open, ready for a fight.

Nobody was there. For a brief moment he wondered if he had imagined the whole thing. Was he losing his mind?

"You left your door unlocked, Alex," a little boy said.

The voice came from behind him. Inside the house. Alex spun around and saw him. Or it. It was a little boy all right, but it wasn't. It was more like the shadow of a little boy that stood in the hallway, a solid black cutout with no detail and no depth. Yet it was standing there. And it could talk.

"Let's play," he said with a giggle.

Alex turned and ran out of the front door, headed for the street, but he was stopped short by another shadow standing in his way. It looked like a young girl with her hands on her hips.

"Finally!" the shadow-girl exclaimed "Let's have some fun."

Alex tried to cry out, but his throat was squeezed tight by the firm grip of panic. He changed direction and ran across the lawn, headed for the next-door neighbor's yard. He would have smashed right through the hedges that bordered the property if two more shadows hadn't stepped out of the greenery to block his way. They waved, as if happy to see him.

Alex changed direction again and sprinted to the back of his house. Which way to go? Where was safety? Why did his parents have to work and leave him alone all the time? He made it to his back yard where several more shadow-children were waiting. They were everywhere, cutting off escape routes like a flock of sheep that were herding the sheep dog. Alex had no choice but to tear through the hedge that separated his backyard from an empty field beyond.

But the field wasn't empty. Not anymore.

Looming in front of him was the tree. The weeping willow tree. Its dark trunk curved into an "s" shape with gnarly thick branches that reached out like an arthritic old man straining against gravity to raise his tired arms. The limbs were heavy with narrow leaves that cascaded to the ground to form a waterfall of greenery.

Alex turned around to see he was hemmed in by a dozen shadow-children. Trapped. There was no escape, and he knew it.

"Enough," he said with false conviction.

He stood up straight, gathering what little courage he had left, and strode toward the tree. With his hand wrapped firmly around the hammer, he stopped a few feet short of the drooping branches.

"You want to play?" he said defiantly. "Let's play!"

He raised the hammer but before he could swing it, a branch sprang forward and wrapped around his arms, pinning them to his sides. Another branch shot out, wrapped around his leg, and pulled him toward the tree. Alex dug in his heels to pull back, but it was no use. He hacked at the leaves with the hammer, but no sooner did he sever one branch than another lashed out to take its place.

"Help!" he screamed. "Somebody—"

His plea was cut short as the branches dragged him through the curtain of leaves and into the umbrella-like tree.

The last sound that Alex ever heard was the joyous laughter of the shadow children, who finally got him to play.

Turned out that bad things *did* happen on days like that.

"Keep him busy," Dylan commanded.

"What d'ya mean? What are you gonna do?" Travis asked, though he wasn't sure he wanted to hear the answer.

"Just do it," Dylan barked, and walked deeper into the market.

Travis didn't like hanging around with Dylan, or his buddies, but they were the only guys in town his age. Unless he wanted to spend the summer alone with his iPad, he had to go along.

"Hi, Mr. Drucker," Travis said as he approached the front counter.

"Travis! Welcome back. Good to see you!" Mr. Drucker said. "How're the folks?"

"You know, same old," Travis said with a shrug.

Travis Lockwood and his family lived in Stony Brook, Connecticut but rented a lake house every summer in the small town of High Pine, Vermont. Travis loved being on the lake, but the older he got the harder it was to find kids his age to hang with. When he was six it was all about playing and swimming and making forts in the woods. But at twelve he had to deal with the strange new world of teens and testosterone. Suddenly playing "Marco Polo" wasn't an exciting option.

"Stocking up?" Mr. Drucker asked.

"Uh, what?" Travis replied.

He had to force himself from glancing down the aisle to see what Dylan was up to. Travis liked Mr. Drucker. The old guy knew the name of every person who lived in High Pine or visited in the summer. He hated the idea that he was helping Dylan do something Drucker wouldn't like. But he hated the idea of Dylan and his pals freezing him out for the summer even more.

"Oh! You mean for the lake house," Travis said. "No, I'm just looking for--" he scanned the counter. "A Milky Way." He grabbed a candy bar from the rack. "My favorite. Candy that is. Perfect candy bar. Nothing else like it. Nope. The good old Milky Way. How much is it?"

If Mr. Drucker knew that Travis' nerves were making him babble, he didn't let on.

"First one's on me," Drucker said with a laugh. "Summer's just getting started. You'll be back."

Drucker's generosity made Travis feel even worse. Before he could refuse the offer and pay anyway, Dylan walked past him, hurrying for the exit.

"Let's go," he said curtly and left the store.

Travis gave a quick look to Drucker, who was eying Dylan. He'd lost his warm smile. Dylan lived year-round in High Pine. Drucker knew him well and wasn't a fan.

"Thanks Mr. Drucker," Travis said as he backed toward the door.

"You're okay, Travis," Drucker said. "Make it a good summer."

Travis felt as though Drucker knew exactly what Dylan was up to, and that he was an accomplice.

"Thanks, I will," he said and went for the door.

As he was about to push it open, his eye caught something on the far end of an aisle of groceries. He thought he saw a fleeting shadow move past the freezer along the back wall. But nobody else was in the store. Weird. He didn't give it a second thought and headed out.

Dylan was waiting for him in the parking lot.

"What was that all about?" Travis asked.

Dylan was wearing a raincoat, though there wasn't a cloud in the sky.

"Supplies," he said. From out of the coat's pockets he pulled two 16-ounce cans of Budweiser.

"You stole those!" Travis exclaimed.

"So what?" Dylan barked and gave Travis a shove that nearly knocked him over.

"Because it's robbery, that's so what," Travis said.

"Jeez, Lockwood. What are you? A Boy Scout?"

Truth be told, Travis *was* a Boy Scout. But he wasn't about to admit it just then.

"I just think Mr. Drucker's cool, is all," Travis said.

"Cool? He's an old fart who charges too much for his crap because he's the only store in town," Dylan said.

"Yeah, but—"

"Meet us at the boathouse. Sundown."

Dylan jammed the stolen beers back into his jacket pockets and hurried off.

Travis wasn't so sure he wanted to go, but without friends it would be a very long summer.

~~~~
~~~~

The ancient cabin in the woods was a one-room, ramshackle structure that for decades was used by fishermen to warm up while ice fishing. In warm months it lay empty except for the kids in High Pine who used it as a secluded getaway to smoke and drink and hook-up. It was close enough to get to by bike along a dirt road, but far enough away from town so adults wouldn't make surprise visits.

The last light of day seeped through the pine trees that surrounded the building, creating long shadows that wrapped around the wooden cabin like dark tendrils. Dylan kicked open the door and entered. He was followed by his friends, Richie, and Dinger. Last in was Travis.

"I'm starting a fire," Dylan announced.

Dylan was bigger than the other guys and at twelve years old, big meant power.

"Get wood," he commanded to no one in particular.

Richie and Dinger obeyed instantly and ran back outside. Travis didn't move. He didn't like being ordered around and was still ticked at himself for helping Dylan rob Mr. Drucker.

Dylan took off his backpack and pulled out the beer, along with a canteen and a butane lighter.

Travis inspected the ancient, stone fireplace. "That thing hasn't seen a fire since the turn of the century" he said. "The *last* century. The chimney's probably blocked."

"Your whining's getting old," Dylan said with disdain.

The more time Travis spent with Dylan, the more he realized what a tool the guy was. A summer spent with his iPad was starting to look more promising by the second.

The others came back with armloads of split wood.

"Nice!" Dylan exclaimed.

"Somebody's been stocking up on wood for the winter," Dinger said. "Nice of 'em to save us the trouble."

Travis was beginning to think Dylan's friends were just as much losers as their ringleader. Weren't there any non-criminal kids in this town?

Richie dumped his pile of wood into the hearth.

"Whoa, you gotta start it with kindling," Travis said. "After that catches you put on bigger pieces."

"Why?" Richie asked.

"Because big pieces are harder to light."

As he talked he picked up Dylan's canteen. He unscrewed the cap and was about to take a drink when he smelled what was inside and gagged.

"Whoa! What the hell?" he yelled.

The others laughed. Dylan grabbed the canteen.

"Or you could do it the easy way," he said as he splashed the liquid from the canteen onto the logs.

"Is that kerosene?" Travis asked.

"Kindling is for girls," Dylan replied.

He pulled the trigger on the butane lighter, touched the flame to the logs and with an instantaneous *WHOOF*, the kerosene ignited, and the logs were ablaze.

"Yeah!" Dinger yelled.

"Sweet!" Richie chimed in.

They were both drawn to the flames like cavemen who had just discovered fire.

Travis wished he had a good excuse to leave.

~~~~

An hour later the sun was down. Though the outside temperature dipped, it was sweat-lodge hot inside the cabin due to the roaring fire. Dylan dropped another log onto the inferno, sending out a spray of sparkling embers.

"Not hot enough for you?" Travis asked.

"Shut up," Dylan replied.

Travis wondered why he ever thought it would be fun hanging out with this goon and his two minions. They passed around the beer as if it were some precious elixir, each taking sips. Travis didn't like beer, but knew he'd catch flack if he didn't drink a little.

"Who's got a ghost story?" Dinger asked.
~~~~

"What are you, six?" Dylan said with a sneer.

"Hey, what else do you do around a fire?"

"Drink!" Dylan said, and took another swig of warm beer.

"We've probably heard 'em all anyway," Travis said.

"Bet you haven't heard the one about our local legend," Dinger said.

"I'm sick of that stupid story," was Dylan's comeback.

"Yeah, but it's *our* stupid story," Dinger argued.

"So tell it," Travis said. He wanted to add, *because sitting here doing nothing but watching you three clowns getting drunk on a couple of sips of beer is torture.* But he didn't.

Dinger let loose with a deep, resonant beer-belch and began.

"Okay. It's called The Weeper. It's about an old man who lived around here about a hundred years ago. He had a cabin on the far side of Hillegas Lake. I guess you'd call him a hermit. He was a nasty old cuss who made money by brewing moonshine. The sheriff left him alone because people liked his shine so much they'd go all the way out to his cabin in the woods to pay him to fill up their jugs."

"A regular captain of industry," Travis said.

"He was a strange old coot. Always dressed in ragged clothes and he didn't smell so hot. Whenever he went into town the kids would make fun of him, calling him *hillbilly* and *mountain man* and what not."

"Because he was," Dylan commented.

"Maybe so, but those kids only made him meaner. One day a couple of teen-guys went out to his cabin to get moonshine. When the old guy wasn't expecting it, they shoved him down his cellar stairs and locked him in. They grabbed a couple of jugs and took off, figuring somebody would come by and let the guy out. But hermits are called hermits for a reason. They don't get a lot of visitors. Nobody went out there again for the whole winter. It wasn't until spring when nobody'd seen him for a long time that the sheriff went to check on him. He found the guy still in the cellar, dead. Mummified."

"More like pickled," Dylan said with a chuckle. "You know, from the moonshine."

"That's a lousy story," Travis said. "It's not scary, it's just sad."

"I haven't gotten to the scary part. Outside the cabin there was a huge weeping willow tree. Must have been a couple hundred years old. When the sheriff found the body, the tree was gone. But not just gone, there was no sign that it had ever been there. It just disappeared. This is where it gets seriously weird. Soon after, kids in town started going missing. But before they disappeared, each one of 'em talked about being haunted by black shadows and having nightmares about a weeping willow tree."

"The Weeper," Dylan added. "That's where the title comes from."

"Yeah I figured that," Travis said.

Dinger added, "And the kids were never seen again."

"Creepy, huh?" Dylan said, and took another swig of beer.

"So, the legend is the old man's ghost haunted the tree and got revenge on the town by stealing their kids?" Travis asked.

"Not all kids. Just the kind of kids the old guy hated."

"You mean d-bags," Travis said.

"Hey," Dylan snapped. "Not everybody's a Boy Scout."

He let out a huge, rumbling beer-belch that made Dinger laugh. Even Travis had to laugh at the impressive boomer. Dylan beamed proudly, as if he'd accomplished something special, making them laugh even harder.

"It's not funny," Richie said, finally speaking up.

All eyes went to him.

"Sure it is," Dylan said and let out another belch.

Travis and Dinger tried to keep from laughing because they saw that Richie was dead-serious.

"I'm talking about the hermit story," Richie said.

"It's just a dumb story," Dinger said.

"You think? People tell that story like it's made-up, but bad things really happened. My sister's friend had an older brother. Alex was his name. About ten years ago he talked about seeing shadows, and had dreams about a tree. Everybody thought he was kidding because he'd heard the story. But then he disappeared. For real."

Silence fell over the cabin. The only sound came from the crackling fire.

The fire.

"Whoa!" Travis shouted and jumped up.

Flames were licking up out of the hearth, licking the ancient wooden frame that looked ready to ignite. Smoke billowed down from the chimney and quickly filled the cabin. Dylan grabbed his pack and was the first out the door, followed by Richie and Dinger. Travis glanced around for something he could use to kill the flames, but it had gone too far too fast. The smoke burned his eyes and made it hard to breath. There was nothing he could do so he followed the others out. The four stood outside the cabin, watching dark smoke and sparks spew up and out of the crumbling chimney.

"I knew we shouldn't have made such a big fire," Richie said.

"Why didn't you say something?" Dylan argued.

"Because you never listen to what anybody says," Richie shot back.

"We gotta call somebody before it spreads to the trees," Travis said.

"You do that," Dylan said as he picked up his bike. "If the cops think I was anywhere near here they'll blame it on me."

He quickly pedaled away.

Richie said, "And they'd be right."

"We gotta get to a phone," Travis said.

The three boys grabbed their bikes and followed Dylan. Travis got only a few yards away when he stopped and glanced back to see flames licking up out of the windows of the old wooden structure. The cabin was a goner. He knew he'd have some explaining to do, but it would be a lot worse if the fire spread to the forest. Without a cell phone, he had to get to a land line, fast.

As he stood astride his bike, he saw something that made him catch his breath. It looked as if three figures were standing in front of the cabin, silhouetted by the flames. He rubbed his eyes, thinking the firelight was playing tricks. When he looked back, the silhouettes were gone. A chill ran up his spine. He jumped on his bike and rode hard, quickly catching up with the others. When they reached the main road, Richie and Dinger went one way while Travis and Dylan went the other.

"You live closer," Travis said. "We'll tell your parents, and they can call 911."

"My mother's not home. She works nights," Dylan said.

"Okay, then we'll call it in ourselves."

"No, *you'll* call it in. I'm in enough trouble. One more strike and I'll get sent away for good. You can be a hero but I ain't gonna say I was anywhere near that place."

"Fine, I'll do it myself," Travis said and pedaled on.

The two rode in silence and soon arrived at Dylan's home. It was a double-wide trailer that was smaller than the cabin Travis' family rented for the summer, with more dirt than grass surrounding it and a few junker cars in front. They dropped their bikes and ran straight inside.

"Phone's on the counter," Dylan said as he grabbed a can of soda out of the refrigerator. "I'll kick your ass if you tell anybody we were there."

Travis dialed 911 and wandered back toward the front door as the operator answered his call.

"Hi," Travis said. "I was riding my bike out by Hillegas Lake and saw smoke coming from the woods. Near Seton's cabin I think. It might be on fire."

Dylan gave him a satisfied thumbs-up, took a swig of soda, and went into his living room.

"Travis Lockwood," he said to the operator. "My family's here for the summer and—"

There was a quiet knock at the front door. Travis put his hand over the receiver.

"Dylan, somebody's at the door," he called out.

Travis then heard a voice coming from outside the door.

"Can Dylan come out to play?"

It sounded like a little girl. It was both sweet…and wrong. It gave Travis goosebumps.

"No!" Dylan cried out and slammed his soda can down on a table.

It made Travis jump. He hung up the phone and joined Dylan in the living room.

"Somebody's at the front door," Travis said. "Sounds like a little girl."

Dylan wasn't interested. He was too busy staring out of the sliders that led to a back patio.

"No way," he said, stunned.

"No way what?"

Travis followed Dylan's gaze out to the back yard. The expanse of dirt and grass was lit by the light of a full moon. There were a few more junk-cars, a picnic table, a rusted barbeque and at the back of the property, a tree.

A massive weeping willow.

"Yeah, so?" Travis asked.

"You see that tree?"

"Yeah."

"That wasn't there this afternoon."

"Get outta here!" Travis said, skeptically.

Dylan slid open the glass slider and headed outside. Travis was about to follow when another knock came at the front door.

"Time to play, Dylan," the young girl said.

Travis wanted nothing to do with whoever was out there. He ran after Dylan, who was striding boldly, straight for the tree.

"How is that possible?" Travis asked.

"Either somebody's messing with me or…"

He let the thought trail off.

"Or what? It's the Weeper?" Travis asked. "That's just stupid."

"Then how did a full-grown tree suddenly show up in my back yard?"

Travis had no idea, but he didn't think for a second that it could be the ghost of an angry old moonshiner who was taking revenge against delinquent kids. Though Dylan definitely qualified.

"I've been hearing that story for years," Dylan added. "I want to know if it's true."

He went right up to the tree and stood boldly in front of the curtain of branches that were waving lazily in the breeze.

"So?" he called out with bravura. "You got a problem with me? C'mon old man. I ain't afraid of—"

A leafy branch whipped out and wrapped around Dylan's neck.

"Whoa!" Travis screamed and backed off in surprise.

The vine-like branch pulled Dylan toward the tree. He struggled against it, wrapping his fingers around the branch that gripped his neck trying to free himself. It was futile. He twisted his head around to make eye contact with Travis and mouthed, "Help!"

A second later, he was pulled through the veil of drooping branches and was gone.

Travis took a few steps back, fearing that the tree might come after him next.

"He was a bad boy."

Travis shot a look to his left to see a shadow child standing there.

"Now he'll play with us, forever," the shadow said.

That got Travis moving. He sprinted for the house while trying to focus and think. What the hell was happening? What should he do? How could he help Dylan?

He blasted into the house and ran straight through to the front door. He was about to pull it open when he heard another knock.

He froze.

"Can Travis come out to play?" the little girl asked.

Travis' knees went weak. Now they were after him!

"Who are you?" he screamed.

"We're from the tree. Come play with us."

Travis was near panic. He went for the phone, but who was he going to call? The police? What could they do? He needed help now. The police probably wouldn't believe him anyway. Something had to be done fast, or Dylan would be lost, and he'd be next.

Travis spotted Dylan's backpack on the floor. Maybe there *was* something he could do. He grabbed it and ran out the back door, headed for the tree. He stopped directly in front of the waving branches, dug into the pack, and pulled out Dylan's canteen and butane lighter.

"Let him go!" Travis shouted. "He didn't do anything to you."

He began to unscrew the cap, when a vine-like branch whipped out and wrapped around his ankle. It instantly went taut, pulling him off his feet. He landed hard and dropped the butane lighter. As the branch dragged him toward the tree, Travis flipped over onto his belly and reached for the lighter. With a desperate lunge, he grabbed it just as he was yanked through the curtain of hanging branches.

Travis was pulled into a different world. He was under the drooping branches of the tree, but the space was impossibly huge, as if he was inside an immense leafy cathedral. The twisted, black trunk was in the center, with thick gnarled branches reaching out at all angles. The sheer size of the space was the least strange and frightening sight for perched on the branches above him were dozens of shadow children. The black cutouts peered down at him like hungry vultures.

They chanted, "Travis! Travis! Tavis!"

It was a surreal nightmare that only got worse as Travis was dragged to the base of the tree where more branches reached out to snare him.

"Travis! Help!'

Dylan was tied to the tree. Vine-like branches had wrapped him up against the trunk like a fly snared by a hungry spider.

Realizing he was about to meet the same fate gave Travis a shot of adrenalin. He fought off the attacking branches with the hand holding the lighter while fumbling for the canteen with the other. If he dropped either, they'd be done.

The branch pulled him up against the tree trunk, while others wrapped around his ankles. Travis stayed focused. He got the cap off the canteen and splashed kerosene onto the tree.

"Hurry!" Dylan yelled.

Travis fumbled with the lighter, curled his finger around the trigger and was about to pull it when a branch shot toward him, whipped it out of his hand and flung it away.

"No!" Dylan screamed.

Travis fought against the predator branches to get to the lighter, but it was no use. He was held tight. The Weeper was about to claim two more victims.

"I'm sorry, Travis," Dylan said, crying. "This wasn't your fault."

Dylan's apology didn't make Travis feel any better for the vines were already tightening around his neck, choking him. He looked up to see the dozens of shadow children looming over them, all victims of the Weeper. They glared down, waiting to welcome two more kids into their haunted club.

"He's right," a tiny voice said.

Travis looked down to see the shadow of a little girl standing in front of him.

"It wasn't your fault, Travis," she said. "You don't belong here."

In her dark little hand was the butane lighter.

She added, "None of us belong here. Not really."

She held the lighter out for Travis to take.

Travis struggled against the branches and grasped the lighter. For a brief second, he feared that if he set the tree on fire, he and Dylan would burn too. But he was starting to lose consciousness. The ever-tightening branches told him they had nothing to lose.

"Burn it!" Dylan screamed a moment before a vine swept across his mouth, gagging him.

Travis took a nervous breath, pulled the trigger and a small flame appeared on the tip of the lighter. He fought against the vines that yanked at his arms in a desperate attempt to keep him from igniting the kerosene.

The vines pulled hard.

Travis pulled harder.

He touched the flame to the tree and the kerosene ignited. A wave of heat hit Travis as the flames spread quickly, travelling up the trunk, fueled by the kerosene. The branches holding Travis and

Dylan retracted, releasing the boys. They both fell to their knees, gasping for breath. The ghost-branches swatted at the fire to try and extinguish the flames, but instead of snuffing out the fire, the branches ignited.

Travis grabbed Dylan and pulled him to his feet.

The flames moved up the trunk and quickly spread to the thicker branches where the shadow children sat. Strangely, none of them reacted.

Travis pulled Dylan back the way they had come, headed for the curtain of branches. Above them, the canopy was ablaze. Burning leaves rained down. The heat was growing unbearable. They were seconds away from being trapped by the rapidly spreading fire.

With one last burst of effort, Travis jumped through the hanging branches, pulling Dylan along with him out into the cool of the night. They kept running until they got to the house, where they finally felt safe enough to turn around, and watch.

"Oh man," Travis said in stunned wonder.

"I think I'm losing my mind," Dylan said.

Every last branch of the tree was ablaze, creating a massive torch that lit up the night. They were witnessing more than the fiery destruction of a tree; it was a spiritual cleansing. The leaves quickly burned away to reveal a tangle of dark branches that moved as if alive and in pain. They writhed and twisted into what looked like the face of a man. Its mouth was open in agony, the hissing flames its cry. It shook, it grimaced, but the hungry flames would not be denied. From out of its mouth came the shadow-children, rising on a plume of heat. The spirits gently floated up amid the burning leaves to disappear into the night sky as their laughter drifted away on the breeze.

Once the last of the shadows were gone, the mouth opened wide to give off one final anguished roar as the entire burned skeleton of the tree collapsed. An explosion of sparks erupted from the impact, followed by a cloud of smoke that filled the back yard, but only for a few moments. Once the last wisp of smoke blew away, the yard returned to normal. There were no ashes, no scorch marks, no sign whatsoever of the dramatic fire that marked the last chapter of the tale of The Weeper.

"Thanks, man," Dylan said sincerely.

Travis nodded.

As they went inside they heard the distant sound of a siren.

"You think it's coming here?" Dylan asked.

"I hope it's headed to the cabin."

The two looked at one another, not sure of what to say when…

A knock came at the front door.

Travis' mouth went dry.

Another knock came.

"It's over, isn't it?" Dylan asked fearfully.

"Who is it?" Travis called out weakly.

"We're going home now," the little girl said.

"Good," Travis called out. "Thank you."

"Maybe we're not so bad after all," the girl said with a giggle.

It was the last they heard from her. It was the last anybody heard from the shadow children.

"How are we gonna explain this?" Dylan asked.

"We aren't," Travis replied. "The story's over."

~~~~

The story may have been over, but the legend lived on. Parents used it as a cautionary tale to keep their children from misbehaving. Kids continued to tell the tale around campfires. But they all slept soundly at night knowing it was all just a made-up story.

Though one mystery remained. It had to do with a tree that appeared on the far shore of Hillegas Lake. It was a beautiful tree. A lush, mature weeping willow. People pointed to it from a distance and laughingly called it The Weeper. But nobody truly thought it was a ghost tree. Nor did they want to know the truth. If they did, they might have discovered that behind the tree, hidden deep in the forest, were the ruins of a forgotten cabin covered by years of dense growth. It was as though the tree was standing guard, waiting for
~~~~

someone to trespass on sacred ground to re-ignite the fury of a restless spirit who in the end, was denied true vengeance.

All it would take is one curious kid who wanted to play.

<u>THE END</u>

THE PAPER TRAIL (VERA)

Early morning sunlight spread across the fall-colored forest of rural Wisconsin. The sole sign of civilization was the winding ribbon of black asphalt that had travelled this same route for over a century, changed only by infrequent repaving. It was a road used mainly by tractors and pick-up trucks, which is why the sight of a long black limousine gliding elegantly along, starkly incongruous. The sleek car navigated the turns with ease, respecting the overly conservative speed limit. It passed a large, road sign which had been erected by the WPA decades before and only occasionally updated.

TOWN OF GLENVILLE, WISCONSIN
POPULATION 10,000 (OR SO)
WELCOME!

Glenville was a small, gray town that sat directly on the way to somewhere else. It was a place to stop for gas, a meal, or for directions to a far more interesting place to find cheaper gas or a better meal. There were no Tesla charging stations or Airbnbs. It was a destination solely for those who lived there, and the number of people who called Glenville home was in constant freefall. Its boom years peaked in the 1950's when the town boasted several low-tech industrial businesses including a pulp mill, a foundry, and a tool-and-die manufacturer...all of which became obsolete when the world transitioned from low to high tech. There remained enough work to keep the town alive, barely. It held on because the idea of tearing up deep roots in search of a better life was not an option that most people in this neck of the woods embraced. Glenville may have been trapped in another era, but it had been home to many families for generations. For those who remained, that was enough.

The town hadn't yet woken up when the limousine turned on to the aptly named Main Street, which was a five-block stretch of throwback shops without a single franchise. There were only two traffic lights, one of which functioned maybe half the time. The elegant limousine stopped at the first light as it turned red, though at this hour of the morning there wasn't much need to follow traffic rules. Once the car eased to a stop, the rear door opened, and its lone passenger emerged.

While the luxurious vehicle may have looked out of place, its passenger was a downright unicorn. He was black, stood well over six feet tall and looked to be somewhere in his fifties. The years had been kind to this slim, handsome gent who had a dusting of silver in his dark hair. One might have likened him to having aged like "a fine wine", though in this town, the bar for what wines were considered to be fine wasn't very high. He wore a black, perfectly tailored three-piece suit, carried a black walking stick with an ornately carved ivory handle, and sported a dark bowler hat. His throwback style screamed "Carnaby Street" though few people in Glenville would have made that connection.

He stood with perfect posture next to the limo and gazed about the quiet street, taking in its tarnished charm with a bemused smile. If there had been anyone there to listen, he might have said something mildly condescending like: "How endearingly quaint". The expected next move would be for him to slide back into the car, issue a curt "drive on" command, and continue to his true destination.

Instead, he gave a slight nod to the driver and the car pulled away, leaving him alone in the center of the intersection beneath an ancient traffic light that swayed in the breeze. He turned a graceful three-sixty as if to orient himself, then let out a resigned sigh. He grasped his walking stick by the handle, lifted it to chest level and as if staking a claim, brought it down hard on the pavement. The surprisingly loud crack of sound reverberated off of the surrounding buildings. It was the only sound that broke the early morning quiet of the sleepy village.

Vera Holiday woke with a start.

It was the sound that did it, but not the sound created by the early morning visitor.

Vera had lived her entire life in the same modest house that sat a few blocks from Glenville's downtown. It had been built by her parents in the 1950's. When they passed in the mid 90's, ownership fell to her, their only child. She didn't particularly like the house, or have many cherished childhood memories, but she lived alone and being the pragmatic sort, she had no desire to trade up or down.

One of those needs was absolute quiet and while Glenville had an over-abundance of that, her property was insulated by a thick ring of pine trees making it particularly secluded which is why an alien sound, no matter how subtle, wasn't missed.

The sound that woke her, was scratching. It was muted by the thickness of the old-school plaster walls so she couldn't pinpoint exactly where it was coming from, but there was no mistake. Something was alive inside her walls.

"Damn," she muttered aloud.

Vera had had similar issues in the past. A squirrel once found its way into the house through a damaged vent near the chimney and set up housekeeping in her attic. Birds made nests in the eaves of the roof. The most annoying were the crickets who slipped in through unknown crevices and proceeded to chirp incessantly through the night. Each time she had a local handyman get rid of the interlopers and make the requisite repairs, but the next round of persistent critters would eventually find their way in. It didn't happen often, but it was no less irritating when it did.

Vera irritated easily.

Without getting out of bed, she reached up to the wall and gave a few sharp bangs with her fist, hoping to scare off whatever creature had found its way inside. The scratching stopped and Vera dared to think that she had solved the problem.

Until the scratching began anew. Distant yet incessant.

"Shit," she said and sat up. She would have to call Dennis the handyman to find and repair the entry point. The idea that she might trap some unsuspecting critter in her walls to die of starvation was the least of her worries. She was more concerned about some varmint starting a family and encouraging other visitors who might chew through wiring or damage plumbing.

"Can't catch a break," she grumbled and got up to start her day.

~~~~

The Rx Diner was the hub of early morning activity in Glenville. Most every customer was a local who would stop by each morning before work for coffee, breakfast, and gossip. (Mostly for gossip). The décor was straight out of the 1950's. Literally. Very little had been updated, upgraded, or replaced since a cup of coffee cost fifteen cents.

"Ow, Jee-zus!" screamed Ben Daniels, the diner's only cook, and one of its two owners. He was behind the counter next to the microwave. (The one nod to modern technology in the Rx. Welcome to the 80's.)

"What happened?" Holly Meade asked. Holly was back from college after earning a degree from Northwestern in "Now what do I do?" Her short-term answer was moving back to her hometown and working the morning shift at the Rx.

"Damn thing gave me a shock," Ben cried. "What did you do to it?"

"Nothing," Holly said patiently. "I didn't do anything. Morning Terri!"

Terri Hirsch, the town's Sheriff settled into a seat at the counter. Terri was born in Glenville, but her mother moved her to Chicago when she was still a young child. She grew up in the Windy City, graduated from the police academy, got married, had a daughter, and promptly got divorced from an amiable fellow who she married way too young. She moved back to Glenville with the idea of raising her
~~~~

child quietly, away from the city hubbub. The moment she set foot in town she became the most experienced law officer available, so she was anointed sheriff and quickly became mother-hen to the community.

"Morning Holly," Terri said, then turned to Scott Wilson, a beefy guy in work clothes who sat at the counter finishing a heavy breakfast.

"Morning Scott. You in a hurry?"

"What'dya mean?" Scott asked.

"You left your car running."

"I did?"

"You did."

"Dang!" Scott exclaimed. "I'm losing it. Thanks Terri."

Scott dropped a few bills on the counter and hurried out.

Terri looked to Holly and said, "And with that one noble gesture I've earned my pay for the day."

Holly poured a mug of coffee for the sheriff. "That's why we love you, always looking out for us."

"That's me," Terri said. "Ever vigilant."

George Daniels, Ben's brother, and co-owner of the Rx walked behind Holly and groused, "Full house. Stop socializing."

"Morning George!" Terri said, overly bright.

"Morning Sheriff," George growled without stopping.

"Give the poor girl a break."

"Arrest me."

"Don't tempt me."

Vera Holiday sat alone in her usual booth. It was the one furthest away from the front door of the diner. Vera had been coming to the Rx for her morning bowl of oatmeal for as long as anyone could remember, and as far as anyone could remember, she always ate alone. Ironically, she knew most everyone who lived in Glenville for she owned the town's pharmacy. She was also the pharmacist which meant she knew who suffered from diabetes, hypo-thyroid, attention deficit disorder, high blood pressure and erectile dysfunction. Vera was discreet. She didn't share any of that information. Then again, she didn't have many friends to share it with.

As she sat staring at the newspaper (she refused to read the news on her iPhone 6) and savored her gruel, she heard something that made the cereal catch in her throat.

It was a scratching sound coming from inside the wall next to the booth, not unlike the sounds she had heard at home.

"Damn varmints," she groused and leaned into the wall to get a sense of where the critter might be.

The front door of the diner opened. Another customer had arrived, though not one of the regulars. It was the tall man in the sharp suit.

All eyes went to the newcomer. It wasn't often that a non-local arrived this early at the Rx, especially not one who looked as though he'd just strolled out of a movie. First off, he was black. His skin-color a deep-ebony. That alone caused heads to turn. There were no black residents of Glenville. Not that they weren't welcome, but over the past few decades far more people moved out than in. People had deep roots in the town and those roots were decidedly white. Besides his skin color, his suit and mannerisms did not scream "country". And the bowler hat! Not one person in the diner had ever seen one, other than in some old-timey movie.

If the man felt uncomfortable being the center of attention, he didn't show it. He glided with grace past tables and booths to the last unoccupied booth which was a few spots away from Vera, who was busy listening to the wall.

Holly had spotted him the instant he stepped through the door and was right there with a menu in one hand and a pot of coffee in the other.

"Morning!" Holly said cheerfully. "Coffee?"

"Tea, if you please," the man said with a decidedly aristocratic British accent. "Earl Grey?"

"Uh, no, it's Holly Meade."

He gave her a warm smile and said, "Of course. Any tea will do. Thank you so much."

"My pleasure," Holly said and turned away to fetch his tea.

"Miss Holly?" he called after her.

She stopped and turned back to him.

"Yeah?"

"Might I bother you for a recommendation? I'd like to speak with someone in order to learn a bit about your lovely town."

"Why?" Holly said with surprise, then realized it may have been rude, so she backed off. "I mean, what do you want to know about Glenville?"

"Nothing specific. I'm an author in search of local color and such".

Holly nodded thoughtfully. "Well, you came to the right place," she said as she gestured around the room with the coffee pot. "Local color is our specialty. But if you want to know where all the bodies are buried, I'd talk to Sheriff Hirsch."

She gestured the pot toward Terri.

"Brilliant. Thank you, Miss Holly. I will."

Holly smiled, a bit flustered. The man certainly was charming. And handsome. Nothing like any of the men who lived in Glenville.

George Daniels rushed out from his office near the booth where Vera sat with her ear to the wall. He was in a hurry. George was always in a hurry, but no one ever knew why. Vera got his attention by raising her hand and snapping her fingers. George stopped and took a deep breath to calm himself. Vera was always complaining about one thing or another and the last thing he wanted was to debate the correct temperature to serve oatmeal.

"Can I help you with something, Vera?" he asked, overly and falsely solicitous.

"You've got a rodent problem," Vera snapped.

George stood up straight. She might as well have said that his food had given her Salmonella. He took a quick look around to see if anyone had heard her.

"What are you talking about?" he asked in a strained whisper.

"Listen," she said and tapped the wall.

George leaned in, putting his ear to the wall.

"I don't hear anything."

"It's gone," Vera declared. "Probably got spooked by us talking. But you've definitely got something in there. I don't know what. A squirrel. Or maybe a rat."

"A rat!" George exclaimed, then realized he shouldn't be shouting out "rat!" in his restaurant. He looked around quickly, hoping nobody heard.

"A rat?" he asked again, back to a whisper.

"Or something," Vera said. "If I were you I'd call an exterminator before somebody calls the health department."

"Let's not go there. I'd appreciate it if you wouldn't mention this to anybody."

"Who would I tell?" Vera said.

That was enough to satisfy George. Vera may have been annoying, but she was discreet. It was confirmed when she made a zipping motion across her lips.

"I'll handle it," George said and moved on.

Vera put her ear back to the wall.

The man in the dark suit stepped up behind Terri. Though he had removed his bowler he looked no-less out of place in this blue-collar eatery.

"Pardon me, Sheriff Hirsch?" he said. "Forgive the intrusion."

Terri hadn't seen him enter the diner. She spun around, gave him a quick up-and-down and nearly spit out her coffee. She sat up a bit straighter and though she would never admit it, she felt a twinge of embarrassment for wearing a decidedly un-feminine and un-flattering khaki uniform. Without thinking she smoothed her hair, though it didn't need smoothing.

"No problem," Terri said.

The man gestured to the stool next to Terri.

"Might I?"

Terri nodded to the stool and replied, "You might."

"Most kind of you," he said while sitting. "My name is Paper. Fitting, I suppose, seeing as I am an author. Non-fiction, mostly."

"Paper? Is that your first or your last name?"

"Last. My first is decidedly less interesting."

Terri had gathered her wits. Though she was intrigued and a bit intimidated by the handsome gentleman, she was still a professional and needed to act like one.

"What can I do for you, mister author Paper?"

"The lovely Miss Holly tells me you are the one who knows where all the bodies are buried in your charming town."

"Did she now?" Terri said and shot a quick look to Holly, who was behind the counter pretending not to be listening. "Well, if you want to know who lost their cat or how much we collect in parking fines, yeah, I'm a font of knowledge."

Mr. Paper chuckled amiably and said, "No, nothing quite so dramatic. I'm here simply to observe and soak up the atmosphere for a book I'm writing about America through the eyes of an Englishman."

Holly placed a brown paper "to-go" bag in front of Terri and said, "Your usual: egg-white omelet, dry white toast, and a carton of milk. I'll put it on your tab."

Terri gazed at the bag, wishing Holly hadn't given the gastronomic run-down.

"And there's your first observation," she said to Mr. Paper. "We're not exactly epicureans here."

"Who am I to judge?" Mr. Paper said, "As I've revealed, I'm an Englishman."

He gave Terri a charming smile. Terri and Holly exchanged looks. Both were taken by the gentleman. Holly broke first and focused on Mr. Paper.

"We don't have Early Grey tea," she said. "Is Lipton okay?

"That would be lovely, thank you."

Holly went back to work as Terri grabbed her bag-of-breakfast and stood up.

"Well, Mister Paper," she said. "Come by the station and I'll tell you everything there is to know about our little town. It'll take about two minutes. Tops. It's on the north end of Main Street."

"Thank you, Sheriff," Mr. Paper said. "I most certainly will."

Terri gave him an awkward smile and headed for the exit.

Holly was writing up Terri's tab with her back to the counter. She shook her pen. Out of ink. When she reached for another, she saw reflected in the stainless-steel tiles above the workstation that someone else was now sitting next to Mr. Paper. It was a woman with long, flaming red hair who sat with her back to the counter.

"Be right with you, ma'am," Holly said over her shoulder.

"Pardon me?" Mr. Paper said.

Holly turned around to see that no one was sitting next to him. The stool was unoccupied. She glanced around with confusion.

"I thought I saw—"

"Is there a problem?" Mr. Paper asked.

Holly shook it off. "No. It's nothing. Weird. Do you want your tea here or should I bring it to the table?"

"I'm quite comfortable here, thank you."

Vera gave up listening at the wall. With a shrug she placed a few dollar bills onto the table and moved to slide out of the booth as a single, loud thump came from inside the wall. It was so sharp that it made Vera jump and her spoon clatter about in the empty bowl of oatmeal. She let out a small, surprised yelp and looked around to see if anybody else had heard. Nobody had. She tentatively reached toward the wall, as if drawn to it. Her breathing was heavy from anticipation, and curiosity. She hesitated a moment, then touched her fingertips to the wall's surface. Nothing happened. After a few seconds she pulled her hand away, grabbed her purse, and hurried out of the booth.

No one gave her a second look.

~~~~

Vera's pharmacy was only a few blocks from the Rx Diner, which is pretty much what could be said about every business in downtown Glenville. For decades she ran the place on her own, which suited her just fine. The few times she hired help it proved to be more trouble than it was worth for she spent more time correcting their mistakes
~~~~

than she would have if she had just done the task herself. At least that's the way she saw it. Vera wanted things done her way, which in her mind was the only way. None of these hires lasted more than a few weeks, whether Vera fired them, or they quit in frustration.

Now that Vera was in her mid-60's, she was more set in her ways than ever, but was beginning to have trouble doing some of the more physically demanding tasks like stocking the higher shelves or keeping a slick polish on the linoleum floors. Enter Mikey Harper. Mikey had graduated high school the year before and had no desire to continue his education. He was a simple kid who lived with his parents. That was perfectly fine with him, though less-fine with his parents. He took the job at the Pharmacy thinking Vera was getting up in years and would be retiring soon. If he proved himself to be valuable, she might one day consider leaving the business to him. And why not? She had no family that anyone knew of. Or friends. Who better to leave the business to than someone who helped her to keep it running throughout her golden years?

Though proving himself to be of value was more challenging than he expected, due to Vera's rigid standards and her lack of respect for any opinion that wasn't hers. Still, Mikey had managed to last a year without being fired or quitting in anger, not that he hadn't considered it more than once. He kept telling himself that if he was smart, one day the business could be his. Trouble was, he wasn't all that smart and there was little chance that Vera would leave her business to anyone, but other than an obsession with Minecraft, it was all he had going on in his life, so he sucked it up and clung to the dream.

"Morning Ms. Holiday," Mikey chirped.

He only dared to call her "Vera" once. It didn't go well. He had to endure a painful lecture about how young people no longer showed proper respect.

She always arrived at the store at 7:30 sharp so he made sure to get there at 7:20 and begin work on some project that made it look as though he'd been there much longer. On this morning he was up on a ladder, dusting the blades of the overhead fans.

"Don't you dare fall," Vera groused as she walked by him.

She wasn't concerned for his safety. It was all about her liability.

"I won't," Mikey said brightly.

Vera walked on, nearly tripping over the store mascot, a fat, gray tabby tomcat of indeterminate age that had wandered into the pharmacy one day and never left. Vera named him Bobcat.

"Bobcat!" Vera shouted. "Go away!"

Bobcat gave her an annoyed meow in response and Vera kept walking. The cat didn't budge. He looked up to Mikey and meowed again.

"Don't look at me," Mikey said. "You tripped her."

Vera went straight for her tidy office in the back of the store. She kept her world in military-like orderliness, which was another issue she had with every one of her previous employees. Nobody could live up to her strict standards. At least Mikey came close. She carefully put her coat on a hangar and hung it in the office closet, with a few inches separating it from the other clothing. She pulled out one of her five arctic-white lab coats and removed the plastic wrapping from the cleaners. She always wore a lab coat at work. After all, she was a pharmacist and wanted to look the part. Each day after work she'd drop that day's coat at the cleaners to be laundered and pressed. She never wore the same coat two days in a row.

Before donning the day's uniform, she'd fill Bobcat's food bowl and change his water, which was probably the main reason Bobcat stuck around. She would then make a stop in the rest room to wash her hands, relieve herself, wash her hands again, and apply unscented moisturizer. She was then ready to don the uniform and begin the day's duty of seeing to the pharmaceutical needs of the people of Glenville.

On that morning, once Bobcat was fed and watered, she entered the restroom, took one look, and screamed: "Mikey!"

Mikey was so startled he nearly fell off the ladder.

"Coming!" he shouted and scrambled down.

He ran to the back corridor to see Vera outside of the restroom with her back to the wall, breathing hard.

"What's the matter?" he asked.

She looked at him and if looks could kill, well…

"You tell me," she said, seething, and motioned with her head toward the restroom.

Mikey walked cautiously toward the room, opened the door with trepidation, and immediately realized where this was headed. The smell told him. The toilet must have backed up because there was the unmistakable odor of sewage that wafted from the small room. Part of him didn't want to go in, but he convinced himself that Vera was so fussy, she might have overreacted. It might not be that big of an issue.

And it wasn't. At least it wasn't as bad as it might have been. What he saw was more of a disgusting mystery, than a hazmat-worthy emergency. The toilet hadn't backed up. But there was shit everywhere, and not a small amount. There were unmistakable brown streaks smeared across the floor, the walls, and the mirror. There were even a few spots on the wall that looked as though wet turds had been flung about. A few still clung there.

"How the hell…?" was all Mikey managed to say.

"Don't pretend you didn't know," Vera said, accusingly.

"I didn't!" Mikey shot back defensively. "It was clean when I left last night."

"You're saying you didn't do it?" Vera asked.

"Seriously?" Mikey shot back indignantly. "Why would I? I'm the one who's gotta clean it up."

Vera downshifted and caught her breath.

"No, I suppose not. But then who did it? Are you sure it was clean when you left last night?"

Mikey thought back. "I don't know. Maybe not. I mean, I probably went in an hour or two before closing."

"We were busy," Vera said. "There were some out-of-towners poking around. It must have been one of them, or their annoying children. Little animals."

Mikey surveyed the carnage and said, "Whoever did this really meant it. They took some time to do it right."

"Right?" Vera asked sarcastically.

"I mean it's like they were angry or something. Were any customers angry?"

"Who knows?" Vera said. "I don't pay attention."

Mikey thought: *And maybe that's why they were angry.* But of course he didn't say it.

"I'll clean it," Mikey said. "You should go out front to open up."

"No," Vera said. "We're not opening until it's completely clean. This is disgusting. I'm leaving to do some errands. Make sure that room is immaculate."

"Sure," Mikey said with no enthusiasm.

Bobcat was oblivious to the drama as he casually ate his breakfast.

Vera headed straight for the front door, leaving Mikey to the dirty work. Literally. He took another look at the mess and had a thought he chose not to share with Vera. *This hadn't been done the night before.* It was all too fresh, and wet. It had happened that morning, which meant it was done by somebody who had access to the pharmacy.

But who? And why would they do it?

Vera had the same thought but convinced herself that it was the out of towners and their demon spawn. Children were small, filthy animals to Vera. She used that opinion as an excuse for never marrying, not that she ever had the opportunity. The idea that some undisciplined child would smear feces on the walls of her spotless bathroom fit her image of children perfectly. Besides, she preferred to place the blame on random strangers rather than to think it was done by someone she knew. That would raise disturbing issues that couldn't be scrubbed away with a little 409 and bleach.

Once she left the pharmacy, she turned her attention to her other problem: the unwanted visitors in her walls at home. She considered bringing Bobcat to her house to be a mouser, but decided it wasn't worth the risk. Animals were creatures of habit. Changing their environment wasn't always the best for them and despite her constant complaints, she liked Bobcat and didn't want to stress him out.

No, this was a job for her trusty handyman, Dennis O'Malley. She gave him a call and asked him to meet her at the house.

Dennis was a classic jack-of-all-trades. He could build, fix, re-build, paint, landscape and pretty much handle any issues that a homeowner didn't have the skill or desire to tackle themselves. His business was one of the few in Glenville that boomed. His wife had died a decade before and Vera briefly considered pursuing a relationship with him, but decided it wasn't wise to mix business with pleasure, which was a convenient excuse to not open herself up to change or anyone else's annoying habits. Dennis was the closest she came to having a friend in Glenville, though it was tempered by the fact that she paid him for his services.

She made the call, and he was there within an hour.

"I've checked the entire house," Dennis told Vera shortly afterward as they stood on the lawn outside of her home. "I didn't hear nothing, and I don't see where any critter got in. That doesn't mean they didn't. I just can't figure out how. They can be sneaky."

"So, what do I do?"

"I baited and put out a couple traps. Three outside, one in the kitchen near the sink in case they found a way in by the plumbing. If they're hungry, they'll come sniffing around and we'll catch 'em."

"I don't want to run across some filthy animal with its neck broken," Vera said.

"Not that kind of trap. It's a cage with one way in and no way out. Very humane. If we catch something, I'll take it out into the woods."

"And kill it," Vera said with a touch of revenge-anger.

"No! I'll set it loose."

"I'd just as soon you killed it," she said. "I don't won't it coming back."

"It won't come back, trust me. I'll take it far enough away. All you've gotta do is relax and let me take care of it."

"Good," Vera said. "I don't need this kind of grief."

"It'll be over before you know it," Dennis said. "I'll come back tomorrow morning to check the traps."

"Good," Vera said. Then as an afterthought added, "Thank you."

"You're welcome. See you tomorrow."

Dennis got into his rust-bucket of a pick-up truck and rumbled off. Vera considered walking around the house to see where the traps were set but decided she wanted nothing more to do with the problem, so she went inside. Though it was only mid-morning she already felt end-of-the-day-weary. She decided to take a catnap and give Mikey time to sanitize the pharmacy bathroom.

The house was quiet, as usual. She stood in the center of her living room and listened. She heard nothing and felt relieved enough to lie down on the couch, close her eyes, and do her best to forget about annoying critters, both the two-legged and four-legged kind. Within minutes she was asleep. It wasn't a deep, nighttime sleep, but more of a light power-down nap where one hovers just below consciousness. It's a place where thoughts bleed into dreams with no way of knowing where one ends, and the other begins. Vera thought (or dreamt) of a time when she was lying in a field not far from her house. It was a place she often went to as a little girl to be alone. It was a happy place. She felt the warm sun on her face and a slight breeze that tickled her bare toes. It was a lovely feeling that brought her back many years.

The dream-breeze picked up. In her semi-conscious state she worried that a storm might be headed in and didn't want to be caught in the rain. It was enough of a concern that it pulled her out of the sweet memory and back to the reality of the moment.

But the breeze didn't stop. She could still feel it tickling her toes. The confusion got her conscious mind working again. She was still lying on her back, just as she always did in the field so she could feel the warm sun on her face. She opened one sleepy eye and looked to her feet…

…to see a fat brown rat licking her toe.

A surge of adrenalin blasted the last bit of dopey sleep away as she screamed and pulled her knees to her chest. The rat was just as surprised. It let out a squeal and jumped off the couch, its worm-like tail slithering across the arm before disappearing. Vera sat up and pulled her feet under her. She broke out in a sweat as her heart pounded. What should she do? She didn't want to put her feet down on the floor in case the rat was under the couch, waiting to pounce. This time it might use its teeth rather than its tongue. She sat there for a long minute, near panic. Once the shock had subsided, she realized that she wasn't entirely sure of what had happened. It all went down so fast. Was it an actual rat? Or part of her dream, brought on by the scratching in her walls?

She relaxed, took a few deep breaths, and convinced herself that there wasn't a rat lurking under the couch, ready to tear the flesh from her bare feet. She actually chuckled at how she had reacted like a frightened child. It was time to get up and get back to work. All was well…

…until she heard the snap of a metal-cage trap and the terrified scream of the animal it had captured. The sound came from her kitchen. It wasn't a dream. The rat was real. Her pulse spiked again. She quickly found her shoes and slipped them back on. At least she knew that the rat had been captured. This nightmare was over, thank-you Dennis O'Malley. Now that she was fully awake and back in control, she wanted to see the monster that had dared enter her home.

She boldly strode for the kitchen but took a moment to collect herself before entering. The high-pitched squealing of the terrified animal continued as it thrashed against the metal cage, desperate to escape. It was trapped and it knew it. If it had been up to her, it wouldn't be alive much longer and maybe that's what the rat feared. It couldn't have known that Dennis intended to humanely release it into the wild. She stepped into the kitchen and went straight to the sink where Dennis had laid the trap.

The terrified squeals ended abruptly. The trap was empty. How was that possible? Vera looked around quickly, expecting to see the angry beast cowering in a corner, but it was nowhere to be seen. She looked back to the trap and noticed that it wasn't empty after all. There was no rat inside, but something else was. Vera approached it cautiously and knelt down to get a closer look. What she saw inside was both familiar, and impossible.

It was a six-inch long black, plastic plaque with white block lettering, the kind used on the door of an office. It read: **"Vera Holiday – Director"**.

Vera hoped she was still dreaming.

She wasn't.

~~~~

"Why in hell would I do that?" Dennis O'Malley argued. "The only thing I put in that trap was dried fruit and peanut butter."

He was faced off against Vera outside of her house. Sheriff Terri Hirsch was there as well, having been summoned by Vera. She was the arbiter who stood between the two of them. She wasn't worried that Vera would take a swing at Dennis, but Vera was known to have a temper, so Terri wasn't taking any chances.

"It was a name plate?" Terri asked. "With your name on it?"

Vera reached into her jacket pocket and held the name plate out for Terri to examine.

"It was from an office I had years ago," Vera said. "It was stuck in the back of a kitchen drawer. The only person who could have found it was him. Nobody else has been in the house."

"I never seen it before," Dennis said defensively. "And I don't go rummaging through your drawers. You know me better'n that!"

"Check it for fingerprints," Vera demanded.

Terri looked at the plaque that she held in her bare hands, realizing the fingerprint ship had sailed.

"Lotta people had their fingers on this," she said. "Including you, Vera. I doubt I could pull a clean print."

Dennis grabbed the plaque away from Terri.

"There!" he shouted. "Now it's definitely got my prints on it."

Vera was ready to explode. She hadn't told them about her toe-licking run-in with the dream rat. She feared it would make her sound even crazier. But she was angry, and scared.
~~~~

"Whoever did this has it in for me," she said. "Maybe it was the same person who smeared their feces all over the bathroom at the pharmacy."

"Now you're accusing me of smearing shit on your walls!" Dennis exclaimed. "What is wrong with you, woman? Have I ever done anything to make you think I'd do this?"

Vera backed down. Dennis had always been a good friend, and quite possibly the only person in town she hadn't offended in some way. At least until then.

"Well, somebody's got it in for me," she said, deflated.

"It is strange," Terri said. "I'll head over to the pharmacy and check it out. I'm not exactly a CSI, but maybe something will jump out at me."

"Just hope it isn't a rat," Vera said.

"Why would a rat--?" Terri asked.

"Skip it," Vera said quickly.

"The best thing you can do is calm down and think about who might have an issue with you."

Vera snickered because that could be a long list. But she honestly didn't think she'd done anything to anybody that would justify the kind of harassment she'd gotten.

"And lock your doors," Terri added.

"What's this world coming to?" Vera said. "I've never had to lock my doors."

"Start," Terri said. "And Dennis, maybe it would be best if you steered clear of Vera for a while."

"No problem there," Dennis said, still angry. "I'll be back for my traps when I'm not so hot."

He turned and strode to his pick-up.

Vera had lost herself a handyman. And a friend. She felt a slight twinge of remorse because truly liked Dennis and hated to have accused him of doing such things, but there was no other plausible explanation. At least not one she could come up with.

"You okay?" Terri asked.

"No, I'm not," Vera snapped. "Someone's been invading my privacy and I don't like it. Would you?"

"I would not," Terri said. "Let me ask around. In the meantime, keep your doors and windows locked."

"And you be a sheriff," Vera said.

That stung Terri, as if Vera were accusing her of shirking her duty. But Terri knew enough not to argue with her, especially since she had every right to be upset. She backed toward her official County SUV and said, "I'll stop by later to check on you."

Vera gave her a dismissive wave and headed back into her house.

Terri got into the SUV. Waiting there for her in the passenger seat, was Mr. Paper.

"For such a small hamlet you have quite the mysteries unfolding," he said.

"Yeah, we're a regular hotbed of intrigue," Terri said sarcastically as she started the engine and pulled away from Vera's house.

Mr. Paper said, "At the risk of sounding ominous, I've found that inexplicable mysteries are often indicative of a larger issue."

"What's that supposed to mean?" Terri asked.

"Are there any open cases on your books? Crimes that have yet to be solved? Unanswered questions? In my experience, unsettled business can often lead to seemingly unrelated conflicts."

Terri looked to Mr. Paper with a curious frown.

"And what exactly is your experience?" she asked.

"I'm an observer by nature, and by profession. Most authors are."

"And what do your observations tell you?"

"Of course, there isn't enough information to form a definitive opinion, but from the little I've seen, I'd say that your earlier sarcastic comment might not be far from the truth."

"What comment was that?"

"Glenville may actually be a hotbed of intrigue. Eyes on the road, please."

Terri realized she'd been staring at Mr. Paper and not watching where she was going. She quickly faced forward.

Though she worried that Mr. Paper's observation might have some validity, part of her was excited at the prospect of finally getting the chance to do some real detective work rather than spend her days being the public servant whose principal function is to write parking tickets and shut down rowdy keg parties.

Vera Holiday, on the other hand, was a raw nerve. Her orderly life had suddenly become decidedly messy. She had no idea why or how someone would have gone through her kitchen drawers to find that old nameplate and put it in an animal trap. Was it to frighten her by demonstrating how easily they could move in and out of her house? Why would anyone want to scare her like that? She wasn't exactly a beloved figure in town, but she had no serious enemies. At least none that she was aware of.

The idea hit her that if somebody had gotten into her house, they might have stolen something. At least a robbery would make sense. The robber could be a psychopath who needed to leave a calling card and that's why they used the nameplate. The thought didn't give her comfort but at least it was a theory that made some sense.

When she entered the house, she took a quick inventory to see if anything was missing. She peered into the living room to see that the flatscreen was still on the wall and the old-school Marantz stereo components were still in the bookcase beside it.

In the dining room she checked the cabinet for the "good" china that had been handed down from her mother, but she had never used. She also checked the drawer where she kept the silver flatware, also from her mother and equally unused. Nothing was missing. She went upstairs to her bedroom and to the dresser where she kept a few pieces of valuable jewelry that were as unused as the china and silverware. She had her mother and father's wedding rings and her mother's diamond engagement ring, along with a string of pearls from her grandmother that hadn't been worn since the pre-Beatles 60's. Everything was there. She thought about anything else in her house that might be worth stealing and came up empty. Her robbery theory wasn't holding water.

And she once again heard scratching coming from inside the walls.

She gasped in surprise.

The sound was louder than anything she had heard before. It was insistent, as if whatever creature was in there was desperately trying to dig its way through the wall behind her bed. Her surprise turned to anger, and she banged on the wall.

"Get outta here!" she yelled.

The scratching stopped for a few seconds, then began again, only now it was coming from the wall opposite her bed. There was no way an animal could have travelled that quickly from one side of the room to the other which meant the bold toe-licker had a friend.
Vera ran to the opposite wall and banged on it.

"I hear you! I'm gonna get ya!"

The scratching stopped. Vera backed toward the bedroom door.

"Forget the nice traps!" she shouted. "I'm getting the kind that'll snap your scrawny little necks!"

She stood in her doorway and listened. The room was silent.

"Yeah, you better be scared," she said, taunting.

The scratching began again. It was coming from the wall right next to where she stood. Vera leapt out of the way and banged her shoulder into the door frame. She stumbled out into the hallway as the scratching continued. Whatever it was, was on the move. It was now in the hallway wall.

"Bastards!" she screamed and hurried down the corridor, headed for the stairs.

The scratching grew louder. Vera also heard shuffling and faint squealing. The creatures in the walls kept right up with her as she made it to the stairs and hurried down, clutching the banister so she wouldn't trip and fall. She had to keep from screaming as she imagined a dozen varmints tripping over one another, chasing her through her own home. They were now in the wall next to the stairs, moving quickly, rattling the framed pictures. Vera had to hold back terrified tears. Her focus was on getting to the bottom of the stairs and out through the front door before the little monsters found a way out of the walls and into her world.

She made it to the bottom and hurried straight for the door. She grabbed the doorknob and felt a sudden surge of indignation. How dare these creatures drive her out of her home? She let go of the knob and turned with her back to the door.

"Don't you go anywhere," she said with rage. "I'm coming back. With poison gas."

She listened. All was quiet.

"Oh? So that scared you?"

Her answer came from what sounded like dozens of animals in the walls surrounding the front door. They squealed and chattered and clawed in a move that was every bit as intimidating as Vera's threat.

Vera threw the door open and ran out, moving to get as far away from her infested house as possible. Once she was a safe distance away, she stopped to catch her breath. What was her next move? She'd go to the pharmacy and make calls to find an exterminator. No more humane traps. Or any kind of traps. She wanted her house fumigated. She wanted it to be a kill-zone. She wouldn't set foot back inside until every last varmint who dared to enter was dead. And she wanted to see the bodies. Whatever exterminator she found would have to be willing to clean the place out afterward, even if it meant tearing into some walls. That would be fine with her. Walls could be patched and repainted. She wanted to see proof. She wanted carcasses.

The pharmacy was a short walk away, made shorter by Vera's quick pace. The sooner she found an exterminator, the sooner this nightmare would be over. She reached the front door to discover it was unlocked. Had she forgotten to lock it? She went inside to see a customer at the cash register buying Tylenol and a toothbrush. Ringing the customer up, was Mikey.

Vera had a moment of calm. Mikey had actually opened the store for business, which is something he didn't normally do. He must have finished the clean-up and took the initiative to allow customers in. For a moment she genuinely appreciated the kid and thought he might be worth keeping around.

"Thanks ma'am," Mikey said as the woman customer left the cash register.

"Morning Vera," the woman said as they passed each other.

"Morning Maggie," Vera replied. "How's the arthritis?"

"Not going anywhere," Maggie said with a shrug and headed out.

Vera approached Mikey at the counter.

"It's all cleaned up," Mikey said tentatively. "Like it never happened. I thought you'd want me to open."

He braced himself, ready to be chastised for having somehow blundered.

"You thought right," Vera said. "You did good."

Mikey beamed, as if he'd just been named employee of the year. Not that there was any competition for the title.

"Would you mind staying up front?" Vera asked. "I've got some business that needs doing."

"Sure!" Mikey said. He enjoyed helping customers. It was far more interesting than mopping floors, stocking shelves, and wiping down shit-covered walls.

"I'll be in my office," Vera said.

As she walked to the rear of the store, her confidence grew. She had a plan. She was being pro-active. She'd call on Terri Hirsch to recommend a qualified rat-killer because that's what she wanted. A killer. No monkeying around. She might have to spend a few nights sleeping in her office while the poison did its job, but that would be okay. She was ready to go scorched-earth. With renewed confidence, she opened her office door, stepped inside…

…and screamed.

Mikey came running. He found Vera on her knees inside the office door.

"What the matter?" Mikey cried for the second time that day. "Are you okay?"

"Why?" Vera said through tears.

"Why what?" Mikey asked.

He looked into the office and saw it. Vera's desk chair had been moved to the center of the room. On the seat, resting upright against the backrest was a wooden board. Nailed to the wooden board…was Bobcat. Dead. He hung there, belly-out with all four paws nailed to the board. The animal had been sliced open from neck to its abdomen, revealing its guts. The poor cat wasn't torn apart, it had been surgically splayed open up like it was being dissected.

Mikey took one look, turned away, and puked his breakfast onto Vera's freshly polished office floor.

"Why did you do it?" Vera cried.

"I didn't!" Mikey sobbed while wiping his chin. "I swear Vera. I didn't."

Vera struggled to get to her feet and dragged herself closer to the grisly scene. Though she never would admit it, she liked Bobcat. The stray cat reminded her of the cat she had when she was a child. She hadn't had another pet until Bobcat showed up. Now he was gone, having suffered a gruesome death. Vera couldn't help but think that all the horrors of this day were somehow tied together. It all centered around her, and she had no idea what she had done to deserve any of it.

She stood in front of the grisly scene, mesmerized by the tidy array of entrails that had been left perfectly in place within the shell of Bobcat's crucified carcass. She had performed necropsies on many animals, including cats, but never on one she cared about. Or had a name. Other than the fact that it was there, there was nothing unusual about the display, except for one thing that caught her eye. Tucked between Bobcat's duodenum and transverse colon was a foreign object. It stood out because of its color (white) and its sharp-angled edge. Only the tip showed. The rest was buried in Bobcat's guts.

Vera's scientific curiosity took over and she reached for it. She grasped the corner between her thumb and forefinger and gently pulled. With a wet, sucking sound, the foreign object came out. It was plastic, a few inches long and a half inch wide. Vera took a close look and let out a gasp.

"What is it?" Mikey asked, still sitting on the floor near his puddle of vomit.

Vera took a few involuntary steps backward, her mind racing to nowhere. She backed into the easy chair she used for reading and fell into it, still staring at the plastic strip.

"Ms. Holiday?" Mikey whined.

Vera let her hand drop onto the arm rest as she stared into space.

Mikey managed to stand up and go to her. He knelt down to get a look at what she'd pulled out of Bobcat, with no intention of touching it.

"*Vera Holiday – Director*," Mikey read.

It was an employee I.D. badge.

"I swear to God, Vera, I didn't do this."

"I believe you," she said quietly.

Vera was remarkably calm. Mikey couldn't tell if she had regained control or had plunged off the deep end.

"This is really fucked up," Mikey said. "Sorry."

"You're right, it is," Vera said.

"I'll call Sheriff Hirsch. She'll figure out who did this and—"

"No," Vera said abruptly.

"C'mon Vera!" Mikey said, momentarily forgetting decorum. "This is serious. Somebody's got it out for you."

"I want you to call her, but not yet," Vera said. "I need to face this myself."

"How? And do what?"

Vera stood up. She was back in control.

"Wait one hour," Vera said with certainty. "Then call the sheriff and tell her to meet me at the High Point Institute."

"What is that?"

"She'll know."

"This is crazy," Mikey said, his voice shaking. "If some nut case is out there who kills and guts cats, who knows what he's capable of?"

"Or she," Vera said.

"Whatever. We should call the Sheriff right now."

He started dialing his cell phone, but Vera gently put her hand over his to stop him.

"Please," Vera said. "I don't know what's going on, but whatever it is, it's on me to deal with it."

"Then I'll go with you to this High Point place," Mikey said, trying to sound more confident than he felt.

"No. I told you; this is on me. But call the sheriff in an hour. Would you please do that for me?"

Mikey wasn't happy with the plan, but he knew that once Vera got something into her head, there was no getting it out.

"One hour," he said with authority. "I'll leave Bobcat like that so the sheriff can see him, but I'll clean up my puke. Sorry for that."

"No need to apologize. Thank you, Mikey. You're a good kid."

Vera left the pharmacy and headed back to her house. Fortunately, she had her car keys in her coat pocket, so she didn't have to go inside. She wanted no part of whatever was going on in there until an exterminator cleared the place out. She opened the garage and got into her ancient Saab. She couldn't remember the last time she'd driven it and feared that the battery would be dead. But the trusty car sputtered, chugged and the engine turned over.

"Let's go," she said to no one. "This has to end, now."

~~~~

Ben Daniels, still wearing the greasy-stained whites from his shift cooking at the Rx Diner hurried along Main Street toward one of the two crosswalks that was controlled by a traffic light. He was on his way to the bank to deposit the cash they'd taken in that morning. Though Glenville had exactly zero-incidents of serious crime, he hated carrying around that much money. The job fell to him because his brother was stuck at the diner, waiting for an electrician to come and check out the microwave that had given him such a vicious shock that morning, and for the exterminator who would rid the
~~~~

place of any rats. Reluctantly, Ben agreed to make the deposit. As far as he was concerned, the sooner it was done, the better.

He stopped at the curb and reached for the lamppost and the metal button that would trigger the crossing signal. He touched it and was jolted by such a strong shock that it knocked him back a step.

"Oww!" he yelped. "What the hell?"

Ben rubbed his stinging hand and looked up the lamppost as if he might actually see a telltale clue as to why he'd been shocked for the second time that day.

"What are you looking for?" Holly asked as she walked up. She'd finished her shift as well and was headed home.

"I got…" Ben said, flustered. "There's a…"

"A what?"

"Touch the button," Ben commanded, pointing to the crosswalk control.

"Why?"

"Just touch it."

"You are a strange man," Holly said.

She stepped up to the lamppost, reached out, and touched the button.

Nothing happened. There was no shock.

"I'll be damned," Ben said.

"Let me know if you need me to do anything else for you," Holly said. "You want me to hold your hand and walk you across the street?"

"Don't be a wiseass," Ben said with a snarl.

"Just trying to help. See ya!"

She gave him a short salute and continued on her way.

Ben stood staring at the button. He looked to the top of the pole, then back to the button. He reached out to try it again but thought better of it and stepped away.

"Screw that," he said and stepped off the curb to cross the street, directly in front of an oncoming car. The driver jammed on the brakes, screeching to a stop a few feet from hitting Ben.

"Idiot!" the driver shouted.

"Screw you!" Ben shouted, threw him the finger, and hurried on.

Holly heard the screech and turned in time to see Ben flipping off the driver. She hadn't seen what happened, but figured whatever it was, it was Ben's fault. He'd never admit it though. Ben was expert at assigning blame to everyone but himself.

Holly's feet hurt from having been on them all morning. She couldn't wait to get to her apartment to lie on the couch and pretend as though she didn't hate the direction her life had taken. Still, she couldn't resist stopping in front of Kaplan's, the one clothing store in Glenville that carried clothes she'd consider wearing. What caught her eye was a mannequin wearing a pretty, flowered sundress that she could imagine wearing on a date. That is, if she ever went on a date. The pickings were slim in Glenville, both in stylish clothing and eligible young men. Still, she could dream. She knew she wouldn't be stuck living there forever, it only felt like it sometimes.

As she stood in front of the store window to admire the dress, she saw the reflection of a woman standing behind her, though Holly hadn't seen her walk up. The woman had a tangle of fiery-red hair that cascaded to her shoulders and partly obscured her face. Holly spun around to ask the woman not to stand so close, but when she turned, the woman was gone. Holly quickly looked back to the store window but saw only her own reflection.

"Window shopping?" Terri asked as she walked up.

Her voice made Holly jump in surprise.

"Whoa, sorry," Terri said. "Didn't mean to scare you."

"You didn't," Holly said, flustered. "I mean, you did but…did you see a woman standing here a second ago?"

"You mean besides you?"

"I could have sworn someone was here. I saw her reflection in the window."

Terri looked at the window. "Maybe it was one of those mannequins. Pretty dress. I'd buy it myself if I were twenty years younger and lived in Chicago."

Holly looked back to the window, trying to understand how she could have been so mistaken.

Terri sensed Holly's genuine concern and said, "Tell me what you saw. Exactly."

"It was a woman. I guess it could have been a mannequin, but she sure looked real. She had long, red hair that covered most of her face. I didn't see her walk up, she was just…there, looking over my shoulder. Looking at me. When I turned around, she was gone."

"I'm guessing it was a mannequin," Terri said, though she wasn't exactly sure how that was possible.

"There's something else," Holly said nervously. "Please don't think I'm weird. But the same thing happened to me this morning, in the diner. Right after you left. I saw the same woman's reflection in the mirror behind the counter. She was sitting next to that Mister Paper guy; on the stool you were sitting on."

Terri felt a cold chill go up her spine. She had been trying to humor Holly, now she was suddenly a player in the drama.

"I…I'm not sure what to make of that," Terri said honestly.

"You and me both."

Terri's cell phone rang. "Sorry," she said and answered it. "This is Sheriff Hirsch".

She listened for a moment then said, "Okay, okay, calm down, I'm not far away. I'll be there in two minutes."

She punched out of the call and looked to Holly. "Is there a full moon today?"

"That would explain a lot," Holly said with a weak smile. "I guess."

"I should go, but we'll talk more about this."

"Go, I'm okay," Holly said.

"Honest?"

"Yeah, sure, I'm fine. And I think you'd look great in that dress."

"Liar," Terri said with a laugh. "But thanks. We'll talk."

Terri walked away, leaving Holly alone. She was about to look back to the window but the last thing she wanted to see was the strange woman with red hair staring back at her. The dress wasn't pretty enough to risk that, so she turned away, dropped her head, and hurried off.

<div style="text-align:center">~~~~</div>

The High Point Institute was situated in a wooded area two miles to the north of downtown Glenville. Vera knew the way without having to think. She'd driven it for the better part of ten years. It sat on a huge parcel of undeveloped woodland that had been deeded to the institute, which was why there were no other structures anywhere nearby. The turnoff from the main road once had a tasteful wooden sign to mark it, but that was long gone. The turnoff itself was almost long gone as well. The bushes to either side had grown wild, nearly choking off the turn with weeds that poked up through the cracked asphalt. It went unnoticed by most everyone who passed by.

Vera knew exactly where it was. She made the turn and winced as branches scratched at her car's finish. Fortunately, once she drove past the bushes that obscured the entrance, the roadway was clear. Though it was technically a public road, there was no reason for anyone to be driving on it unless they were visiting the institute. It was a barely two-lane road that wound through a thick forest of pine trees on the way up to the crest of a hill, upon which sat the High Point Institute. It was always a breathtaking moment for Vera when her car emerged from the dense forest to come upon a view of the impressive building.

It had been built in the 1920's in what was considered the Gilded Age of architecture. It was an era when American barons of industry built fabulous European-style mansions to showcase their wealth. High Point was a five-story, sprawling structure built mostly of red brick, with several round turrets that gave it the feel of a medieval castle. It was designed and built to be a hospital and operated as such for the entirety of its functional existence.

That existence ended decades before when High Point shut its doors for good. When the last of the staff left, the doors were locked, and the grand old building was abandoned. Years of litigation hadn't settled the question of responsibility for the structure, so there it sat. Empty. Crumbling. Waiting for a savior that was not soon to come.

An imposing wrought-iron fence circled the property, with tall brick pillars spaced twenty yards apart to anchor it. The entryway was through massive iron gates that were fixed between two of the tallest pillars. Vera feared that the gates would be closed and padlocked but found them wide open, as if someone knew there would be a visitor.

Vera drove through the pillars, across the brown weeded grounds that once sported a manicured lawn, and onto the circular driveway to park directly in front of the main entrance. She got out and looked up at the imposing wooden doors. It was an entrance she had rarely used. Normally she would park around back and enter through a much less dramatic side door.

"Such a beautiful old hell-hole," she said to no one.

She climbed the ten marble stairs and once again worried that she would be locked out. But not only were the doors unlocked; one was slightly ajar. It was both a relief and slightly unnerving. Did someone actually expect her?

Vera gently pushed the door open and entered the building's foyer. It was still a breathtaking atrium that reached up the entire five stories. This had once been an impressive first look at the interior opulence of the building, complete with massive stained-glass windows and intricately detailed Venetian tile floors. A grand marble staircase faced the entrance that led to a second-floor balcony that ringed the entire atrium. The centerpiece of the foyer was an immense marble fountain that once had a constant flow of water that cascaded from multiple tiers of Roman-style cisterns. Now it was filled with dirt and debris that had fallen from levels above.

It made Vera a bit wistful to see how this showplace from another era had fallen into such a sorry state of disrepair. It was a fleeting sentiment, for there was no love lost between her and anything that had to do with High Point. Few of her memories were good ones.

When she left for the final time, she vowed never to set foot in the place again.

Yet here she was because ghosts from her past were beckoning.

Vera left the atrium and walked deeper into the tomb-like building. The only sound came from the broken bits of plaster that were crunched beneath her shoes. With each step, more vivid memories of her time there returned. Memories she had suppressed for years.

She had been hired as a researcher out of grad school and went to work in the institute's lab that was primarily geared for live animal research. She was fascinated by the biology and thrilled to be on the forefront of research to produce pharmaceuticals that would one day improve the quality of health care.

Her boss, a Doctor Abernathy, was a jovial old man who she enjoyed working for, but he retired two years later and died soon after. The lab became Vera's domain by default.

Once Abernathy was gone, her once noble pursuit devolved into a dark journey.

At any given time, there were several hundred animals involved in multiple projects. There were bins and cages filled with rats and mice, dozens of rabbits, dogs, cats, pigs, and monkeys. More arrived every day to replace the animals that had died by design, euthanasia, or as a direct result of testing. Death and suffering were constants that Vera became inured to. While her interns might have blanched at the task of exposing a monkey's brain in order to attach electrodes that would monitor the animal's reaction to pain, Vera only saw the science.

The management of the lab was her sole responsibility, and it was a challenge. When faced with budget cuts, she routinely skirted government regulations she considered to be counter-productive. Not everyone agreed. Many interns resigned over disputes regarding Vera's callous treatment of their subjects. Others were fired.

Her questionable practices were never challenged by the institute's administration for their contracts with big pharma were incredibly lucrative and helped keep the lights on. The fact that the institute's board of directors turned a blind eye to the way she managed the lab made it all the more devastating for Vera when they threw her under the bus the moment the state came knocking to investigate multiple complaints that had been filed against the lab, the institute, and her directly. During the inquest, Vera argued that the state only focused on one side of the story and didn't appreciate the value of the work being done. Who cared if some unnecessary regulations were skirted?

The state did. Vera was fired and the lab was shut down. Soon after the entire institute was shuttered. It was one of the last major employers in a town that was struggling to remain relevant. Fingers were pointed at Vera, but she was unfazed. She truly believed she had done nothing wrong.

Once her tenure at High Point ended, Vera re-invented herself. Using the money that she had been saving since high school, she went back to school to obtain a degree in pharmacology. She then returned to Glenville and opened her pharmacy. The history of the lab at High Point was mostly forgotten.

Though apparently not by everyone. The mysterious appearance of Vera's office name plate and the I.D. tag pointed directly at her and her time at High Point. The evisceration of her cat elevated the taunts to a threat. She felt certain that someone had arrived through the mist of time who held a grudge against her. There were plenty of suspects who had it out for her back then. The self-important animal activists, the disgruntled employees, even the state investigators. They treated her as though she was a villain, but she would not apologize for having done her job.

She had no idea why this person chose this moment to re-surface.

The lab was in the basement of the East wing of the institute. It was tucked away, out of the sight of the rest of the building. Out of earshot as well. No one else who worked there had ever heard a peep, screech, or howl coming from Vera's domain. She descended into the depths of the building with trepidation. What would she find there? Was someone lying in wait? She cursed herself for not thinking to bring a flashlight. Without the overhead lights she had to rely on the slight bit of daylight that found its way through to the depths. It was a dark, gray world that met her when she hit the bottom of the stairs. She had to rely mostly on her memory to show her the way.

She also wished she had thought to bring her gun.

The lab was on the far end of a long corridor, a short distance from the crematorium where the carcasses of thousands of dead animals were disposed of. Vera approached the door of the lab with trepidation. She had not been back since the day she was fired. Oddly, there was enough light to navigate. That didn't seem possible, given the depth of the corridor. It wasn't until she neared the lab that she saw light seeping out from under the door. Somehow, the lab had light.

Before she could take another step, she heard a sound that instantly shot her back to decades before. It was an intermittent, mechanical clatter that came from inside the lab. Though she hadn't heard it in forever, she knew exactly what it was.

It meant she wasn't alone.

~~~~

Terri Hirsch parked her SUV directly in front of Vera's pharmacy. Always finding a parking space in front of a destination was one of the few benefits of living in a dying town.

Mikey ran out of the pharmacy to greet her.

"She told me to wait an hour before calling you," he said, breathless. "She'll be pissed, but I couldn't wait that long."

"Calm down, take a breath," Terri said. "What's this all about?"

"I wish I knew. You gotta see this."

Mikey led her inside. On the way he told her about the shit-mess that someone had blessed the bathroom with, and the later discovery that was more gruesome.

"It must have happened while I was cleaning the bathroom," Mikey said, frantic. "I was in there a while, but the front door was locked. I don't know how somebody could have gotten in, done that, and left without me knowing, but they did."
~~~~

"Okay, I get it," Terri said. "Show me."

"Brace yourself," Mikey said. "It isn't pretty."

He opened the door to Vera's office and Terri's eyes immediately went to the splayed Bobcat.

"My God," she said with a gasp.

"That smell is my puke," Mikey said. "I was going to clean it up, but I couldn't stand being in here with Bobcat like that. Sorry."

Terri looked to Mikey. She instantly deduced that he was either innocent of this ghastly crime, or an incredible actor. She'd known Mikey for a while. He was a good kid. There was nothing about him that made her think he could have done anything as depraved as this. She decided to buy his story, at least for the time being.

"Where's Vera?" Terri asked.

"Gone. That's why I called you. When she saw Bobcat, she was upset at first but then she got all calm. It was weird, like she went numb or something. She told me to call you in an hour and tell you to meet her at the High Point Institute. She said you knew what that was. I couldn't wait the whole hour. She's gonna be pissed at me but…too bad."

"It's okay, you did the right thing. I'll try to get her."

Terri grabbed her cell phone and called Vera's number. She heard the phone ring, live, only a few feet away. Vera had left her cell phone in her desk.

"She never carries that around," Mikey said with a shrug. "I don't think she gets the concept of a phone being portable."

Terri punched out of the call.

"Did she say why she was going to High Point?" Terri asked.

"No! She wouldn't even tell me what it was. She said you'd know. Do you know?"

"Yeah, I know High Point."

"This is freaking weird, Sheriff."

"Lot of weird scary stuff going on today," Terri said, more to herself than to Mikey.

But Mikey heard it.

"There is?" he asked. "Like what?"

Terri ignored the question and said, "Don't touch anything, all right? I'll go meet Vera and bring her back here. Then we'll all sit down and try to figure out what's going on. You okay with that?"

Mikey nodded quickly, though he wasn't truly okay with anything that was going on.

"I'll be back as soon as I can," Terri said. "You can go home if you want."

"No, I'll stay. It's kind of my job."

"You're a good kid, Mikey. We'll figure this out."

Mikey gave her a weak smile that said, "I hope so."

"Don't touch Bobcat," Terri added.

"Don't worry."

Terri strode back through the pharmacy and out the front door, headed for her SUV.

Standing on the sidewalk in front of her vehicle, was Mr. Paper. He stood tall with both hands resting on his walking stick.

"Yet another odd occurrence?" he asked.

"Something like that," Terri said as she opened the car door. "Don't go writing any of this stuff in that book of yours, all right?"

"No promises," Paper replied.

An older man wearing coveralls, Karl, walked up quickly, focused on Terri.

"Sheriff!" he called out. "Yo, Sheriff! I got a bone to pick with you!"

Terri acted as though she hadn't heard him. She started the car, and quickly pulled out of the parking spot.

"Hey! I'm talking to you!" Karl yelled.

Terri drove off, leaving Karl frustrated.

"Perhaps she didn't hear you," Mr. Paper said.

"Ah, she heard me all right," Karl said angrily. "She don't want to deal with me is all. What else is new?"

He continued on in a huff.

Mr. Paper watched him for a moment, glanced to the rapidly departing SUV, gave a slight smile, and casually strolled off.

~~~~

Stepping into the lab was both a strange and familiar feeling for Vera. Familiar for obvious reasons. This had been her second home for years. Strange because the overhead fluorescents were on. It made no sense for there was no electricity coming into the ancient building.

The plastic bins that once held hundreds of small rodents lay empty, as did the large and small cages. A thick layer of dust covered the counters.

None of that mattered. Vera was focused on the clattering sound that was coming from the room that had once been her office. She moved with trepidation toward the closed door. It proved her instinct to come to the institute was the right one, though she felt no sense of victory. She didn't want to be there. She wanted to see who was in her office even less.

Vera stepped up to the door, gently pushed it open and looked in to see an elderly man in a white lab coat sitting at the desk behind an old-school Royal typewriter. He was hammering away at the keys, hunting-and-pecking out the letters, just as she remembered him doing so many times in the past. Terri's knees went weak. Like the rest of the lab, the sight of this man was both familiar and impossible.

"Doctor Abernathy?" Vera managed to say.

Abernathy looked up over his half-glasses to see Vera standing there, clutching the doorknob in a death-grip.

"Vera my girl! So good of you to come! Close the door please."

Vera's head swam. As she closed the office door she held on to the doorknob for fear she might pass out.

"You can't be here," she whispered as she closed the door.

"And why not? I used to run this place, remember?"

"But…you're dead."

"True, but do the dead ever truly leave?"

Abernathy was a jovial old guy with a thick head of white hair, a twinkle in his eyes and a quick smile.
~~~~

"I'm dreaming," Vera said and fell into a dust-covered wooden chair next to the desk.

"If only that were true," Abernathy said as he typed a few last letters. "It isn't."

"What's happening to me?" Vera asked numbly.

"That's the wrong question, my dear. What you should be asking is what *happened* to you."

"I don't understand."

"When I hired you, you were an idealist with a marvelous, inquisitive mind. The idea that our work here could lead to bettering people's lives was what brought you to me. But that didn't last, did it?"

"It was far more challenging than I anticipated," she said, hesitantly.

"Challenging," Abernathy repeated as if trying the word on for size. "Yes, that's one way of putting it. But we weren't only dealing with scientific protocols; we were charged with the care of living creatures. Many of whom lived in, shall we say, less than ideal circumstances."

"There were so many," she said softly, as if her mind had floated back to a dark memory.

"They weren't just numbers though, were they?"

"But they were," Vera argued. She was less disturbed about having a conversation with her dead boss than about being challenged over how she ran the lab. "If we cared about them, treated them like, I don't know, pets, it would have driven us insane."

Abernathy chuckled, "Your word, not mine."

"I treated them well enough," Vera said with confidence.

"You say that as if you believe you had compassion for our charges," Abernathy said.

"I did!"

"Well you certainly had an odd way of showing it," Abernathy shot back. He was becoming less jovial by the second. "By all accounts you lost sight of the fact that we were dealing with living beings that experienced pain and suffering."

"They were animals."

"Animals that were undernourished and lived in their own filth." He flipped through some papers on the desk and said, "What was it you said at the inquest? Yes, here it is. I quote: "*I had a budget that was reduced each year. I couldn't meet it without cutting some corners. Knowing these creatures would soon be dead, I didn't feel the need to feed them as if they would have normal lifespans. I only did what was expected of me and a big part of that was hitting my budget numbers, which I always did.*"

Abernathy dropped the pages and looked straight at Vera.

"You must have been so proud," he said, dripping irony.

"I did what needed to be done!" Vera shouted.

"Did that include torture?"

"I didn't torture the animals!" Vera protested. "Not beyond any discomfort that was expected and accepted within the parameters of the experiments."

"Is that so?" Abernathy said as he flipped through a few more pages until he found the one he wanted. He read, "*At times when she became overly stressed, she would take one of the larger rats and literally squeeze it until it either suffocated or until she broke its neck. That always seemed to calm her down.*"

"That was testimony from a disgruntled employee I fired," Vera said defensively.

Abernathy found another page and read, "*We had one monkey, Old George, who had electrodes planted into his brain for a biometric study. Miss Holiday would often send electric impulses into poor George's brain that had nothing to do with the study. She simply wanted to see him twitch and squirm. She actually seemed to enjoy it and giggled with each involuntary spasm as if George was a puppet to play with for her amusement.*"

"I didn't design the experiment," Vera said.

"No, and you didn't follow the protocols either. Do you deny that?"

"I'll tell you the same thing I said at the inquest, I did what the experiment called for. I have no regrets."

"None at all?"

Vera started to answer but held back.

"There are pages of testimony here, Vera," Abernathy said. "All recount a pattern of abusive behavior toward these animals that resulted in suffering and premature death. Treating them like numbers might have actually been the best they could have hoped for. You went out of your way to abuse them."

"They were animals!" Vera repeated.

"Not that it will change anything, other than to satisfy my own curiosity, but what was going through your mind when you intentionally hurt these creatures?"

Vera held back as if she didn't want to answer, but finally couldn't hold back any longer.

"It was their fault!" she blurted out.

"Please explain," Abernathy said coldly.

"They weren't here to be treated, or cured," Vera spat out. "They were here to die. I was constantly dealing with pain and death. It was overwhelming. I resented them for that."

"Are you saying you felt it was somehow their fault for being here?"

"I saw them as the cause of my own agony. I had to reduce the stress and did it the only way I could think of."

She took a deep breath and added, "I'll admit. I'm not proud of everything I did, but given the circumstances, if I had to do it over again, I'd probably do the same thing. They were animals. My peace of mind was more important."

Abernathy stared at Vera with a mixture of pity and disdain. He then pulled the paper from his typewriter with one quick snatch.

"Yes, well, this will all be documented in my report."

"What report?" Vera asked. "What are you doing here? Did you smear the shit in my bathroom? And kill my cat?"

"Me? No. Perish the thought".

"Then who did?"

"I'm afraid you'll soon find out."

Vera heard the sound of a cage rattling in the lab. She shot a look to the closed door.

"Who else is here?" Vera asked with fear. "Is there another ghost haunting me and—"

She turned back to Abernathy, but the ghost was no longer there. Neither were the pages of his report. Vera's office looked the same as it did on her last day of work. It held nothing but dust and memories.

A cage outside of the office rattled again.

Vera snapped a look back to the closed door. Who was out there?

Terri wasn't sure if there was any urgency in meeting Vera at the High Point Institute or not, so she didn't turn on her flashers and speed out of town, but she didn't take her time, either. It had been a strange and disturbing day. Glenville was a sleepy, rural town where the dramatic events never escalated beyond the occasional barfight or car accident. Now there appeared to be a disturbed person lurking about who had killed and eviscerated a cat after having desecrated the pharmacy bathroom. And Holly Meade was seeing ghosts. And the Daniels brothers had nearly been electrocuted.

The arrival of the odd man from England, Mr. Paper, only added to the overall weird vibe of the day. She would have considered him a suspect in the cat-slaying, if not for his solid alibi. If Mikey's account was accurate, Mr. Paper had been with her when the cat was killed. She couldn't begin to guess who else might have done such a horrid thing. She hoped it was a transient. With any luck this disturbed person would already be miles away and somebody else's problem.

That brought her around to Vera's strange behavior. She'd already complained about hearing odd scratching noises in the walls of her house, and at the Rx diner. Now, after having seen her mutilated cat, she suddenly decided to drive out to the High Point Institute. Why? Undoubtedly it had something to do with the nameplate she found in the trap in her house, and the ID tag that Mikey said they found inside poor Bobcat's guts. Could the same sick person have been responsible for planting both those clues? Did Vera have a theory as to who was doing this? Or was she just searching for answers? Whatever the case, Terri felt it was important to get to her, so she stepped on the gas.

She knew exactly where the institute was, though she had only been there a few times. Someone had tagged an outside wall of the old building and she worried that the abandoned structure would be vandalized. Worse, she didn't want curious kids going in to explore or to party, and get hurt. The place was far enough outside of town and secluded enough that most kids didn't even know it existed. Still, she didn't want to take any chances, so she put a heavy-duty padlock on the front gate. Since the wrought iron fence was too tall to scale, the locked gate was enough to deter the curious. Or so she hoped.

When she drove out from the woods to see the institute building, a cold shiver ran up her spine. Both previous times she had been there, she felt as though the place was giving off an unsettling vibe. This time was no different. Terri was a pragmatic woman. She didn't believe in anything she couldn't see, hear, feel, taste or smell. But there was something about the building that gave her the creeps. She chalked it up to having seen too many horror movies. In those stories, nothing good ever happened in abandoned buildings. Though she knew those were works of fiction, Terri never enjoyed a visit to the High Point Institute.

She drove up to the front gate and was relieved to see that it was closed and locked. The padlock she had put there was doing its job. She got out of her vehicle and walked to the gate to see something that didn't make sense. Vera's Saab was parked at the bottom of the stairs leading up to the front door. It was inside the locked gate. How did she drive in there if the gate was padlocked? Did she have a key? If so, where did she get it?

"This day just keeps on getting better," she said to herself and headed back to her SUV to fetch the ring that held the key to the padlock. Unfortunately, the ring also held several dozen other keys to various padlocks, door locks, bike locks and equipment locks that had been entrusted to her. Many people gave her duplicate keys in case theirs were lost, or she had to break up some major crime that was being committed, neither of which ever happened. All it meant was that if she needed to use one, she had to go through the painstaking process of trying them all until she found the one that worked.

"And…here we go," she said as she tried the first key.

It didn't work. Finding the right key might take seconds, or she might end up having to try them all. As she worked she couldn't help but wonder how Vera got her car through the gate, and what she could possibly be doing there.

Vera kept her eyes on the closed office door. The cage-rattling sound continued and was soon joined by another. And another. Within seconds it sounded as though an earthquake was rattling all the cages. After having a chat with her dead boss, she had no desire to find out who was beyond the door. But the only way out was through the lab.

"This isn't happening," she said to herself.

While she didn't think she was dreaming, she knew that none of what was going on could be real. Her mind had to be playing tricks on her. It had happened before. When she worked in the lab, she often felt as though the animals were watching her. Sometimes she heard whispered voices, as if the creatures were talking to one another. She could never make out exactly what was being said, and didn't question how animals could be whispering, let alone in English. But she heard them.

She made some of them pay the price for conspiring against her. All it took was a not-so-gentle neck-squeeze.

Vera knew she needed help. Not in that moment, but beyond. She would find a therapist. Someone who had no connection to Glenville. She'd tell the truth, about everything. Even if it meant losing her pharmacist license. She needed to get right and calm her brain.

Having made that decision, Vera's confidence grew. With some work she felt certain she could exorcise the ghosts that had been haunting her for decades.

The sound of rattling cages grew more frantic. It didn't bother her for she now had a plan. She stood up and strode boldly for the door, ready to walk straight through her hallucinations and out of the institute, for good this time. She'd get in her car, drive home, and start the process of healing. Yes. It was a good plan. In that one sweet moment, Vera felt ready to start on the road to a new and healthier life.

She grabbed the doorknob, yanked the door open and stepped into the lab.

The sound of clattering cages died instantly. There wasn't so much as a fading echo from the cacophony. All was deathly quiet.

But Vera wasn't alone.

The cages were occupied. All of them. There were rabbits, Beagle dogs, and a few kittens. And rats. Lots of rats, both white and black. Larger cages held monkeys of all sizes. Even Old George was there with the top of his skull exposed to reveal his brain and the electrode terminals that had been fused to his skull. Larger cages on the floor held a few goats, some larger dogs, and several small pigs. Vera looked to the white-plastic bins to see silhouettes of mice, gerbils, and hamsters. There had to be several hundred animals. None moved. None made a sound. They were all stock-still.

And they were all staring directly at Vera.

The only thing that kept her from screaming is that she knew it couldn't be real. Animals didn't have the capacity to focus like that, and certainly not as a group.

"I have no guilt," she said to the assemblage, though in reality she was saying it to herself, trying to convince herself that everything she had done in the past was justified.

She forced herself to walk for the door, moving slowly, not wanting to provoke any reactions. She didn't believe for a second that the room was actually filled with animals, but she moved as if it was. She tried to keep her eyes on the floor but couldn't help stealing a few quick glances to see that the animals kept their gazes locked on her, following her movement. While she was convinced that the scene was being conjured by her mind, she was grateful that the cages were latched. There was nothing these animals could do to harm her.

That's when she heard the unmistakable, metallic squeak of a cage door opening.

She stopped and turned slowly to see that one of the cages was indeed open. Inside was a Rhesus monkey. Vera stared at the little primate, who opened its mouth and hissed at her.

Vera gasped. Was it going to jump out at her? She took a step backward, getting nearer to the door out of the lab. Her eye caught movement on the other side of the room. One of the rats had pushed open its cage door. It was followed by another, and another. Tops of plastic bins were pushed up as sniffing rat noses poked their way up and out.

Old George pushed open his cage door. His eyes were locked on Vera's.

What was going on? Why was her brain creating this impossible scene? Vera still couldn't believe it was actually happening.

That's when the Rhesus Monkey let out a scream. It was a signal. A battle cry. More rats pushed up and out from their bins and jumped to the floor. No sooner did they hit the ground than each and every one got to its feet and scurried toward Vera. Other cage doors flew open as animals jumped out of confinement, headed for Vera.

Hallucination or no, Vera wasn't about to stand there and let these dream-animals attack her. She ran for the lab door, threw it open and escaped into the corridor, slamming the door behind her. She backed away as the door was immediately pummeled from inside by dozens of the animals. Vera stumbled along the dark corridor with one goal in mind: get out of the building and to her car.

Behind her, the lab door crashed open.

Vera didn't stop or look to see what was coming out. She ran, stumbled, fell to a knee but got back up and kept going. She heard the sounds of hundreds of clawed paws scurrying across the linoleum behind her. Chasing her. If she fell again, they'd be on her.

Vera turned the corner at the end of the hallway and for the time-being was out of sight of her pursuers. She kept moving but was still a long way from the stairs that would lead up to the lobby. Too long. She feared the animals would catch her before she reached the top. There had to be another way.

She spotted an open door and made a snap decision. She jumped through it and quickly closed and locked the door behind her. She stood stock still and held her breath. If any of those beasts had seen where she went they'd surely batter down the door, just as they did at the lab. But if they hadn't seen her, perhaps they'd pass by and hunt for her through the rest of the building, giving Vera enough time to sneak out behind them and get to her car.

She leaned into the door and put her ear against it. The sound of the approaching animals grew louder. The taunting screech of monkeys joined the scuttling of claws and hoofs on the hard floor. Vera held her breath. They'd be at the door in seconds. She had the brief, sickening thought that they might smell her. After all, they were animals. She cursed herself for being so stupid and thinking that she could hide from them simply by being out of sight.

Glancing over her shoulder she saw that she was in a closet. It was large and lined with empty metal racks. It looked to once have been the domain of the janitorial staff. Most important, there was no way out other than through the door she was leaning against. She prayed that she hadn't trapped herself in a dead end.

She heard the wave of animals approaching and had to force herself not to whimper in fear. They were nearly at the door. If they smelled her, she'd certainly feel the thump of their bodies being hurled against the door. She closed her eyes and prayed to a God who had never heard from her in the past. She braced herself…

…but the barrage didn't come. The sound of the animals receded. They hadn't seen her go inside. They hadn't smelled her. Her desperate gamble had worked.

Vera instantly thought ahead to her next move. She'd wait a few seconds to make sure there were no stragglers. She'd then leave the closet and hurry back the way she'd come. There was a loading dock past the lab where the animals were received. It was the last sight the creatures had of the outside world. Now it would be Vera's escape route. She took a shallow breath and listened for any animals that might be in the hallway. She didn't hear anything coming from outside the closet.

What she heard was on the inside.

Scratching.

It came from the walls, just like in her house, and the Rx Diner. Something was in the walls, scratching furiously. It wasn't until that moment that she realized there might be a connection between the scratching she heard elsewhere and the impossible events that had been happening at High Point. Had she imagined those earlier scratching noises as well? Had this hallucinatory odyssey begun the moment she woke up that morning? It made sense, but it raised the question: why now? Why was this the day that her mind decided to torture her? Why not yesterday? Or the week, month, or year before? What was different about today?

The scratching grew more incessant, bringing her back to the situation at hand. There would be plenty of time to dive into those questions in therapy. It was more important to be diving into her car and getting the hell out of there. Vera gave one last listen at the door. Confidant that the pursuers had passed by, she moved to unlock the door, but froze when she felt something drop on to her hand. It was a dusting of plaster that had fallen from…where? She slowly looked up.

In that instant, the ceiling crumbled directly over her head. Whatever had been digging from inside the walls, had broken through the ceiling. Vera was hit with chunks of plaster. Dust got into her eyes, blinding her. She quickly rubbed away the debris and looked up again to see that broken plaster was the least of her worries. Directly over her head was a large, dark hole that had been eaten, clawed, and torn open. She stared up in wonder, only to have a waterfall of small mice drop from above. They landed on her head and got tangled in her hair. They fell onto her shoulders and clawed at her blouse. Several found their way to her collar and slipped down along her neck. They slithered inside her blouse, and they bit. Their teeth were tiny but sharp. Vera was hit by what felt like hundreds of bee stings that pierced her flesh.

She swatted them away, tore them off of her clothes and pulled them from her hair. In spite of the vicious attack, she had the wherewithal not to scream which would reveal where she was to the wave of animals that had passed and bring them back. She continued to tear the mice off with one hand, while fumbling to open the door with the other.

The mice kept falling. Hundreds of them cascaded out of the hole in the ceiling. Most hit the floor and moved to climb up her pants. Vera kicked at them and stomped them under foot, crushing their tiny skeletons and squirting blood out from under her shoes. She was oblivious to the gore, and their squeals of pain.

Finally, she managed to open the door and half jumped, half fell out of the closet. She stayed focused and turned to head back toward the lab and the loading dock, but she was stopped by a waterfall of mice that came tumbling out of another, larger hole they'd opened up in the ceiling of the corridor. She was cut off from that escape route and had no choice but to run in the opposite direction. She continued pulling mice off of her and had the brief thought that for a hallucination, it was all so very real.

She now had only one way out. Through the lobby. That was okay. Her car was waiting at the foot of the stairs outside the front doors. As long as she could avoid the wave of beasts that had been chasing her, she had a chance. She threw the last mouse off and sprinted for the stairs at the far end of the subterranean corridor. She reached them in no time and ran up, taking two at a time. It was the most exercise her 60-year-old body had been through in decades, but she didn't falter. Adrenalin will do that. And fear. She bounded up the stairs and covered the short distance to the lobby. She didn't see a single animal along the way and dared to think that they were searching for her in other parts of the hospital, or maybe her brain had simply given up on conjuring the nightmare.

The light ahead meant freedom. She was nearly at the lobby and soon to be out of the front door. Her hopes rose. She was going to get out of this. She even allowed herself a moment of anger. These animals had been the cause of her anguish decades before and were doing the same today. In her mind this only justified what she had done to them years ago. They were beasts then and they remained beasts today. Her only regret was that she couldn't make more of them suffer for what they had done to her. Thoughts of revenge weren't far off. But she first had to get away.

She hurried into the warm light of the lobby and immediately realized she had made a grave mistake. The animals hadn't given up. They were not hunting for her throughout the rest of the sprawling institute.

They were waiting for her.

Vera ran into the large room and stopped near the dry fountain. She was surrounded. She looked around for an escape route and realized there wasn't one. The animals were everywhere. Mongrel dogs stood menacingly in front of the exits. Rats swarmed the floor, taking up most every inch of space, crawling over one another, all looking to Vera. Monkeys had climbed up onto the fountain and looked down on her, screeching. To Vera it sounded like taunting laughter.

On the wide stairs that led up to the second floor was Old George. He sat on the first landing overlooking the lobby like a stoic judge, surrounded by several other monkeys. He had the air of being the wise old leader of the group. While every other one of the animals was agitated and ready for action, Old George sat calmly, gazing at the scene.

Vera focused on him. The two held eye-contact.

It had all come to this.

Terri grew more frustrated with each failed attempt at finding the right key. There were at least fifty on the ring, most of which weren't labeled, or had some useless markings like: "Front #1" or "Padlock" which meant absolutely nothing to her. She was as much at fault for the poor markings as any of the people who gave her their keys. She made a mental note that she wouldn't put another key on the ring unless it was clearly labeled. Better yet, let everyone keep their own damned keys.

"I know it's going to be the last key I try," she said to herself, then chuckled, realizing that of course it would be the last key she tried. Why would she keep looking after finding the right key?

As frustrating as it was, there was another emotion at work.

Dread.

She took a break to look through the fence at the imposing structure that was the High Point Institute. It gave her the same uneasy feeling she'd experienced the few other times she'd been there. There was no practical reason for her to have that feeling, other than the fact that Vera's car was there. Still, there was something about this decrepit building that quite simply, gave her the creeps. While she wanted nothing more than to jump back in her SUV and get the hell out of there, her job description forced her to do otherwise.

She had been trained to work as a sheriff in Cook County Illinois, which included Chicago. After her divorce, she made the choice to move back to Glenville to raise her daughter in a safer, less hectic environment. The trade-off was that being a sheriff in a small town may have been safer, it was a step below boring. She knew what she was signing up for, but it didn't keep her from occasionally lamenting that her skills were going to waste, and she was losing her edge. She missed the action.

As she stood in front of the pad-locked gate, part of her reveled in a slight adrenalin boost she hadn't felt in quite some time. It felt good. But she couldn't shake the feeling of dread, and it wasn't just about this spooky building. She couldn't help but wonder if what was happening right now, here, and elsewhere in town, was only prelude to something bigger.

Be careful what you wish for, she thought, and continued searching through the keys.

Vera stood frozen, surrounded by hundreds of angry animals. Trapped. Strangely, she was no longer afraid. She was angry. Being cornered by these varmints was a validation of how she felt about the creatures back when she ran the lab. The animals had her trapped back then as well. Her resentment may have gone dormant since she left High Point, but it never left her completely. It not only came flooding back, but it was also compounded by the fact that these animals had dared to band together to physically torment her. It didn't matter that it was a conjured hallucination, it was evidence of her deeply seated hatred of these beasts.

Back then, her only way to alleviate the anger was to lash out. To torture. To strangle the life out of the monsters. It was always so simple. A single squeeze would snap a neck, though death wasn't always instantaneous. Those were the most gratifying times. She didn't want it to be quick. She wanted them to suffer. She wanted to see it. Those precious moments would quell her anxiety for a while, but it would inevitably build again until she would need another release.

The ultimate relief came when she was fired from High Point. She resented the fact that the administration had turned on her, seeing as they were guilty of far worse atrocities. She enjoyed a slight measure of revenge when the institute itself closed shortly thereafter. In the years since she managed to push the memories and emotions of those dark days deep into her subconscious, knowing full well that one day they would resurface.

Today was that day.

Vera locked eyes with Old George. He sat there calmly, as if he knew he had the upper hand. It only intensified her rage.

"What do you want?" she said through gritted teeth. "Revenge? I won't give you the satisfaction."

She walked slowly toward the stairs while rats skittered around her feet. A few nipped at her ankles, Vera winced at the sharp jabs but continued on.

"I suppose some therapist will tell me this is all just a manifestation of my guilt, but they'd be wrong. I have no remorse. If anyone should feel guilty it's the companies that wanted the testing done, and the institute that accepted their projects. And their money. I had no choice. I was as much a victim as you were."

The mongrels that guarded the exits let out deep, guttural growls. They were on a hair trigger. Vera had no doubt that if she made a break for any door, the dogs would attack. The fleeting image of being brought down by a pack of angry dogs, followed by what would surely be a swarm of rats tearing at her flesh killed any thoughts of escape. Her mind may be conjuring the situation, but the pain she felt from the nipping of the rats felt all too real.

She made it to the foot of the stairs, directly below Old George and his minions who watched her dispassionately.

"How is this going to end?" Vera called to Old George. "With an apology? Is that it? Do you want me to acknowledge that I treated you badly? No, that's too simple and you know full well it wouldn't be sincere. I have no regrets. The next move is yours. What is it you want from me?"

As if in answer, the circle of animals drew tighter around Vera. The dogs closed in. The rats swarmed over her feet and clawed at her pants leg. Though she had convinced herself that this was all happening in her mind, Vera was once again afraid. The idea of being set-upon by vengeful beasts with sharp claws and teeth was too horrifying to imagine. Yet she did. Though it was all being created in her mind, she couldn't bear to give these creatures the satisfaction of getting revenge on her.

There was only one way out. A way she was all too familiar with.

"I choose my own fate," she said to Old George with determination.

She slowly raised her hands as the dogs drew closer and the rats climbed up her pants legs.

"And I choose to kill every last one of you, once and for all."

As she had done so many times with the creatures under her charge, she wrapped her fingers around a neck.

"Got it!" Terri said triumphantly.

She had to go through nearly the entire ring of keys, but she found it. The lock was slightly rusted but opened with no problem. Terri pulled it off of the latch and pushed the heavy gate open. She didn't bother getting back into the SUV and driving to the entrance. The walk was a short one.

When she got to Vera's car, she looked in to see that the keys were in the ignition. That wasn't unusual. People in Glenville left keys in ignitions. And didn't lock front doors. They only put padlocks on valuable equipment. That's what they cared about. It's why Terri had a ring full of keys. As she was peering into the car, she heard the unmistakable sound of a lock being thrown. She stood up quickly and looked over the top of Vera's car to the front door of High Point.

The door was slightly open. Had it been open a moment before?

"Vera?" Terri called out.

No reply.

Terri circled Vera's car and climbed the stairs. She thought about pulling her service Glock, but a quick assessment told her to keep it holstered. Eerie feelings didn't justify drawing one's weapon. She got to the top of the stairs and gently pushed the front door open with her foot. The last time she'd been there, the door had been locked. Again, did Vera have a key?

"Vera? It's Terri," she called.

Still no response. Terri took a cautious step inside and waited for her eyes to adjust. As when she had been there in times past, she was hit with a wave of sadness. This was once an elegant building. The giant stained-glass windows alone were breathtaking. She had no idea of when to expect that someone would take over, but she hoped that whoever it was, they wouldn't immediately raze the building but instead restore it to its former glory. Realistically there was no chance of either happening. Glenville wasn't a dead town, but it was on life-support. There was no realistic commercial future for the old mansion. Unless someone with more money than sense wanted to refurbish the place into a modern-day castle where they could live in opulent solitude, the likelihood was that the High Point Institute would remain empty until time and the elements reduced it to rubble.

"Vera! It's Terri Hirsch!"

Terri had no idea of where to look for her. The message was to meet her here, not where she'd be once she got here. The last thing Terri wanted to do was search the sprawling, spooky building. She walked further into the lobby, gazing up at the stained-glass windows that had colorful, idealized depictions of green pastures complete with herds of sheep and cattle. There were horses trotting across manicured, grassy plains and trees in full, colorful springtime blossom. Though the glass was crusted with dirt and dust that had been accumulating for decades, the beauty of the craftmanship shone through. Terri had the silly thought that she would like to come back with a portable power-washer to blast away the grime to see these windows in their full glory.

It was a lovely moment,..

…that ended quickly when Terri nearly tripped over something.

She looked down and let out a scream.

She'd found Vera. The woman lay on her back with her eyes bulged open. Her two hands clutched her throat.

Terri didn't need to examine her. The truth was obvious.

Vera Holiday was very dead.

~~~~

An hour later, Terri sat on the front steps of the institute looking and feeling shellshocked. A woman exited the open front door. She was short, powerful and wore blue coveralls with the words County Coroner stitched over a breast pocket.
~~~~

She sat down next to Terri and said, "Bet you're missing Chicago about now."

She looked to Terri for a reaction but got none.

"What the hell, Terri?" the Coroner went on. "I thought Vera was too mean to die."

"Any thoughts about what happened?" Terri asked.

"Not a whole lot. We're photographing everything before moving her out. I can't say for sure until the autopsy but by the looks of things it was self-strangulation. Nice, huh? Not something you see every day. Or ever."

"There's no rush," Terri said. "She has no family that I know of. I'll do some digging to make sure."

"One thing's a little strange though."

"Only one thing?" Terri asked and the two actually chuckled.

"At least that I could see at first. The cuffs of her pants were all torn up and shredded, like she'd been walking through a pricker bush."

"What do you think that means?" Terri asked.

"Damned if I know," the Coroner said as she stood up. "That's your job to figure out. I'll be in touch."

The Coroner headed back up the stairs leaving Terri with more questions than answers. She drove back to town and went straight to Vera's pharmacy. She needed to tell Mikey that his boss was no longer his boss.

Terri had no idea what would happen with the pharmacy. As she told the Coroner, Vera had no known family. It would fall to Terri to trace any possible relation to inform them of her death. Ideally, she'd find someone who would want to know, and take care of Vera's burial. They might even lay claim to the pharmacy. Whether she found someone or not, she would shortly turn the issues over to the county to sort out.

What she couldn't turn over was the investigation into what had happened to Vera, and why she had choked herself to death.

When she parked in front of the pharmacy, she found Mr. Paper sitting on the bench outside the door. His hands were resting on his walking stick, his eyes were closed, his face turned up to the sun.

"I'm glad someone's enjoying the day," Terri said as she approached him.

"I take it that you are not."

Terri sighed and looked both ways, up and down Main Street as if seeing it in a new light.

"You came here to observe a normal American town. Before today I'd have said you came to the right place."

"And now?"

"Something's going on," she said thoughtfully. "Something…odd. I hope I'm wrong and I probably am. But if I'm not, I damn well better be able to deal with it."

She looked to Mr. Paper and added, "I don't know why I'm telling you this. I have no idea who you are and to be honest, your being here makes things that much stranger."

"Forgive me for adding to your worries, Sheriff. I do apologize for that. I know very little about your town, but in the short time I've been here I too have sensed that all is not…normal as you put it. Would you like to hear my thoughts?"

"Please," Terri said. "Objectivity is a good thing."

"The world is remarkably symbiotic," Mr. Paper said. "Call it Karma, Ying Yang, water seeking its own level or to use a more scientific analogy, for every action, there is an equal and opposite reaction. Or so says Sir Isaac Newton."

"And what does that have to do with Glenville?"

"Something is amiss in your town, Sheriff," Mr. Paper said. "It goes beyond the tragic death of an individual. If that were the case, this would be over. There would be no more inexplicable incidents. From the look on your face, I'm guessing that there have been others."

Terri didn't respond, which was her response.

"As I thought," Mr. Paper said.

"What am I supposed to do about it? They don't teach *strange* in the academy."

"In order to understand what is happening, you'll have to take a step back, look at the entire picture, and try to find the common denominator. I believe those in your line of work would call it an investigation. That is something that was taught in the academy, correct?"

"Sure," Terri said.

"Brilliant," Mr. Paper said jovially. "Then Glenville is in very good hands."

Terri couldn't take her eyes off of Mr. Paper.

"Part of any investigation is to look for anomalies," she said.

"Indeed."

"I consider you an anomaly, Mr. Paper."

Mr. Paper stood and fixed his bowler hat.

"I'm sure you do," he said. "In your position I would as well. But consider this: I've only just arrived in your lovely village. In my experience, these types of issues don't suddenly commence by chance and the answer is far more complex than can be attributed to the appearance of a single individual. But if it makes your job any easier, I don't plan on leaving just yet. The research for my book has taken a decidedly fascinating turn."

"I'm sure it has."

"If I can be of any assistance to you, please do not hesitate to ask."

"Because in your experience, I'm going to need it?"

"Perhaps. Perhaps not. But as I said, I am very experienced."

Mr. Paper tipped his bowler to Terri and said, "Be seeing you."

He turned and walked off with his head held high and his face turned to the sun.

"I'm sure you will," Terri said to herself.

<u>NOT THE END</u>

About the Author

D.J. MacHale – Is the #1 New York Times bestselling author of the book series *Pendragon – Journal of an Adventure Through Time and Space* as well as the spooky *Morpheus Road* trilogy and the sci-fi thriller trilogy *The SYLO Chronicles*. In addition to several other published works, he has written, directed and produced many award-winning television series and movies including *Are You Afraid of the Dark?, Flight 29 Down,* and Disney's *Tower of Terror*.

D.J. lives with his family in Southern California. Visit him at **djmachalebooks.com** as well as on Facebook, Twitter, and Instagram.

Selected titles by D.J. MacHale

PENDRAGON – Journal of an Adventure Through Time and Space

The Merchant of Death
The Lost City of Faar
The Never War
The Reality Bug
Black Water
The Rivers of Zadaa
The Quillan Games
The Pilgrims of Rayne
Raven Rise
The Soldiers of Halla

MORPHEUS ROAD

The Light
The Black
The Blood

THE SYLO CHRONICLES

SYLO
STORM
STRIKE

Website: DJMacHaleBooks.com